The Finger's Twist

The Finger's Twist

Lee Lamothe

RavEN STONE

Published by Ravenstone
an imprint of Turnstone Press
018-100 Arthur Street
Artspace Building
Winnipeg, MB
R3B 1H3 Canada
www.TurnstonePress.com

Turnstone Press gratefully acknowledges the assistance of the Canada Council for the Arts, the Manitoba Arts Council, the Government of Canada through the Book Publishing Industry Development Program, and the Government of Manitoba through the Department of Culture, Heritage, Tourism and Sport, Arts Branch, for our publishing activities.

Cover design: Jamis Paulson
Interior design: Sharon Caseburg
Printed and bound in Canada by Friesens for Turnstone Press.

Library and Archives Canada Cataloguing in Publication

Lamothe, Lee, 1948-
The finger's twist / Lee Lamothe.

ISBN 978-0-88801-347-7

I. Title.

PS8573.A42478F55 2009 C813'.6 C2009-905018-8

For Lucy K. White, Katy and Michelle.

The Finger's Twist

Prelude

My old man was the last rag-and-bones man. Like his own old man who had roamed the neighbourhoods in a horse cart, he trolled networks of laneways and alleys in a broken-back pickup truck looking for the rags and bones of lives: discarded appliances, three-legged tables, bedsprings, yellow-stained mattresses, coloured glass bottles, and sheets of metal. Blind busted lamps, amputated chairs and hollow radios. His hands were always coated in black grease; his fingers always had nicks and cuts in various stages of healing. His back was wide and his arms thick: alone he could lift a refrigerator—not the lightweight flimsy tinfoil models you find now, but the real metal monsters encasing motors that dragged you down into gravity if you didn't grab them just right. After lifting the fridge—or stove or chesterfield or old porcelain toilet—he could wrestle it smoothly onto the bed of the truck or onto the cart like a skinny man dancing a jitterbug with a fat lady, finding her point of balance and just rolling her off her feet, across his back, and onto the danceboards as though it was nothing at all.

My old man followed his old man's secret map that let him harvest vast portions of the city, even out beyond the neighbourhood, without appearing on an actual street. The main avenues were the rivers of the city. His alleys and laneways were streams and creeks that fed them. He was the man nobody saw, who took what no one wanted, who looked beneath the surface of things and found an invisible value. Behind the house where we rented a half-a-flat he had a leaning shed where he kept an arsenal of tools, bits of wire, welding guns, touch-up paint, and buckets of washers and screws and nails and bolts. When my mother vanished he disappeared for days into the shed—his workshop, he grandly called it when he was feeling grand—dodging the rain drips, resisting winter with a pot-bellied stove that he nourished on wood scrappings and wadded newspapers. He became increasingly erratic and the neighbours noticed—his wanderings and mumblings reinforced the belief that he'd done in my mother and made her parts vanish.

Maybe he had.

One cold smoky morning he awoke me with a glint in his eye: a washing machine was jammed up a cramped alley and he couldn't get the truck in.

"Charlie, I need a tipper." His voice was rough but had finally found life after a month of solitary grief. "It's gold. New rubber wringers and we're in business. The Pollack will pay fifteen, maybe twenty."

He made me my school lunch, baloney and bread, while I dressed. I hated the half-a-flat we lived in; even with my mother gone it was crowded. It smelled of leaking gas, roach powder, and the odours of two people who hadn't mastered the skills of personal maintenance. When we went down the stairs he whistled. The truck took a while to start and he had to spend some time under the hood, tinkering but still whistling. It turned over and he jumped in.

We cruised through the pre-dawn streets, just the two of us; the only heat in the cab was our sour breath. His head never stopped moving, looking for treasure that fools had left on lawns or curbs. We gathered a tube of linoleum. A bookshelf with no shelves. A coffee table with a hole punched through the top. A twine-bound stack of magazines.

He stopped the truck at the top of an alley; in the long gloom glowed the squat washer. "That's her. You ready to put that school wrestling stuff to good use?"

He'd only seen me wrestle once—a high school match where I'd been disqualified for going into a blind rage that had me punching and kicking my opponent. "Your old man collects turds from toilets," he'd whispered. "Garbage boy." And we were off, and I was out.

"Let's get 'er done, Dad."

Somehow that morning it came to me that I was bigger than him, strangely not because I was growing, but because he was shrinking under the weight of time, and perhaps something else. We rolled on our feet down that alley and together manhandled that fucker out and up onto the bed of that truck. While I caught my breath, he wandered to a metal garbage can, lifted the lid and looked inside. I heard his breath go in, then come out in a rush that was like a sob.

He reached in and took out a child's doll, a blonde head like my mother's, a ripped dress, a leg on backwards. A murderer's discard. I think he forgot about me for a long time as we stood there, him cradling the doll in his big greased hands, his thumb running repeatedly across the face, pushing back the stiff blonde hair.

Then he got into the truck and I climbed in beside him. He laid the doll on the dash, but couldn't stop looking at it bouncing as we navigated our way to my school. He turned it face down; the bumps in the alleys made it juggle about.

When it was face up, he turned it face down. It turned again, face up. He turned it and finally put a canvas work glove on it. He drove the rest of the way to school with his jaw clamped and his nostrils pinching tight as he sucked in air.

A week later my dad cribbed together a handful of wrinkled bills and bought himself a bus ticket to Florida. For a week or two, he said. But he never came back.

When the children's assistance folk came to get me I cleaned out the shed—my dad's workshop, I told the man and woman who waited patiently—and found the broken blonde doll wrapped in one of my mother's old but elegant English bandannas. I took it with me and later gave it to one of the orphan girls who lived in the brooding foster home across the street.

Elodie's a bit of a broken doll. I'm sure that if my dad had met her he'd have stood back a few feet to look her over, then run his hands over her legs, examined her teeth, and pronounced her fixable to a point. He'd say: "New job of paint, a couple of pop rivets, she'll be good as new. Almost."

Sometimes when I feel like a busted boy I sense Elodie is the rag-and-bone man of me, looking at me glowing in the gloom at the vanishing point of a long foggy alleyway, a broken item that might be worth salvaging.

1

Even with the riots, the condo was ideal for our needs that year. A few blocks from the provincial legislature with a clear view to the immaculate vast grounds, we'd found the fifth floor condo after months of indifferently looking at more expensive, smaller places with balconies the size of a closet. Inside, it wasn't much bigger than the other apartments we'd looked at—two bedrooms, two baths, fully accessible for both the handicapped and the drunk; one of us was one, one of us was both—but what immediately sold us was the terrace, a flagstoned affair measuring fifty-odd feet by eighteen with chest-high thick marble walls, a lilac tree, a mulberry tree, a twenty-foot rock garden and trellis work that would hold dazzling blooms in the warm months and in winter would create perfect snow sculptures.

We'd moved in in late spring. The first few riots were amusing. I bought a powerful telescope of German glass and watched the havoc and mayhem on the lawns of the legislature all that spring and summer, gaining a pretty good understanding of how the cops made a perimeter and stuck to it, could tell the masked girl demonstrators from the masked boys—the famously dreaded and earnest Black Bloc—by their style of throwing clumps of the lawn. At one point I actually recognized one of my daughters, unmasked, racing between two police horses, taking a glancing whip from a baton across her back. Go, kiddo, I said aloud, giving Elodie the 'scope so she could try to see the Mouse. I could spot the undercovers by how they made themselves available to witness and assist, but not get confused in the melee and clubbed into the ground by their own guys in the fervour of enthusiasm, before the arrest teams moved in. The hollow echoes of horses' hooves on the concrete sidewalks, the yells, the rhythmic clacking of baton on shield, chants of *No Justice No Peace,* all rode in a complex acoustic air tunnel between the surrounding buildings, delivering a soundtrack clearly onto our swank terrace, the aural dynamics of the tall buildings magnifying the sound as much as the telescope did the visual.

By the end of that first season of discontent neither the demonstrators nor the cops were fooling around anymore: the fun had become work, the ski masks became gas masks, the clods of earth had become paving stones, and the riot squad and equestrian units took on a Cossack precision.

I had to bail the Mouse out twice and visit my other daughter, Allie, at Toronto General where they'd put stitches into the skin over her right cheekbone. They were twins in age only: the Mouse was smaller and more agile and blonde like her mother, visceral and sly. Running was never an option for her. She owned the ground she stood upon.

Allie was somewhat taller, a little smarter, almost brunette where her hair wasn't purple, with a tendency to examine and parse. Her reasonableness and craving for perspective sometimes made her a little less quick than her intuitive darting sister, thus the three-quarter inch of tiny railway track on her cheekbone.

But after a while it all became one big fist fight, the funnery in the park. You had to have absolutely nothing else to do, and even if you didn't want to watch the movie, that screaming, clack-clack-clacking soundtrack was unavoidable.

I was grunting in the declining sunshine on the terrace under too many weights, to the singsong of chants at the legislature. Inside, through the sliding doors, Elodie was clacking away at the computer keyboard and gabbing into the telephone, trying to find a man named Wong in Yunnan province, a daunting task when southern China was wall-to-wall with them.

Elmer Wong had gone into the wind with one of Elodie's clients' money, an advance payment scheme that had left his victim pool out about a million-eight, total. The point-eight belonged to one of Elodie's contract clients, a merger-acquisitions guy to whom the concept of due diligence was clearly alien. Unless he wanted me to stomp over to Yunnan and put the grab on the guy, it was a job that had nothing to do with me. I wouldn't have minded though: in my tramping I'd discovered the spice and climate of the southern provinces and had gotten into enough trouble over there to look forward to going back. Someone said, once, something like: China is where you accept a friendly drink in a bar, then wake up with a bleeding tattoo, a broken nose, a beard, and a pregnant wife complete with a whole new set of in-laws.

Inside, Elodie stopped chatting and stopped clacking. The tires of her wheelchair squeaked—the humidity's effect on the air pressure in the inner tubes—as she rotated away from her desk. Her voice came through the open sliding door. "How much you got on there, stud?"

"Two-twenty." I spoke casually, but my hands were

sweating inside the gloves and I was actually a little fearful, my skull swollen. Not having a spotter was a dangerous enterprise. I was a little nervous beneath it all but casually racked the weight as though I'd stopped only to talk to her. "About three times your weight, my pretty." This was almost exactly true: she was a bone rack. I'd never seen her standing upright but she swore she was five-nine and had once weighed a sleek one-fifteen. I sometimes asked her brother how tall she was before her accident and, depending on his mood, he variously said five-six and one-hundred-fifty, five-eight and one-hundred-ninety, and, once when she'd pissed him off at dinner, said five-five and a healthy two-ten. Photographs her aunt made me endure from the family album showed a variety of Elodies, ranging from lean and tall in elegant black cocktail attire, to significantly heavy after a graduation trip a year before the accident, upon a tour of beers of Germany and butters of southern France. In any case, she was no dumpling now; if she grew her hair another inch she might tip seventy-five pounds.

I sat up and rotated my shoulders, looking for messages in the creaks and pains. But I felt pretty good, almost as I had wrestling in my first and only year of high school when the joys of both victory and defeat soared through my body like the laughter of abandon. Or, not regularly but often, the soaring of bitterness when the coach leaned over me on the mat and whispered, "Pretend you're your old man wrestling a stove off his horse-cart." The resulting laughter of the other wrestlers made my head swell with purple worms.

I looked at the angle of the sun and said to Elodie, "It's beer o'clock."

"What's the hey-rube about today?" Through the window she could hear chants and the squealing bullhorns. She liked the old carnival terms I had picked up in my tramping days.

Hey-rube for a dust-up, *squaring the mark* for winding up a con victim, *kee-a-zops* for cops. I'd spent a drunken night once talking for hours in Be-aza-be-za-bop. She thought it was cool: *Kee-a-zool.*

"Dunno. They're mostly all in wheelchairs. Accessibility, maybe. Benefits, maybe."

She rolled away and said over her shoulder, "Oh, poor dears."

She clearly hadn't found the gone Wong and was looking to get her mind off it with a bit of combat. The first time it happened it rubbed me wrong. I told her that if she didn't have a family fortune under her ass she'd likely be in a warehouse for broken dolls someplace, growing pasty and pale, waiting for mommy government to send her a cheque so she could buy dented cans of risky food at a seconds outlet. I think that was about our second month together and the first time she called me a cocksucker.

Ke-a-zok-ze-a-zuk-er.

We'd both learned separately in our travels that civilized dining took place after nine o'clock. We filled the hours after my workout drinking a little, talking a lot, and idling our way through hands of cards.

Elodie updated me on how the hunt for the gone Wong was progressing. I told her about a Harley Davidson I'd looked at that morning and we discussed the asking price. We went over some sketches my friend Tommy the Biker had drawn up for sidecars that would fit the wheelchair. My dream was to thunder her along the Burma Road.

I pumped up her tires and used four-in-one oil on the caster locks. At eight-thirty she squinted at me and said, "Charlie, you're stubbling."

I went into the bedroom and found the buzzer and a bottle

of none-shine emollient. I sat on a milk stool with my back against her dead legs. Her fingers sketched over my skull like cold electricity. The four-in-one oil made the room smell like a rag-and-bones man's workshop and I took a deep sad breath of it.

After the children's assistance folks had installed me with the first of a series of families that took in what they called *the needy,* a policeman came to the house and said my old man had indeed made it to south Florida but while fishing had failed to both secure himself to the fishing chair and to let go of the rod when a fish struck. Police down there hadn't found the body but the witnesses said there was no question he'd hit the water pretty hard and had gone to where the fish went. A day or two later a detective came by the house and asked if, now that my father was gone, there was anything I wanted to tell him about my mother. He left, unsatisfied, and a few days later I left, too, first to a circus job scutting out animal stalls, doing heavy lifting, sometimes looming near barker stands and because I was big, leaning on dissatisfied ring-tossers. When the circus moved on, I moved with it.

Disjointed cubes of time somehow arrange themselves into a life like a multi-coloured square twisted in your fingers until they accidentally become organized, or at least sensible. Years were made up of seasons of carnival work. When I tired of breaking down and putting up, there were short-order cooking jobs. There was a funny gig working as a dummy running backwards from second-rate boxers. I cooked at a seaman's home and was ensnared by the romance of the endless ocean and the slurred tales of sideways pussy, bug-eating tribes, headhunters, and firewalkers. I sailed away off the edge of Vancouver and found there is no sideways pussy, that people did eat bugs, that headhunting was seasonal, that firewalking was no big deal.

A swami in New Delhi greeted me with the oldest Eastern con: "Ah, I've been waiting for you." A Chinaman in Fuzhou laughed as he stuck a bicycle spoke through his face, in the left cheek and out the right. A beggar in Rangoon made room for me at his post near the *Shwedagon* and offered to painlessly cripple me for ten American dollars. I got drunk with some Italian sailors in Bangkok and wound up working for free, for passage to Gioia Tauro in southern Italy. Somehow, drunk, I crossed the Strait of Messina to Sicily and realized it was my twentieth birthday. I celebrated with an African woman who decided my skull was perfectly formed. "And you have," she added in a sexy guttural French accent as she slipped a bone-handled straight razor from a leather case, "the flat ears of the Mongol warrior. I promise you you'll be very attractive and evil too. Or the night is ... free." I sat naked on a three-legged milking stool balanced on the piece of the rocky hill that served as her patio. In town, just below us, the baking ovens were exhaling a last puff of yeast smoke, cooling down for the night. In front of me, far beyond, was Africa with its purple clouds of dark smoke, and that dark smoke just sucked me up and I somehow landed at home, wherever that was anymore.

I heard Elodie put some cascading strings on the CD player. I wondered how she felt, listening to ballet music, remembering when she could get up and whirl through a room for the pleasure of herself and others. Dancing was a big thing into her late teens. Her aunt has a photograph of her and her old man, a stiff-looking mustachioed dude with a strong cleft chin and a wide mouth, he in a tuxedo and she in a crinoline dress that looked like spun sugar, winning a father-daughter dance contest; another of her in her ballet gear, one position off-centre in a formal class presentation. Her aunt had many, many other pictures she showed when tearfully drunk: Elodie riding Pesky, her horse, Elodie in ski goggles and designer gear, Elodie in parachute, jumping, thumbs up, from the door of a plane, the camera obviously a remote, mounted on the wing. Elodie completely in the air at school, her lacrosse stick in scoop with the ball, another private school wench of similar breeding with her mouth open and Elodie's elbow in her chest. I'd have hated her then, I knew, the blue-eyed blonde with the dent in her chin and all the wealth of the world in her eyes.

I took a potted jade plant off a stool and sat with my back to her. She massaged my scalp for a few minutes, rubbed in the emollient, and clicked on the buzzer. She kept the fingers of her left hand on my neck. They were cool and long. The first time she really touched my bare skin, her icy fingers gave me a sharp shock that actually made me jump.

We were so vastly different we had to take turns at almost everything we wanted to do, or do them separately, together. When we ate in I usually shopped and cooked. Even this was a little complicated because I like all manner of food, particularly what she called dirty foods, organ meats that are the interesting basis of the cuisine of poverty. Like the Cantonese, I believe the only thing with legs you don't eat is the table.

"Tonight, Madame," I'd say, unloading bags from Kensington Market, "it is our pleasure to serve you calves' liver and onions, the appetizer is scallops wrapped in pro-shoot, a salad of fennel and arugula with a hint—a hint!—of *balsamico*." And she'd put her hand on my arm and say, "Sounds deee-lightful, Charlie. Only on mine change the liver to steak, frites instead of onions, and I'll have brie and apples for the appetizer and a naked green salad. Pour the vinaigrette in your ear." After dinner we'd alternate doing the dishes and here too differences emerged. I scraped, then rinsed and hand-washed in scalding water, then dried the plates and glasses and put them away. On her nights she crammed everything into the dishwasher, slammed the door, hit some buttons and rolled away, serene. Pleasure followed, of course, by ease.

"You know, Charlie," she'd offer, "the pleasure of food doesn't have to be followed by the pain of cleaning."

My hands scalding, I'd silently say: "Yes. It does."

It was an out-night, it was a my-night and so I hadn't shopped. I slicked my hand over my scalp, feeling for burrs, and found none. I changed out of my workout clothes and had a fast shower while Elodie clicked her progress report on Wong into the computer. Drying off, I looked over her shoulder. She'd been into his credit cards, a series of pretext calls, trying to track the money offshore, or back to Hong Kong. She'd emailed—"contacted sources in Asia"—a former private school girl reporting for the *South China Morning Post* in HK, and fed Wong's information to her. She'd conducted several interviews with people in the mergers and acquisitions community, looking for other as-yet unidentified victims, hoping to find someone who could provide any data on Wong or his personal and business activities. She added the updated information to her now-voluminous but ultimately unsuccessful report, and signed off.

The CD player stopped and late-evening traffic came softly up through the terrace doors. No sounds from the legislature. I heard a wild cat sly its way over the trellis separating our terrace from the neighbour's.

"Are we sure Wong's gone back to China?" I massaged her shoulders, stuck my thumbs into the base of her skull and she rotated her head slowly, sighing.

Elodie had very erect posture. Two stainless steel rods were imbedded in her back, one on each side of her severed spinal cord. They gave her a mien of alertness and a regal stature that, when combined with her sometimes imperial way of speaking, could piss me off. "His house is sold, cars are sold, his kids are out of school and they told the teacher they were going back home. No activity on his or his wife's accounts. No activity on the credit cards. No new phone listing."

"Who'd he sell the house and the cars to?"

She leaned forward and flipped through her notebook. "Folks named Tsu bought both Mercedes a month ago, folks named Yip bought the house at around the same time."

I read Wong's full name, date of birth, and his address off her notes. "DMV?"

"Driver's licence to the old address. Same for Mrs. Gone Wong. The young Gone Wongs aren't old enough to drive. This one might be a wash, Charlie." Elodie hated it when her engagements didn't have a conclusive ending, when the doer and the money both made away, when she had to tell the client it couldn't be done, that in spite of buffed-up and wordy reports, the bottom line was: Sorry and here's your invoice.

"Hey, everybody is someplace, right? Just have to find out which place."

"Well, let's go eat."

While she took an extended visit to the bathroom—paraplegics have complicated procedures for personal maintenance and hygiene—I called the detective office at York Regional Police and spent five minutes talking to the detective-sergeant about a kickboxing tournament coming up the next weekend; he was reffing and his youngest son was in the lineup. Then we chatted about mutual friends, and he asked after Elodie.

"Ah, hell," I said, "she's after a Chinaman used to live up in your neck of the woods, can't find him and she's giving me a hard time."

He said, "Gutsy girl, your girl." He knew the game, and everyone liked Elodie. "This Chinaman, used to live up here? What's his name? They all fucking live up here, one time or another. Maybe we know him."

I read off Mr. Wong's information. He put me on hold for a few minutes and came back on the line. Mr. Wong, it emerged, had three moving violations in the past two weeks, all rolled stops between eight-thirty and nine in the morning at intersections along the same stretch of Markham Road, all written by traffic guys targeting violators near a school. The DMV address was the useless old one; the car, a black 5-Series BMW, was registered to a leasing company. He read off the licence number. I jotted down the information.

Elodie came out of the washroom looking fresh, if a little tired. We put on light jackets and rode the elevator down to the lobby. The night man hustled out from behind his command centre to operate the automatic handicapped door buttons, an over-achievement that Elodie found either charming or patronizing, depending upon her mood, and he wished us a good evening. I steered us south, towards Chinatown, holding hands, she gently correcting the steerage with her other hand.

"Hey, Charlie, how 'bout Italian?"

"Sorry, kid. My choice tonight, and my choice is ... Vietnamese, the food of my peoples."

"Linguine'd be nice. You could have the clam sauce. I could have lasagne."

"Next time, sport. Tonight it's sea garbage and noodles. The dreaded pho. Ten bucks including tip, leftover breakfast soup for the next day."

"C'mon. I'm really hungry. Let's go Italian."

"It's a longer walk. Have the mystery meat soup. Good, cheap. Plus, I don't have a lot of dough. I didn't make any money today."

"How 'bout, how 'bout I buy? White wine, gelato. Maybe some mussels for you, clammies in the red sauce. Thick crusty bread. The food of your other peoples. Eh? C'mon, be a sport. I had a hard day."

"You buy? The whole shot? No splitsies?"

"On me."

"And, amaretto? And, grappa? Coffee and *sambucc'*? And, and, and ... and later?"

"Don't be greedy. But you play it right, you got a shot."

We headed along Dundas Street, past the mosque and the police station. It was a warm night and couples and groups idled around the art gallery. Be-suited drivers leaned on gleaming limousines in front. A hot dog vendor did a surprisingly brisk business with the uptown trade. Hot dogs and a grand preview, donors and patrons only. There seemed to be a whole lot of bums on the streets lately, some kind of trickle-down from barbered smoothies operating their blue cult out of the legislature. You couldn't, I thought, take a piss in a doorway without soaking a bum or a bag lady or a mental outpatient bundled up in the shadows.

Standing apart from the chattering aficionados and mavens were an older white-haired woman and a man wearing matching hair that looked bluish under the streetlamps. Both were dressed up for a Manhattan-style night out. She had her hands to her face and he was consoling her, one hand on her shoulder and the other holding both a cellular telephone and her purse. Elodie let go of my hand and rolled across the sidewalk towards them.

"Mrs. Carlson? Mr. Carlson?"

I bought myself a dollar hot dog with 'kraut and hung back. When Elodie runs into the swells it requires at least a half-hour of conversation, who's doing what, who got divorced or remarried, who bought whose place on the Lakes, who admirably adopted an orphan from Asia. How Pipsy is doing, where Poppy and Aggie are wintering next year. And of course, how well you're doing, Elodie, got your own business and your own place, and—even—a man. Sort of. Our plucky little Elodie. What a fighter.

I was two bites into the tube steak when plucky little Elodie motioned me over.

"These are good family friends, Bernard and Alice Carlson. This is Charles Tate."

Mrs. Carlson barely looked at me, her hands were busy applying tissues to her face. She glanced around to see if anyone noticed her distress. I juggled my hot dog to shake Bernard Carlson's free hand.

I said, "Charlie."

"Charlie, they've got a problem, a big problem. Their granddaughter was just arrested."

I pictured a girl much like a younger Elodie in a Porsche doing triple digits down Bayview on the way home from the Granite Club; I pictured her lipping off to the cop about who her family was, talking her way into a visit to the station and some quality time in the cells.

"Yeah?" I said. "Arrested for what?"

"Planting a bomb at the legislature." She stared at me, waiting.

"I think," I said, "I'm gonna need another hot dog."

2

There was a fine mist, almost a fog, in the air the next morning. To the east the tip of the sun glowed gold, nuclear, just out of sight, struggling against heavy broken cloud and the thin gases that created irradiated sunrises. Elodie's complained in the past that everywhere reminds me of someplace else. It's usually the architecture or the food smells or the weather that does it. Tramping in Asia were my best times and walking past a fragrant noodle house on Spadina Avenue transports me into a dream sequence. Garlic softening in hot olive oil with basil leaves can stop me dead in my tracks. It isn't only food. The creamy yellow light of a sunset or the moist air of a spring morning means western Sicily or a seaport on the edge of any ocean.

Like most motorcycle riders I check the local weather first thing in the morning; if it's uncertain I dial up the Weather Channel and examine the day's conditions. It wasn't to be a riding day, anyway, so I opened the terrace doors and took my coffee outside. Below the traffic was thin, but the haze, the damp roads, and the still-lit streetlights made interesting shapes and patterns and reflections. I went back inside and loaded an old Leica with out-of-date black and white film. The neighbour's wild cat examined the soft clicks of the twitching camera curtain as I shot a bunch of mostly nothing—the dim intersection below with a striding man in a flapping trench coat crossing a startlingly white turning-arrow; the throbbing lights of a stopped bus, half-faces and shoulders leaning against the windows; a manhole cover glistening in the morning wet, looking like a round oil slick—but I've put a lot of film through a lot of cameras and knew that between my eye and the darkroom I'd find something, even if it was, as the sages say, a lucky accident.

The first morning newscast was fifteen minutes away, so I took some hand weights out of the wooden shed in the corner of the terrace and did some slow curls, dreamily looking at the ghostly mists swirling in the abandoned battlegrounds of Queen's Park.

Elodie was twenty-five when I first met her, ten years ago. Our initial contact didn't hold much promise for romance: I went home with a broken nose. That first time I saw her was as clear in my mind as a photograph taken by some old bent European wizard who knew absolutely what he was doing: pearly whites and eggplant purple-blacks, and in between every hint of grey known to the human eye.

My circumstances at the time were fluid; I'd been a year back from my wanders and had run through a series of short-term jobs, mostly slinging plates, occasionally picking up a few bucks working charity casino nights. I met my ex-wife, Judith, when a restaurant I worked for catered a fashion media event. After the last plates of dessert were out of the kitchen and onto the tables, I went out back to smoke a joint with the guy who carved up meat. As we smoked and goofed, a tall blonde woman came out of the club, leaned against the wall and began puking with rhythm.

I began laughing. "I told you I thought that pork roast was a little ... grey."

"Fuck you," he said in a thick Jamaican accent, laughing. "White folk devil food." He hissed his teeth in disgust.

The woman went first to her knees, then flat out on the alley floor. She had great legs and wore a press card on a silver chain around her neck. She convulsed.

"She yakking pretty bad, there, Devon. We oughta call somebody."

"We oughta," he said, "scram the purse." He had it in his hands and was off down the alley when the woman began trying to sit up.

"You look like Mr. Clean," she said, slurring. "You gonna scrub me up?"

We hit it off that night. She was working at a monthly magazine that attended to women's issues, fashion, makeup and women's health. We went out for six months, got married, and had the twins. Her boss, Kent, was the owner of the magazine and, I later learned, she had long been his mistress, a circumstance that didn't change much except for the few months after the kids were born.

We double dated with Kent and his wife, Wanda. We had dinners at our homes, at expensive restaurants Kent scouted for his review team, a tasty tax writeoff. Kent listened to my disjointed tales of travels and asked if I wanted to go on the road and write what he called weird stuff. It didn't matter much that I couldn't write too well: that's what editors were for, he said, and added he believed media was too elite-centric. The common voice, he said, go for it. He made a point of finding interesting assignments, for which I thought he was a fine fellow, letting me meet the world again, this time on the magazine's ticket. I thought I wasn't bad, but actually I was just okay, which Kent didn't mind because, not bad or just okay still meant I was absent as well. I supposed I should have felt like a dunce—he knew Judith was high-maintenance and her ego required periodic tuning and regular attention, something he couldn't provide, being married and all—but once I figured it all out, Judith and I settled up on my visitation rights for the girls. I spent as little time in town as I had to and Kent made it easier by continuing to direct the assignment editor to keep me in motion.

When I first saw Elodie I was still with one of Kent's magazines, still married to Judith. I was working a story about how rich goofs get stupid and their smart money buys them out. It was the kind of story Kent, a very rich goof himself, loved. It would allow him to make scandalous at the clubs, and he and his pals could snicker. There was no shortage of examples for the story, there was a host of embittered victims who got out-lawyered and out-spent trying to collect some form of retribution or financial settlement from people with big money. There were the prominent developer's kids who bought themselves out from under a gang rape, there was the boyish prankster who tried to jump his new BMW over a swimming pool and landed in the deep end on top of an elderly couple doing their cautious prescribed laps, there were the three private schoolgirls who played Russian roulette, except they fired daddy's vintage Colt revolver at a passing postal worker, an astounding one-in-six chance that paid off for the shooter although not for the postie who took a wound to the head and was blinded. Witnesses were bought in each case, hush money slid through shadowy channels of cut-out accounts, investigators were transferred or bought, evidence vanished, nasty press leaks horrified the victims' families and shut them up.

Towards the end of my research, a sport powered his speedboat, a sleek Donzi, without lights through a group of inner-city children swimming just before full dark off the end of a dock at a charity summer camp, killing one of them and mangling two others. The young Donzi jockey was a popular party animal and a stickman of repute. I headed up there and hung out at the local watering holes, keeping copious notes on all the nasty gossip people told me. I drank with the best friend of the killer boater. He said he'd visited the accused—who was out on bail—and they'd laughed about the victims.

"Peasants," he had told him, laughing. "They got a shot and they're taking it. I just wish they weren't so fucking greedy."

He said the Donzi boy described the victims' families as lazy fucks who deserved nothing.

I talked to the investigators who did the case and was surprised when one said he'd filed a report that the Donzi was travelling safely away from the dock and with lights ablaze and the swimming kids, apparently entranced by this beautifully lit sight, swam out into the propellers. This was clearly at odds with the witnesses other investigators had interviewed. The chatty investigator turned in his report and almost immediately resigned, going to work for the Donzi boy's old man, who ran an international conglomerate that had exhibited a sudden hunger for sharp young provincial constables looking to jump into the private sector in Europe.

Doing the legwork I stayed at a cheapish motel just outside the high-dollar three-lakes area where the multi-million-dollar cottages were arranged like medieval family compounds, little tribal communities that closed in upon themselves, a population of Muffys and Miffys and Bitsys and Babsies. The motel had a small tavern next door where I sat late each night, eating thawed hamburgers and writing up my notes, blocking out characters, transcribing my tapes through a Walkman, and drinking. I'd become friendly with a waitress who in turn was friendly with the three-lakes crowd and on my last night she invited me to a dock party.

"It's to show support for Brendan."

She jumped on the back of my bike and we were off. The party was held at an estate I'd photographed from a rented plane earlier in the week. The boathouse was bigger than most city houses and the property was larger than most city blocks. The dock was a pattern of eight piers, arranged geometrically to both please the eye and to allow more than two dozen boats to park comfortably. The waitress and I got separated almost immediately by the flowing crowds. Arriving already drunk, I wandered into the main house, was handed a drink, and carried it down to the boathouse where a live band was performing on the upper porch, people were dancing, and there were some naked folk in a hot tub. I caught a glimpse of Brendan the Donzi boy. He was surrounded by all manner of tanned well-dressed guys and women with glowing teeth they showed off with glittery menace.

A woman came over to me and rubbed my head. For luck, she said, but didn't say whose. We went around the corner of the boathouse and there was a lineup in front of a patio table where a black man in waiter's garb was portioning out cocaine with the edge of a razor blade, fashioning each portion into a long line. He had a look of disdain for his clients but they didn't notice. The woman had the waiter cut a line on my head and she snorted it.

"Anywhere you want to snort off me?"

We went upstairs and danced, an activity in which I believe, like fighting, enthusiasm is more important than skill. We made two more trips down to the cocaine table and a few more to one of the bars, sucking oysters she drenched in pepper sauce and washing them down with beer. As I got wasted into darkness and depression I wondered if going insane was a rich man's game, a luxury like killing people by accident. Is there anyone who doesn't want to go insane, if only briefly and without penalty? I took the woman—the same woman, I was almost sure—beyond the lights of the boathouse and the noise and fucked her standing up against a tree, listening to the grunts and laughter of other pair-offs around us. Afterwards she said Wow in a voice with no inflection and went away.

My muscles were jumping and unsatisfied. I went up into the boathouse and looked for someone to dance with or to fight with.

A slim blonde woman was sitting very erect on a divan under an open window, the band's music washing over her. Her head bobbed to the double beat. I spotted her right away, she sat with her legs crossed Indian style, wearing a white men's button-down shirt tied at the waist and the sleeves up to her elbows, white and grey silky harem pants, and bare feet. She had a drink in each hand. I watched as just about everybody stopped to touch her on the arm, the shoulder, on the knee or on the neck. It was like she was a talisman. Some sat for a few minutes of serious conversation into her ear; some walked away with tears in their eyes. Others came and gave her drinks: there were a half dozen coloured things in shooter glasses on the table at her elbow. People paused to sit or chat and a lot of the men kissed her on the cheek or the corner of her mouth.

In spite of all the attention, she seemed to be unattached, and I made my way over to her.

"Dance?"

She looked up at me, the 'man chu, the shaved head, the earring. She shook her head. "I can't dance."

"Everybody dances."

"No, I really can't dance," she insisted.

I took her hand. My mitts are huge and meaty; her hands were slim and ghostly. "Come on, I'll show you." I tugged on her hand to get her to her feet, and stepped back, taking her with me, her lack of weight and balance surprising me. She did a face plant onto the floor. People around us froze. I saw the wheelchair at the end of the divan just as a blond guy in rimless glasses flat-handed me in the face, breaking my nose. People were at me. Somewhere on the way out to the parking lot they dropped me into the gravel a few times; I lost my diamond stud and a boot.

I got on my motorcycle with my broken nose and rode home, shifting with my bare foot.

The rich bastards story, as Kent called it, got good play, even though the high profile of the Donzi boy's family kept the magazine's lawyers busy for several days while they filleted out most of the inflammatory statements, took out the details of the new lucrative career of the investigator, and deleted entirely the reconstruction of the amusing greedy-fuck conversation between the accused and his buddy.

I didn't cover the Donzi trial—it was one of eight incidents I wrote in the story—but one of Kent's brainstorms sent me to write about street crime in Brazil. I ate a kilo of meat a day in São Paolo, rode around the neighbourhoods on a little dinky Vespa and was surprised that most of the people spoke Italian. I stayed out of trouble. At odd times I thought about the little blonde in the harem pants who everybody seemed to want to touch.

When I got back I learned the Donzi boy had been acquitted of criminal charges. But civil courts don't demand the same tough rules of evidence and burden of proof, so the victims' families filed a lawsuit. I contacted their lawyer and offered my assistance. He was surprised that I made myself available without a subpoena. He was even more surprised when I let him copy my notes and transcribe my taped interviews.

The family of the Donzi boy settled out of court for an unreported sum—the lawyer said the dead kid's family got a million, the chewed-up kids got one-million-nine.

Kent called me in and fired me. I was grateful enough not to punch him out. I was by then hating the concept of journalism, although I liked the idea of gathering information, meeting lots of interesting folks, and of course the travel. I still did some freelance writing, enough to keep me in play and aware, but less and less as time went by.

In his life my old man left the city twice, both times to fish in Florida, him being a widower, for marlin and hopefully a rich widow. He died when his anchor belt wasn't fastened correctly and he was too drunk or stubborn to let go of the rod, a funny story to picture in your mind and a strong win for the marlin, but less funny when it was your own dad. I'd been to dozens of faraway places, although I never caught a widow or a marlin. I was in my late thirties, had been a three-for-a-quarter-and-one-for-a dime booth operator in the carney, a short-order cook, a doorman, a chop-man in a midnight motorcycle shop, a running dummy for much better boxers to build their confidence upon, and a stumbling reporter. I was really no better off than my old man, for all of it. I was alone and looking for that one piece of salvage that I could turn to gold under my hands.

I had some dough and was ready to take a year off when the silvery Cornelius Fox, the lawyer for the lawsuit against the Donzis, called up and told me he owed me one and why didn't we start with a big honking steak dinner?

3

The bomb was the lead item on the first newscast. I punched a tape into the recorder, brought my clothes into the living room, and dressed in front of the television. Three people, two females and a male, all seventeen, were in custody and couldn't be identified under the Youth Justice Act. They'd been caught just after dark the day before outside the legislature, and a homemade bomb had been seized. The detective in charge of the case said he couldn't say much, again citing the Youth Act, but he said the bomb was armed, it was the real McCoy, capable of causing massive destruction and the potential loss of human life. He said detectives had seized videotapes from the surveillance cameras around the legislature. He said the investigation was continuing and couldn't say if other suspects were being sought. He praised the alertness of Queen's Park security for preventing what he called a catastrophic event. Behind all this chatter, video showed the Park being sealed off, the bomb squad cautiously approaching the east side of the building, where the premier made his daily entrance, and archival footage of previous bombs or bombing attempts in the city. The reporter at the scene, a cool young blonde with a punkish haircut and black-framed glasses, told us sources said those arrested were part of the Black Bloc of anarchists. She recited, again over file footage, the antics and actions of the Black Bloc at anti-globalization rallies, World Bank meetings, United Nations symposia, and other international financial sector meetings where anarchists didn't believe enough action was taken on Third World debt. She breathlessly said it hadn't been ruled out that the bomb had been an attempt at political assassination.

Outside the art gallery I'd told the distraught elderly Carlsons to call Cornelius Fox. A golden run of out-of-court settlements had boosted his profile and he was in great demand. Mr. Carlson asked if we could do an investigation, find out how the police could have made such a mistake.

"We don't do investigations," I carefully told him. "We take on research engagements. You don't need a PI licence to do it, and you can get a lot more things done. Give Cornelius a call tonight, I'll call him tomorrow."

Elodie used the Carlsons' cellular phone to call 52 Division. She didn't call the detective office, where they were too smart to talk, and she didn't call the sergeant's direct line, where they were too indifferent to talk. Instead she called directly into the area foot patrol office and snagged a guy who couldn't walk past a ringing telephone. She said she was calling from the *Sun* and she did the breathless gee-whiz routine of a rookie reporter, just trying to get a leg up on the competition. "We're on deadline, can't you, please, just give me something, anything?" She said the *Star* was way ahead of her, knowing cops hate the *Star*, and the guy relented. She said, "Perfect, perfect. Oh, look, I really owe you, guy."

In point form she told the Carlsons that identities of those arrested hadn't been and wouldn't be released to the press. "They're saying it's a terrorist act, anarchists. The legislature security cameras have them on video. It's a real bomb. Three in custody. Investigation continuing."

Mrs. Carlson began crying and Mr. Carlson began comforting her. Elodie told them not to worry, to talk to the lawyer, and to call us if they needed anything. We went home and I made Elodie a plate of spaghetti with pepper and butter. We went to bed early.

I popped the tape from the VCR and put it beside the coffee maker. The day planner showed I was free until noon when I had a few hours of bodywork escorting a Russian businessman into a luncheon speech to local tycoons and trade officials. The Russian would have his own bodyguards, but they always arrived drunk and got drunker and either crashed into civilian cars or became hopelessly lost. AFB, the security firm I did some work for, did a brisk little trade tripling up driver, body-man, and fixer. This all meant I had to wear a big suit and find sunglasses. The day planner also showed a dozen folks were coming by for drinks that evening.

I bagged a big dark suit, found some sunglasses, and went into the bedroom to poke the bear. I rubbed at her shoulder. I told her the coffee was ready to go. "I'm going out a while."

She was dozy; mornings were an irritating time and I seldom stayed in the apartment while she was waking up. Her daily regimen of various drugs—Valiums, muscle relaxants, all manner of others necessary to orderly bodily functions—seemed to catch up with her during sleeping hours, making her disoriented and rude. She made a pissed off noise and jerked away, going instantly back to sleep. I took her car keys and went out.

The all-news radio station led their newscast with the bomb at the legislature. Another excited lady read the story and she too had clearly watched the early TV stuff: she had nothing new to report and also referred to the source's comments about political assassination. Radio news is about ninety-nine percent rip-'n'-read, a depressing state of affairs for the journalists I'd met who began their careers behind a microphone. Radio was first with the weather and last with the news.

Elodie's car had hand controls—push down to accelerate and push away for braking. But the foot pedals still operated. I liked the Intrepid, a good, solid, quick car. Elodie wanted a Mercedes convertible and had a little fund tucked away where she stashed money every time we took off an engagement. Our business ran on two revenue streams: corporate clients that required invoices and meticulous accounting, and the dark side—mostly my side of the business—that generated no paperwork at all, particularly reports, invoices, or cheques. Jobs we did for lawyers were protected by work-product privilege and paid for as research. Elodie's side of the business had increasingly leaned towards due diligence, usually researching one side or the other in business deals, a lot of it in mergers and acquisitions. The other stuff was called ratfucking and covered a range of problems people had that required dodgy methods and more muscle than brain. I suspected much of the work we'd do on the bombing engagement, if we were hired, would fall into this category.

I travelled up through the city on surface roads, stopping for a sinker and a coffee at a Tim Hortons. There were newspapers scattered on the counter and while I waited I found the bomb story on the front page of all of them. Not one had a photograph of the arrestees. On the highway I flicked radio news back on but there was nothing new in their report. At Markham Road I went north, watching for the street the

Gone Wong had been stopped on. There was an unmarked police car with a crash bar on the front and emergency lights in the rear deck just east of Markham Road and he had a woman stopped. A half dozen kids made faces in the windows of her van. I looped the block and found a corner to hide behind that had to be on Mr. Wong's approach to his daily traffic ticket.

I ate my doughnut and sipped at my coffee, periodically hitting the wipers to erase the mist. Surveillance wasn't my favourite activity, but I'd done a lot of it and seldom got bored. This morning I watched the momsers who walked their kids to school, checking off the ones I'd bang if I had the chance. Would, would, would, wouldn't, would, would, absolutely, absolutely, absolutely not, not even at gunpoint. Of course in reality I wouldn't in any of the cases; someone once said the fucking you get isn't worth the fucking you get.

With Elodie I was happy, as happy as I'd ever been, and for a change I wasn't wondering if I could be happier. This was a delicate balance for me. I never lost sight of the fact that between me now and me as a stove tipper was a very thin margin, one that could evaporate easily.

"David, you're a rich guy, and that's okay," I'd once told Elodie's brother. "But rich guys can afford to make a mistake or two. Lots of 'em, in fact. But I can't. There's no cushion in most people's lives. A mistake that might seem minor to you, and solvable, can move an entire life just an inch or so and that inch is as critical as balance. I'm like an alcoholic in more ways than one: I can't make just one mistake, I gotta make 'em all. Elodie's the mistake I can't make. I know it, she knows it. So I can't fuck around, I can't call her a fucking twat and come home with a mink coat by way of apology and get away with it. You can. So, I have to be successful in all things big and small."

He laughed. "Fuck you, Charlie. No one wears mink anymore."

The Gone Wong's BMW 5 Series, sure enough, rolled the stop sign. The windows were tinted and I couldn't see inside. The traffic cop had another momser van full of kids stopped and the Beemer rolled the next stop sign, too. We went out onto Markham Road, south to the highway. The Beemer boomed up the ramp, blending quickly and efficiently into the eastbound traffic. It took me four cars before I could get into the traffic stream. Cars were throwing up haze, but the drizzle had stopped. I put a baseball cap on my head, opened the window and stuck my arm out, riding the left-hand broken white line to keep his left rear in sight.

Moving surveillance is very difficult to do, whether traffic's heavy or not. The Intrepid, in downtown conditions, can easily follow a Beemer, wherever it's going. The trick isn't just to stay behind—or in front, taking the target by the nose—but to try to anticipate what the target vehicle is going to do before it does it. Most people do a shoulder check, whether they signal their intention or not, or they hunch a little forward to look into the left-hand mirror to see if the lane is clear. People who ride with their arm across the top of the passenger seat will take it down when they're ready to make a lane change, a turn, or an exit. With the Beemer's tinted windows I couldn't tell, so I had to read the car.

At the first left-hand exit onto the express lanes the Beemer drifted a little, the left-hand wheels touching the white line. I signalled and bullied my way into that lane, left a cushion and waited for the Beemer to get in front of me. The express lanes came to a predictable halt and I noted the tag number and the lease company's name on the licence frame. Traffic picked up—it seemed to have stopped for no reason at all—and we crossed the top of the city. At Avenue Road we left the highway and headed south. After a few minutes the Beemer made a left up a side street and another left behind a block of buildings, crawling along looking for a parking spot. Frustrated, the Beemer jumped up to speed, rounded the block and cruised the metered street parking. It found one on the west side and backed in neatly. I drove on by, turning into the next side street. I changed my baseball cap for no hat at all, took a plastic grocery bag with a camera in it from behind the front seat, and headed out Avenue Road.

A Chinese man was standing at a meter peering nearsightedly at the writing on it, trying to determine if he had to pay and how much. He was five-five, stocky, wearing a black business suit, white shirt, and a tie knotted so the end came five inches above his belt buckle. I stepped into a doorway, leaned the long lens out and photographed him; I photographed the car, and him and the car in the same frame. He fed coins into the machine, took his stub and put it on his dash. He looked at his watch, crossed through the Avenue Road traffic, diagonally, and went to a doorway beside a reuse clothing store. He used a key to open the door and went inside. There were two floors of commercial offices above the reuse store; a few minutes after he went in I watched him open the venetian blinds on the second floor. A sign in that window said Star-Asia Investment Services. When he stepped away from the window I photographed the sign and walked back to the Intrepid, writing everything down in the notebook.

The dash-mounted cellular phone was ringing. I let it ring, took binoculars from the trunk, and drove around the block and found a place where I'd have a clear view of the doorway.

The phone rang again.

"Hey, stud, where you at?"

"If I told you I was sitting on Mr. Gone Wong, would you take me out for Vietnamese food tonight?"

"You got him?"

"Well, I got his car and I got a Chinaman, fits the description." I told her where I was and gave her the company name and the address so she could start a work-up.

"If this is him, Charlie, you could be in for a night of forbidden dee-lights."

"I'd rather have spring rolls and mystery meat soup."

"You say that now."

The mailman did the block just before noon, just as I was about to leave for the body job. He paused at the doorway beside the reuse and stepped in. When he continued on his rounds I crossed the road and found four black tin mailboxes with fliptops. I checked the mail for Unit 2 and Unit 3. Unit 3 was Star Asia. I took everything from the box, then mixed up the other mail and got most of it back into the wrong boxes. If Gone Wong was expecting anything particular that day, he might believe it went awry in one of the other offices. I went back to the car.

The body job was at the downtown hotel near City Hall. I found a parking lot and took the suit bag from the back seat. I struggled out of my working clothes and into the suit. The suit was double-breasted: the firm liked their bodymen wide and massive, and if it looked like you were wearing a bulletproof vest under it, all the happier was the client, who figured he was getting his money's worth of firepower. I made a suitably big knot in my necktie. I balled my morning clothes and tossed them into the trunk on top of a dozen boxes of variously coloured garbage bags, a box of hats, and several cheap jackets of different colours.

There was a one-hour photo shop in the hotel. I dropped in at the Gone Wong film and went to meet Jerry Hamer in the lobby. He straightened my knot and put a small gold star-shaped pin into my lapel, the identifier that let the bodymen know whose side I was on if things began to go sideways.

"Let's go in the coffee shop. We've got a booth, I'm gonna ear you up."

"Is there a credible threat?"

"Charlie, there's credible money. We conducted a threat assessment and they went for it. We're giving them the secret service package."

The secret service package gave the client a looming mass of alert impassive meat, dark sunglasses, and a flesh-coloured earpiece at the end of a coiled wire that disappeared into your collar and hooked into a radio unit. The microphone was fitted up the sleeve. Bodywork is fairly simple: watch hands instead of faces, get rubbies and bums away from the body, and stand with your weight balanced evenly on both feet. You constantly keep your head moving but you don't rock onto your heels and toes, don't blue sky every time a good-looking woman comes by. If the client thinks you're keeping your jacket buttoned up because you've got a vest and shoulder rig, that's okay.

Two of Jerry's guys were sitting in the booth drinking coffee. Both were eared up, both wore double-breasted suits, and both had the gold pin in the lapel. I slid in and Jerry slid in after me, blocking his hands as they rapidly put a unit in my belt, ran the coil up behind my left shoulder under the coat, and pulled the ear plug through to reach my left ear. He clipped a small microphone to the underside of my shirt-cuff.

"It's simple," he said as he fit me up. "He's coming up in front in a three-car convoy, he'll be in the second car. Tommy, you get by the right rear door, open it and get him out, stay on his right; Bobby, you crowd his left; Charlie, you look at windows and rooftops. His guys'll make a security box back and front. He's into the building and I'll take the lead. We're going to the right through the corner of the lobby and onto the escalator and one level down to the ballroom. I got two guys at the escalator, one at the top and one at the bottom. They'll fall in as he passes. Follow the front man, he knows the entrance and approach to the podium. There's another guy at the podium keeping it secure. The room's been swept. Crowd size, about a hundred. Nearest exit from the podium is behind to the speaker's left. The escalator guys'll man that side of the podium and get him out if necessary. Tommy and Bobby'll be in front of the podium, facing out. Charlie, you lean at the back. The body's guys will fall back while he's in the building, but he's their responsibility once he's in the car."

Bobby, an ex-city cop who'd worked VIP security, asked, "Should we be wanding the people coming in?"

"I thought about it, but with that many it'd take hours. And piss them off, besides. There'll be a wand by each door in case something looks really shitty and you have to wand 'em down, but, my choice? Fuck it. Anybody goes for this guy, it's going to be a bomber. Last year they put a device under his car in Moscow and blew up his wife and his driver. Plus, putting up the front today'll show the people he's a straight guy and takes his business seriously. He's a player, risking his life to bring outside investment into Eastern Europe."

I asked, "And after he's finished speaking?"

"We run the movie backwards, except he'll leave the opposite way off the podium. Each of you guys does the same thing as you did when he came in." He thought a moment. "Media. A press release went out about the speech, so there's probably going to be some press people in there. If there's media you can check their credentials, they've been asked to wear them in sight. Anybody without the city police pass is a no-no, unless the organizers vouch."

He looked at his watch. "Showtime."

Except for a persistent bum, who kept stumbling into our security box, the entire thing was predictable. I took out the bum gently, offering him a broken arm or a five-dollar bill, his choice, to leave. I'm a big guy, even when I'm not wearing the big suit, but since being with Elodie I find I'm a lot more easy-going, almost unflappable, friendly, even. The bum took the five and took a hike, holding it to his face and reading it as though it told a secret. Bobby smoothly squared my place in the box until I got back in step and we took the short miserable Russian and his crew of drunks into the ballroom.

His English was rough but serviceable. He spoke about wrestling the economy and indeed his entire country from the hands of criminal entrepreneurs. I kept my head roving the backs of the heads of the packed audience.

Michael Bailey from the *Post* edged into the room late. Before I recognized him, I moved along the wall and checked his Metro Police pass.

"Anybody kill the fat fuck yet?"

"Hey, Michael, he's our fat fuck, okay? A paying fat fuck, in fact. You want to get a seat?"

"I'll stand back here with you. Something goes off, I like to have a lot of beef between me and the shrapnel."

We spoke softly without looking at each other. Michael had covered the adventures of Donzi boy and we'd compared notes. He thought I'd been a bad journalist to give over my notes and tapes to the families' lawyers instead of to him, but he didn't hold it against me. One of the ratfucking services we offered, Elodie and I, was to either leak stuff into the paper or to keep it out. I'd planted stuff with Michael—not wrong information, but information our client wanted out one week instead of the next. Michael didn't really care, one way or another. He had eyes to quit newspapering and write screenplays. And in a town crowded with four dailies and a bunch of freebies, regular lay-offs, and a shrinking pool of advertising money, there was always a Michael around thinking about his future.

"Speaking of bombs," I said, "what was that about last night at the legislature?"

"Black Bloc stuff. Anarchy. Chaos. They just had a presser at headquarters. Public Affairs didn't seem ready for it. Magda the K said she didn't know or couldn't comment twenty-two times. She was pretty guarded. I called the local division and they said all answers would come from the PR chick at the Puzzle Factory. I told them Magda didn't know anything useful and they said, well, tough titty."

Magda Kraznak was an old friend from back in the days before Elodie and I started up. We'd met when Kent assigned me to profile her as the Gloria Steinem of the environmental Left after a front-page newspaper picture showed her being arrested at a landfill site. She looked strong and stunning as two smiling cops carried her through a hole in a fence to a paddywagon. She'd had a business card that said The PR Babe—The Second Oldest Profession. Somehow she wound up doing corporate work, and was later hired to work at the Puzzle Factory by the new police chief in anticipation of a tough fight for a bigger budget. Getting Jack Chu and his law-and-order agenda and his successes into the paper was the K's number one job.

This Black Bloc stuff, I'd've thought, was tailor-made to churn up all manner of new funding, for beefing up the bomb squad and the intelligence unit, and all the equipment that went with it. Crazed anarchists abounding was guaranteed to wake up the sleeping taxpayers, who in turn would wake up their snoozing city councilors, who in turn would wake up the dizzy little guy dozing out his term at City Hall and he'd fork out some emergency funding. I said as much to Michael.

"Beats me, Charlie. I thought the Chinaman would ride this horse 'til it croaked, but ... nothing. So far at least. They're looking for a couple of other people."

"Maybe they'll wrap it all up in one big international conspiracy and get to go ape later."

"Naw. They could go ape twice. Once now and once later when they carry out the well-known double whammy."

I asked if he knew anything about the people arrested. He said there were no names because they were kids, but he didn't know any more than the radio folk had that morning.

The Russian finished his speech to great applause and ovation.

"You know, he had his own wife and chauffeur blown up over there so the government had to support his nutty plans, or be seen as pro-Mafia?" Michael laughed. He was a tall thin guy with a silent laugh and watchful eyes, waiting for something to strike. "If a guy comes running up to him with a gun, Charlie, you want to do the world a huge favour and be tying your shoelace."

When the engagement was finished and the miserable Russian was away in his mini-convoy, Jerry Hamer came up to me on the sidewalk, a white envelope in his hand. I unhooked the radio rig and gave it back. The bum had returned, looking for another five bucks. I shrugged him off. He wandered a few feet away, east, then stood smiling loosely at Jerry. Jerry excused himself for a minute. He walked the other way, west, to where the building is protected by an overhang. The bum followed and both left my sight. A few minutes later Jerry came back and the bum staggered away."You recognize that guy, Charlie?"

"I gave him five bucks on the way in, keep him out of the play."

"That's a job I wouldn't want."

"What, bumming?"

He leaned in close to me and put the white envelope into my pocket. I felt it. It felt like about three hundred bucks in tens and twenties. "He was with the Sisters. Now they got him seconded to Dyas." The Sisters were CSIS, the federal security intelligence folks. Dyas was Dyas Road, the Toronto Police intelligence bunker, where the Funny People worked. In our engagements regarding businessmen from the former Soviet Bloc, Elodie and I had come across numerous instances where the Sisters were clearly shielding and protecting our targets. In one case we'd found an entrepreneur from Moscow was a prime suspect in a murder and one of the Sisters, testifying in camera, made the case go away. The husband, it transpired, was providing the Sisters with information about the movement of black oil money, looted before the 1991 breakup of the USSR.

Bobby came out of the lobby and walked over to us. "I don't know if I'm a bodyguard or an actor in some street theatre." Jerry slipped him an envelope and took his ear rig. "Thanks, boss. You know that guy's guards had guns? They're pretty wound up. I was more worried about one of them going ape than I was about some mad bomber."

The two of them headed for the parking garage.

4

The girl in the film shop said my pictures weren't quite ready, so I went out onto the sidewalk and crossed to Nathan Phillips Square. The mayor's office was on the second floor facing south; in the window hung a blow-up poster from his election campaign: BE A BUDDY FOR BUDDY; THE BUDDY SYSTEM WORKS. I bought an Italian sausage with kraut on a bun and ate it with my face turned up towards the sunshine. A crazy lady had managed to cover herself in cooing pigeons: she stood like a martyr with her arms straight out from her sides and a dozen pigeons perched all over her, one of them sitting on the dirty grey hair of her head, pecking at her scalp. Tourists took photographs. I felt like scratching myself all over. Sightseeing buses idled at the curb. A half dozen demonstrators walked in a tight circle around some kind of an ad hoc shrine of smoking incense. All were men and of Native extraction, they seemed upset with the loony little mayor for something: the smoking shrine would, I assume, allow the Great Spirit to nurture him, or at least seal his mouth shut. A book had been written after Buddy's first term, a quickie paperback that listed and analyzed each of his verbal fuck-ups. My favourite one was when a reporter asked him whether he thought public ignorance or public apathy was the toughest problem facing politicians. He said, "I don't know and I don't give a shit."

There were some cops loitering around the entrance to the hall, each with a plastic plug in his ear, each with his coat buttoned. Up on the walkway surrounding the square, in an area closed to the public, a man with a camera and long lens seemed to be speaking to himself. The curtains on Buddy's office were closed.

I went to get my photographs.

After the night when Elodie's brother busted my nose I didn't see her again for almost a year. The criminal case against Donzi boy eventually went south and the filings in the civil case began. In that year I'd been to Los Angeles to cover the Crips vs. Blood gang wars in south central, had been to Idaho to spend two weeks with the nutty crackpots of the Aryan Nations, and had been back in Italy for the capture of the most-wanted of the most-wanted Mafia bosses. When I got angry about the Donzi case going in the hopper and wandered into Cornelius Fox's office with my evidence, I was pretty much tired out and sick of it all.

"What can you do, Charlie?"

"Not much. Cook eggs, take a punch, ride a bike, and operate a circus concession. I can write a coherent, if boring, sentence. Pretty much without any effort I can make people think I might bang 'em up, and I can make 'em grateful when I don't."

"Perfect."

Two weeks later he invited me out for a steak.

We had a fine dinner at The Ferns and afterwards sat at the

bar with Frank Comeau, who ran a security firm and an employment agency. Strike-breaking was illegal in the province, but that didn't stop Frank from providing employment services and transportation for replacement workers.

"Job's a piece of cake, Charlie," Frank said. "You walk alongside the truck and peel off any assholes that fuck with our people, unless the truck gets 'em first. The way you look, I don't think you'll have trouble."

I told Frank I had a couple of things cooking, but that I'd get back to him. After he left, Fox and I went to the bar; I told him thanks for the intro, but pounding working stiffs into the ground like fence poles wasn't a role I saw for myself. My father, a workingman, would have taken me apart.

"Well, fair enough. You need any dough?"

"Naw. I got a good severance out of the magazine. I'm looking around."

"Frankie's got other work on the go, you know. He's got the security firm, straight stuff, retail and warehouse, and he's got a PI ticket. You ever think about PI-ing?"

A party of six, three and three, came to the host podium at the front of the restaurant. An older couple, a younger couple, a nerd, and a woman in a wheelchair. Elodie was the youngest of the group.

"Who's those?"

Fox knew something about everybody in most places. "Dunno the others too well but the old guy's Colin Gray. I think the old doll is his wife. Mary? Martha? Do-gooder, the arts, the poor, the halt, and the lame. Anyway, I don't know the others too well. Gray runs a foreign exchange thing, mostly offshore, some commercial real estate, some dodgy arbitrage. The girl in the chair's their niece; she survived a bad wreck a few years ago. Her parents burned up. The Grays raised her. Ellen, I think. Maybe Eleanor. The sleek twosome, I don't know, but the guy of the couple is probably Ellen or Eleanor's brother, they look alike. The babe's his wife, dunno her name, but she's at all the swank charity balls. Arm furniture. Dunno who the goofy guy is." He looked at me. "Why, what's up?"

"I interviewed the girl after the Donzi thing. I think the brother's the prick who flat-handed me." I touched my nose.

"If you're gonna bust the place up, Charlie, let me grab my coat and get out of here, okay? Don't make me go under oath and lie for you."

I had no intention of busting the place up. Elodie looked around the room casually. She looked better and happier than when I'd dragged her off the sofa and onto the floor; she looked sober. Her hair was longer, swept up at the sides and held in place with two silver barrettes. She wore a dress of grey silk and had a black silk wrap around her shoulders. Her escort appeared to be a knob with no shoulders and a very long neck and she appeared to be ignoring him.

"You know this Gray guy well enough for us to stop on the way out?"

"If this is going to be trouble, Charlie ..."

"I just want to meet the woman in the chair again. Can you do it?"

He looked at me. They call lawyers land-sharks because of guys like him. "You'll license up with Frankie, work my cases for him?"

"I'll give it a month, we'll see how it goes."

"Deal." He snapped a couple of twenties onto the bar and we climbed off our stools. As we passed the Gray table he acted surprised to see Colin Gray in the restaurant. I loitered while he and Gray stood and schmoozed. I watched Elodie watch me with a faint puzzled recognition. The brother knew right away who I was and moved his chair back a few inches. He wasn't afraid in the slightest, but seemed resigned that if things went really ugly and he was going to the hospital, he wasn't going alone.

After a moment Fox introduced me to Colin Gray, who in turn introduced the folks at his table. The drippy-looking guy had an instantly forgettable name. The brother was David, his wife was Sharon. Colin Gray's wife was indeed Martha. The girl in the wheelchair was Elodie.

I smiled at Elodie and said, "Want to dance?"

She stared at me and her face formed itself into recognition. "You're the guy that screwed Brendan."

"Brendan's a killer. And he can't dance, either."

She kept staring at me without expression and without blinking. "How's your nose?"

"It only hurts when I breathe." Her brother was facing me off, not happy about it but not about to let me straighten his lapels for him, either. He was in some place that took a bit of training to get to. I said to him: "You've got fast hands."

"Tennis, racquetball."

"And, maybe something else?"

He smiled, using half his mouth. "Maybe."

Elodie unlocked her brakes, snapped off her castor locks and wheeled back from the table and said, "Yes."

We went to a gay club up the block where the disc jockey did some wowing, stuttering, and backing up with the turntables, extending the heavy backbeat of the songs out past a half hour. It took a while to get used to spinning Elodie in the wheelchair. The footrest was made of some heavy metal and barked my shins bloody until the pain made me creative. I was jumping about like a monkey every time I spun her. We went through until the last song, the Elton John thing about Norma Jean. The DJ played "Bette Davis Eyes" five times running; the gays got moony and some of them wept. Slow dancing was awkward and I so picked Elodie up in my arms and danced her around the floor. She seemed to weigh barely a few ounces more than her silk dress. She smelled of roses. Her cheek stayed against mine, smooth and dry and hot, and I thought she was holding on for something as dear as life, afraid I'd drop her. Afterwards I wheeled her out to my car and lifted her in. She explained how to deconstruct the wheelchair into pieces and we went to an after-hours place run by an off-duty downtown detective. He clearly thought silk was class and good for the joint and stood us a couple of rounds. I don't remember what Elodie and I talked about, but when the good folks were making their way to work at rush hour, we were sitting over eggs and bacon in the back of Fran's on College Street.

I asked her about the accident. There was probably no way to ask that she hadn't heard before, so I said, "How come you're all fucked up?"

"Car crash. I was thrown out and smashed into a lamppost." She thought about all the angles and details and was deciding how much to tell me. "My parents didn't make it out. They died." I found out much later she'd been driving, drunk, and unbelted, and was thrown from the rolling vehicle while the car carried on into a lamppost down the road. The firefighters arrived at the scene, they extinguished the flames, and the coroner made his obvious pronouncement, all before a cop found a Ferragamo shoe on the roadway, a good thirty-five feet away from the wreck. Elodie later told me she never lost consciousness, beyond the first few seconds, a minute at most, and lay there amazed at the proliferation of stars in the sky. "I found out my size that day, and it wasn't as big as advertised on the container." She shrugged. "You still a writer?"

I told her about being recently fired. "Now," I projected, "I'm a PI, a private investigator." It seemed to matter that she thought I did something beside drag cripples around rooms and get punched out by their friends.

"Cool." She stirred at the eggs on her plate. "What's this about? This dancing and gabbing 'til dawn? Clearly, you got no life, either."

I stared into her eyes. They were cornflower blue and didn't waver. They were like her brother's, ready for anything, hoping for nothing, accommodating, either way. "Can you get past me fucking up your pal, Brendan?"

"Can you get past this?" She gestured at the chair.

"Well," I said, "at least you didn't step on my feet. That's a start."

"Indeed," she smiled, "it be."

Frank Comeau piggybacked me onto his agency licence. Fox, it seemed, had made an awful lot of money and, being disappointed with the rate of return he received on his legitimate investments, had loaned it out to folk who had no credit and no hope of paying it back. This was okay with Fox, as long as the interest kept rolling in; when it didn't he called Frank. Frank had me do a half-dozen skip traces before I figured out that after I found the miscreant debtor, other guys not as nice as me went visiting and powdered jaws. I told Frank, and then Fox, no hard feelings, but I didn't see myself as a finger-man for the busters. We all parted on fine terms.

I was living then in a small flat in the Annex, surrounded by university frat houses and a couple of places that rented short term to speed freaks and old hippies. Most nights I'd carry both Elodie and the wheelchair together up to my second-floor rooms and we'd neck like kids and watch videos.

She said one night: "Hey, how do you make love to a paraplegic?"

"Carefully?"

"I'm busted but I ain't broken." She laughed. "Quickly is how you do it, Charlie. While you still got a shot."

It was awkward, an affair of creams and condoms and positioning. She clung to my neck and I clung to her. She was tiny and easy to move around, but her legs didn't work and my years of learning creative stunts for the woman I'd finally end up with was wasted, like an opera singer who got a job in a school for the deaf. Afterward I laughed and she laughed with me. "Cool, eh?"

"Well, I'm glad you came," I said.

"I did?"

"Absolutely. After all, El, I used to work in the circus. I ..." I said, "could make the hair stand up on the fat lady's back."

Easing into knowing each other was difficult. But she was direct and often humorous. We agreed that when we wanted to know something, we'd ask outright and not be shy.

"Charlie," she said one night. "You got any money?"

"Sure. I could buy and sell the average household cat, not even dent my bank account. You?"

"Rolling in dough. The Grays invented money. Somehow it all passes through the family. We let other people use it for a while, but eventually we have to take it back from them before they get used to having it."

"Elodie," I said one night, "what do you do all day?"

"Nothing. I do some painting. I play some basketball, swim at some club or other."

"How do you do that? Not painting or basketball or swimming, but nothing? You ever think about, like, working?"

"You're a very funny fellow, Charlie."

One night she touched her fingers to the bumps in my face bones and the said, "Hey, Charlie. How'd you get to look like that?"

We moved in together a few weeks after our all-nighter. She told me about the boyfriend who bailed out while she was working her way through rehab, learning to wheel uphill, how she was dumped out of her chair and had to right it and get herself back into it. She was a bad patient, cursing out the nurses and physiotherapists, smoking in her washroom.

"It wasn't supposed to be this way for me," she said in bed one night in her house in The Beach. "I was supposed to marry a stock jockey, be a trophy wife, and fill my time doing good works to keep me too busy to fuck the pool guy or the gardener. I was to be married to Somebody the Third, get a new Mercedes every year or so, and keep myself presentable by working out every day at the Club. If we divorced, my pre-nup would take him to the cleaners—and the Grays own the cleaners. If we stayed together, we'd have perfect little kids doing perfect little things at a perfect little school. But I had to lose a shoe and after that, it was goodbye, Charlie." She reached out to stroke me. "Not literally of course, Charlie."

She told me her brother thought I was a goon. "He said you're the kind of guy that busts other people's legs."

"Well," I said airily, "it's a job. One of us has to work."

She laboriously turned herself to face me. "My uncle Colin said last night a guy conned him out of some money. Think you could find the guy? Get the Gray money back before the guy gets used to having it, thinking it's his?"

And we were in business.

5

I picked up the photographs from the girl at the photo shop, ransomed the car from the lot, and went home. Through the telescope I could see yellow police tape up the side of the legislature; live-eye crews were out with their satellite dishes, waiting to do stand-ups for the six o'clock news. Elodie had set a grey stone buffet table with a white and red cloth, constructed a Zen-ish centrepiece of sand, pebbles, dry grasses, and mixed flowers. A hired-for-the-day woman was arranging a bar at the south end of the terrace. The hired lady took over all the arrangements while Elodie and I sat at the north end. I had a beer and Elodie sipped at a glass of white wine.

"A day," she said, "from hell."

"What, you chip a nail?"

The Carlsons had called several times for her, she told me, and Fox had called twice for me. "The Carlsons are freaking out. Fox made a couple of calls and said the cops told him they have the whole thing—faces, masking up, the bomb, the arming—all on videotape. Little Miss Carlson is laughing and joking on the tape, Fox said the cops said. Fox says this might be a loser, but either way there's long money in it. That's what he said, actually it was long dough. Give him a call." She looked at me critically. "You wearing that tonight? You look like a bouncer at a cemetery."

I waved my hand. "I have," I announced, "been guarding the body. Economic ventures between the two worlds, ventures that will join all in furthering the prosperity, democracy, and security of mankind, both locally and globally. Our brothers in the former Soviet Union have the vast resources, the able manpower, the iron will. But all we need, comrade, is the competent investment of our wealthy and envied brothers in democracy. Then we all march towards paradise. Arm in arm."

"You actually listened?"

"Couldn't help it. I couldn't wear my shades inside, so I couldn't doze. I had only Michael from the *Post* to talk to. Michael thinks the cops weren't ready for the Black Block arrests, they hadn't teed up the K, she wasn't ready to answer questions. And the Big Chu was nowhere to be found."

"Tell me first about the missing wily Wong."

"Well, I'd need another beer to get into that story. But, I must say, it was sterling detective work. If I was a detective."

She stared at me until I went to get my own goddamn beer. I brought back the photographs and the mail I'd collected. "Send the client one without the car's licence and without the name of the company." If it was indeed the right Wong we'd be paid for finding him, plus we could ten-percent some money for arranging an asset recovery firm to slap an injunction on his bank accounts. I didn't want the client jumping the gun and getting stupid and greedy and doing it himself.

Most engagements came in phases. Phase One was basic open-source information—Internet, media, public filings, land titles, motor vehicles, maybe a single pass at the target's residence. We pulled it all together and dressed it up and Elodie analyzed it into what looked like an intelligence report, citing "sources." It was a basic package that cost a few hundred bucks and really only took an hour or two. Phase Two was a little more detailed: we worked bank sources, police sources, international media, and court filings, made some phone calls, and maybe did a little surveillance, which we called visual research so it wouldn't appear we were working as private investigators, unlicensed. Phase Three was the lucrative but more edgy ratfucking, where it got complicated and had to be tailored to the client's needs. Phase Three was purely results-oriented and generated no paperwork. An unsuccessful Phase Three engagement could eat up all the profits in One and Two. Phase Three could be expensive to the client, but the benefit to the client was that if it wasn't successful there was no cost. A lot of victims of fraud have a choice: they can go to the cops and see the perpetrator in jail, or they can get their money back. Most, needless to say, want the dough.

Elodie chose a photograph and went inside to scan it over to her client. I watched the day-hire lady at the other end of the terrace. She didn't exactly wear a uniform—uniformed help was déclassé, I'd been informed—but she wore a starched white blouse, a black pleated skirt, and sensible shoes. She was setting out round crystal and silver bowls that would hold ice to keep the oysters and shrimp cold. She reminded me a bit of my mother, who'd done clean-up work for cash, swiping the odd small object from the customer's house that she would wrap up at Christmas and give me. Between her income and the old man's rag-and-bone business we were almost middle class, maybe at the bottom of it. It was important to both of them that I go to school, that my clothes were clean, and, particularly to the old man, that I didn't take shit from anybody. There was, I recalled, much shit to be had when your schoolmates recognized your old man from his rusted beaten-up old pickup truck, doing his rounds in their neighbourhood on garbage day. He used to tell me, "You got nothing to be ashamed of, Charlie. I work like everybody else. Everybody needs somebody to look down on, and you shouldn't worry about it, just don't do it yourself."

But I was ashamed. I was the rag-and-bone boy. My schoolmates would pile my desk with old smelly tin cans, stuff dead fish into my coat in the cloakroom, and comment on my clothing, saying they didn't mind me having it because their mother threw it out only after it turned raggy, or the cat pissed on it, or it didn't fit them anyway.

I didn't feel comfortable with the day lady, which amused Elodie no end. The first time she had someone in for a cocktail party—forty, I think, of her closest friends—I had picked up a platter of shrimp and carried it to the buffet.

"What are you doing, stud?"

"That's a big platter. She's a little woman. Helping out."

"Charlie, you don't help out the help." As though explaining the economics of the world to a child, she said, "It works like this: I give her money, she does the work. She takes the money and feeds herself and her family. If afterwards there's a little left, she can save it and thereby invest in the economy, or she can spend it, also investing in the economy. A good economy makes jobs. Jobs make money. People spend it and the Grays invest in the companies that accumulate it. And around we go."

"And," I said, "the money comes back to the Grays."

"And why is that, Charlie, my sweet?"

"Because it belongs to the Grays, my love."

"It does, doesn't it, Charlie? All of it."

"Absolutely. Every penny."

"Perfect. Put down the shrimp and I'll tell her to make us cocktails."

I should have hated Elodie and the Grays and felt like I was betraying my parents but I didn't. I actually quite liked them, although I could never get a read on how they felt about me. They were, except for the brother, exceedingly polite. There was a sister, Agnes, who I'd never met: she was on an around-the-world trip and the two times she came home I was out of town myself. Agnes, I'd been told, was a ferocious big sister in the best sense of the word and would, should we wind up within stabbing distance of each other, strip me to the bone and then eat me. "Ag's like you, Charlie. Except tough and better looking," her brother, David, said one night when we were drunk and getting to know each other.

There was another side to the clan, one I didn't pick up on right away. Rich people are generous for three reasons: taxes, guilt, and empathy. The Grays poured money into all manner of causes and it took me a while to figure out why. I asked David once why he funded weekly dinners for the families in the projects. He looked embarrassed a moment, then laughed and said, "If we don't feed the fuckers they'll die in the streets and we might run over 'em. You ever try to get the alignment fixed on a Mercedes? Cheaper this way. Plus we wouldn't have a work force." He made a perpetual circle with his hands and smiled sadly. "Did El tell you about how the money works?"

I picked up Mr. Wong's mail. Six business-sized envelopes, all addressed to Mr. Denton Wong, President, Star Asia Limited. Each contained a reply letter, formally confirming investment in Star Asia's International Development Fund. Each letter said a ten percent refundable "good-faith" fee—the ten percent ranged from $40,000 to $80,000—would be wire transferred to Denton Wong's bank upon the signing of contracts. Each sender looked forward to a prosperous long-term relationship. Mr. Wong didn't care about the other ninety percent of the money he'd never get. The advance fee was what he was after and he was satisfied with that. I took my pad out of my jacket and wrote down the names of the investors. Elodie could contact them and, for a fee, show them the error of their ways. Worst case was that they would go ahead anyway and that would provide a new pool of clients for us.

Elodie wheeled back onto the terrace and poured herself another wine. "He emailed back: bingo. We got the right Wong."

"How does the client want to proceed?"

"He'll let us know. He wants the final report tomorrow and he'll get back." She held up her wine glass and toasted against my beer bottle. "We're pretty good, Charlie. How'd we do it?"

"Ah ha. I tell you my secret ways and you'll dump me for a guy in a blazer and a mouth full of round vowels. I'm protecting my turf, toots." I showed her Mr. Wong's mail and tore off the page in my notebook with the names of the fresh victims. We chatted about how to approach them, then decided to wait to see what our client's next step would be. At the beginning of most research engagements we signed confidentiality agreements that we wouldn't divulge or act upon any information we gathered on behalf of the client. Elodie would have to finesse her client before we could proceed.

At six o'clock I put on the news and we flipped back and forth and watched the day's developments on the anarchist front. Nothing new, which was pretty newsworthy in itself. The three accused had been held overnight and had appeared in young offenders' court, all ordered held in custody pending reports. Detectives cited the Youth Act as a reason for not answering any questions. The Big Chu was strangely absent, having found a crime prevention symposium to attend out of town. Magda the K was shown at a podium, pondering questions and appearing frustrated at the restraints placed upon her by the youth law: Gee I'd really like to alert the public but our hands are tied by that bastard law.

The stand-up reporters too were clearly frustrated at not being able to push this particular rock up the hill; one cited sources who, she said, indicated the bomb was one of several as the Black Bloc geared up for an offensive against the government. There would be, she said her sources said, further developments and all city police officers were on round-the-clock standby. According to her sources. Days off for the riot squad, the bomb squad, and the intelligence bureau had been cancelled. According to her sources. Area hospitals were on alert. According to her sources. Department of Defence explosive experts were available, at a moment's notice, from the federal government. I recognized the magic carpet she was riding, having woven a few of them myself.

I told Elodie I was taking a power nap and asked what the dress was for the evening. She said khakis and button-down were fine, a blazer if I felt dashing. She said we could have sandwiches before the guests arrived. She didn't mention my muchly desired Vietnamese feast—or whatever else she had in mind.

I'd call Fox when I woke up. The day-lady was gently rattling crockery and china outside the sliding doors of the bedroom. She was humming a soft tune I didn't recognize, but thought I'd once sung it to my daughters when they were babies.

My daughters.

The Black Bloc. The anarchists. Bombs and ski masks.

I called out to Elodie to remind me to call my kids.

It got dark a little earlier than the week before, but the warm weather held. There was no movement of air and the sheltered terrace was ideal for entertaining. The cityscape was filling with shadows, at first a faint grey that was mostly pollution and exhaust, then a gradient that could only end in blackness. I stood at one point speaking to a tall slim woman wearing her almost-best jewellery; she faced me and listened with a surrealistic gentle interest, I think, as I explained what I liked about Hong Kong, from whence she and her husband had just returned from something she called a buying trip. I mentioned a restaurant in Kowloon, on Austin Road, and she looked at me blankly and asked where was Kowloon. I felt my eyes glaze over. I faced her, glancing over her shoulder out over the town she owned and didn't know, the town I knew but couldn't own.

For some reason it was important to Elodie that I behave and fit in. Some of the guests were people who'd been condescending to her in the years after the accident, folks who gave her pep talks but, she could see, didn't expect much. A rich shut-in surrounded by all that the Gray money could provide. Nurses, attendants, fitness trainers. They talked about character as if they'd patented it and lent it out for short periods of time to the needy, about strengths they knew she had, how the Gray genetics would overcome this horrible adversity. Money helped, sure, they said, but without character, well ... Elodie had told me she was never expected to leave the Gray houses, never expected to live alone, never have man or child. Living with me, having a job, travelling, all this was seen as either a betrayal of their goodness or an affirmation of their faith. Judgments abounded, Elodie said, as if it all had nothing to do with her and everything to do with the unselfish efforts made to make her, now a victim, fit into their expectations.

"I'm their broken doll," she'd said one night. Elodie wasn't perfect; she cried with self-pity sometimes. "Normally they'd throw it out and get another one, but I'm a Gray doll and no matter how bent or cracked, they can't. So they had these expectations that I'd be in the doll hospital they built, live in the doll world they created, and be an example of how strong they all were. Then came Charlie, eh?" She was drunk that night, self-pitying and drunk, a potent cocktail. Bitterly, she said, "Oh, Charlie, they must hate you."

She said Colin Gray and her aunt handled the accident the best, swinging immediately into making the entire Gray world accessible by ramps and elevators and retrofitting. Martha, the aunt, pushed Elodie to let go of the world before, to look ahead, to fashion the new and different life she was to have. "I became the Gray family cause. When I needed them I didn't know it, but they did, and they were there."

According to Elodie, Uncle Colin was a closed man who said nothing of his feelings, who seemed to go out of his way to convince people he didn't have any, but he made the correct moves without comment, instinctively as he did in finance. "My uncle had to examine himself for heart and emotion. I think he might have found both, but he didn't recognize them. If he did he never mentioned this discovery. But he knew what to do, and how to do it, even if he couldn't say why. He just did it because something, something other than his heart, maybe a basic goodness, made him do it."

She loved her relatives but took childish delight in dragging me to family affairs, to the cottage estates, the condominiums, weddings, the Christmases, the family trips to the Caribbean. "They don't know the world, Charlie, but we're gonna show 'em, eh? We're going to introduce a little Charlie into their lives."

During the party I watched Elodie work the crowd. When I could I passed behind her wheelchair and touched my fingers to her neck, just below where her hair was upswept. She wore ruby earrings she'd had made when she flew to meet me in Bangkok after I'd disengaged a client's activist daughter from the smiling thugs in Burma. I brought the stones out under my tongue. Gold and skill are rampant and excellent in Bangkok. Elodie found a Chinese jeweller who first tried to buy the rubies—they were perfect, he said; a lucky accident of my drunken shopping at the Scott Market—then settled for overcharging her for the craftsmanship. The Grays were certain I was some kind of fool, having Elodie fly across the world by herself—allowing her to do it, they said, as if anyone could permit or force Elodie to do or not do anything. Her brother had suddenly found some business he had to do in Thailand. Her aunt said there was a divine exhibition of Burmese lacquerware she just had to see; it too was in Bangkok. A clerk from one of Colin Gray's commercial real estate firms had to, coincidentally, be in Bangkok that week, and why didn't he accompany Elodie through the plane changes at Chicago and Tokyo?

In the end she told them, Thanks, but no, with some great degree of firmness. But what, they said, if that Charlie person doesn't meet you at the airport when you arrive? Then, she said, I'll have myself an adventure; maybe I'll get laid. She wore the earrings as reminders.

The day-lady, who was assisted in her endeavours by a young man in a white shirt and black pleated pants, moved through the terrace constantly with trays of nibblies. The two might as well have been invisible people, and the platters floating unattended. I was famished and took several items from each platter. Elodie looked around for me, caught my eye, and waved me over to meet the young couple she was chatting with.

The woman was clearly in some distress, but held herself together tightly by her social graces. Her facial features told me what Elodie wanted to tell me: this was a Carlson woman. She had her grandmother's soft eyes and her grandfather's broad, aggressive forehead. With her was, it turned out, her husband. They were so similar I thought he was related by blood, not marriage. Both were curly blond, in their late twenties, and a Caribbean brush had painted them the same expensive tan. Both were in chairs to bring themselves down to Elodie's eye line.

"Charlie, this is Janine and Ted Appleby. You met Janine's grandparents last night at the art gallery, the Carlsons. Janine's little sister, Corolla, is the one with the ... problem."

They both stood and I shook their hands. I never know what to say when it comes to sympathy, beyond, I guess, Shit happens. "I'm sure she'll be fine," I said, thinking the old line: If you want sympathy, you find it in the dictionary between shit and syphilis.

Janine Carlson-Appleby asked if I'd heard anything. Before I could answer, Ted Appleby said the family had hired a tiger lawyer to sue the cops, the security at the legislature, the media, and anyone else who was within pissing distance of the whole thing.

I was careful. Something about him reminded me of the Donzi boy. "Well, I understand there's some evidence that doesn't look too good for her."

Ted was aggressive. "What evidence? It's a frame-up. Those, those fucking cops and their ..." He lost speech and his brown tan went an interestingly dangerous red. He immediately apologized; people around us were looking. He apologized again to each of them. "It isn't right."

Elodie patted his arm. "It'll be alright, Teddy." As if she didn't already know, she said, "Charlie, what evidence?"

"Well, it's rumour so far, but apparently there were surveillance cameras on them as soon as they approached the building. Good clear pictures of them all, with and without masks." I shrugged. "Tough to beat video with a jury."

Ted stared at me a moment, then got up and stalked off.

Elodie said Janine wanted to hire us, to keep an eye on the criminal case and assist the lawyer if we could. She held Janine's hand. "I told her I couldn't charge her for it. She's almost family."

"No charge?" I drank most of Elodie's glass of wine at a shot. She was watching me, waiting. I asked, "Elodie, when your spaceship took off from Jupiter this morning, did you have enough fuel to get all that duty-free home?"

6

I had an early perimeter sweep the next day and left the party before it broke up. I had a wine headache and drank a half-quart of water before closing the terrace doors most of the way and climbing under a duvet. As I drifted in and out of an almost-sleep I heard Elodie making nice goodbyes and thanking everyone for coming, promising to keep in touch. There was a brief verbal exchange and I heard Ted say he was going to take a cab home. He gave his wife the car keys. I awoke briefly when the clock said midnight and could hear Elodie and Janine still out there, talking in low voices.

Elodie, slurring her words a little, said, "He's a good guy. He'll do the right thing."

"He's scary. He even scares Ted, and Ted scares everybody."

"My Charlie's a pussycat. I can take care of him, don't you worry about him."

I dozed with a secret smile on my face and I awoke again when a wine bottle cracked against crystal and crystal hit the flagstones in shatters and laughter. I slipped out of bed and moved so I could see the terrace through the curtains. Janine Carlson-Appleby was sitting on the terrace floor beside Elodie, who had either climbed or fallen from her wheelchair. It was just past two thirty in the morning.

I went into the kitchen in my boxer shorts and a T-shirt. I took a cold beer from the fridge. Elodie called my name, a soft question, and I called hers in answer.

"My sweet," she said gaily. "We're out of wine."

I found an opened bottle of something white and took it out. "Last call, ladies."

"Charlie," Elodie babbled. "You're such a grown-up guy."

Janine Carlson-Appleby was, if possible, even more shit-faced than Elodie. "You're a guy, Charlie. Can I call you ... Chuck?"

"Only if you can fly five stories." I poured them each a temperate measure and went inside to make up the guest room. When I came out they were leaning on each other and Elodie was pouring for both of them. There was a pre-dawn chill in the air; above them the downtown lights in the towers were mostly lit, silvered by a soft fog. Birds, I knew, flew into those windows and killed themselves, thinking they were flying into a promising new sunrise.

Out on the terrace I told the ladies to drink up. I picked up Elodie and sat her in her wheelchair and helped Janine Carlson-Appleby to her feet. Janine leaned on me as I steered Elodie into the apartment and into our bedroom. I took Janine to the guest room, lit the bathroom light, and wished her goodnight.

She put a finger to her lips and beckoned me closer. "Elodie said you're a good guy, Chuck." She planted a sloppy kiss on my scalp. "She said you can help my sister."

"I'll leave the coffee ready to go in the kitchen. Just punch the button. Ibuprofens and ice water by your bed."

"She says you're her rag-and-bone man." She was quite beautiful and drunk. She slurred, "Whatzzat mean? *Ragznbones*?"

She was asleep or unconscious before I turned out the light. I policed up the terrace and found a half-package of cigarettes and a disposable lighter. It was almost three o'clock and my perimeter sweep had to be done before dawn. I decided to stay up and smoke cigarettes and enjoy the views of the city no one, not me and not them, would ever really own. Behind me, after a while, the bathroom light went out and I heard Elodie transfer from her chair into our bed. She called my name softly and when I answered she didn't answer back.

At four o'clock I finished smoking too many of the cigarettes and crept into the bedroom for some work clothes. She was passed out across the bed. I found some plastic gloves in the kitchen and hunted up her keys. I took our household trash, tied the bag into a knot and locked the door behind me.

A perimeter sweep is a fancy name for stealing garbage. It looks a lot better on an invoice and manages to distance the client from the act. My weekly target was north of the city, in Woodbridge. With little traffic it took me less than forty minutes to get to the target's house. I was a little disappointed with the quickness of the drive: I like the radio of the middle of the night and the pre-dawn hours, with the old forgotten songs and the slightly crazy call-in listeners who grapple with issues and beliefs when everyone else is sleeping.

The target was a fellow who had left his previous employer and started his own software business using work product he designed while under contract to our client. He lived in a split-level light brick place with an attached three-car garage. The house was in a cul de sac so I drove past the house quietly and had a peek and came out again.

People who live in areas with significant prowling wildlife tend to use locking plastic containers if they put the garbage out at night. When they do it on their way to work they usually use garbage bags. My target tended to sleep late, past pick-up time, so he put the trash out before going to bed. I drove around the corner, pausing to let a fat raccoon waddle across the street, then popped the trunk and filled a deep green garbage bag with our kitchen waste. I stuffed another bag with newspapers. I sat listening to the end of a sweet Ricky Lee Jones song and wished I had some cigarettes. Listening to Ricky Lee Jones in blue darkness and not smoking or drinking was like wearing a condom when you were still hunting up a date. When the song ended I eased the Intrepid around the corner to the curb in front of the house, and switched garbage bags.

Away from the house I realized I didn't feel like heading home. Instead, I drove until I found an open gas station and bought a package of cigarettes and a cup of thin coffee. Nearby, there was a parking lot of a conservation area and I parked and watched the night creatures making their way home along invisible genetic paths that predated urban development. An obscure love song played on the radio. Slow shadows in the conservation area took shape. I saw a fox wait patiently until a trio of animals that looked like dogs cringed past. Raccoons made their way around the Intrepid. As the sun began to come up a skunk, a hint of darkness with a perfect white stripe, approached and disappeared out of my sight, under the car.

This was my father's world, I realized as I started the car, smiling. Emerging night creatures, the gradations of grey as the day began, the subtle warmth of morning.

Our condo building had a garbage area where the big bins were parked and later pulled out by hydraulic trucks. I parked the Intrepid underground in front of my lonely old motorcycle and took the target's garbage, some extra bags, and some zip-lock baggies from the trunk. Up in the garbage area I pulled on the rubber gloves and cut into the bags. Most of the content was kitchen and garbage waste. There was a tied-off white grocery bag full of shredded paper, long shred, the kind people stupidly thought was secure. I carefully transferred the shred into another green garbage bag, put envelopes and unshredded paper into the zip-locks, and locked it into the trunk of the car. I tossed the household waste into the Dumpster.

Upstairs both ladies were snoring from opposite ends of the condo. I had another cigarette as the sun came up fully. I found an inch of wine left in a bottle and took it out onto the terrace. An early worker at an office building across the street was watching me. I toasted him, or her, with the bottle and the silhouette shook its head.

I went inside and stood in the hallway between the two bedrooms. I lay down on the floor of a living room that was bigger than any home I'd ever lived in. When I was a boy we'd had only two rooms and a kitchen. A mattress acted as a bed and some nights when my old man and my mother were enamoured and fitted like spoons, his hand around her waist and her head back under his chin and her blonde hair in his mouth, I'd try to sleep in the living room on the floor under the window, always open to let the night noises drown out the furtive sounds coming from the bedroom.

It was freeing in a way to sleep on the floor in a swank condo, but cheating a little because I covered myself with a duvet from the blanket box that doubled as a coffee table. How many mornings, I wondered, did my old man get up and creep out before dawn, go foraging, and come home in the still-dark to sleep his way to daytime beside a woman he might one day murder?

Even having been out half the night I was still the first one up. Creakily I hit the coffee and took a couple of Ibus with a lot of water. At nine, Cornelius Fox called and I caught the phone on the first ring. We arranged to have a late breakfast at a greasy spoon, an easy walk halfway between his office and the condo. I showered, then drank coffee until a quarter to ten and went out in the same clothes I'd worked in, that I'd slept in.

Before I was fully seated, I saw a copy of the *Sun* on the leatherette seat, half of a white envelope poking from the fold. Fox affected to look away while I flipped open the newspaper and slit open the envelope. Finder's fee for the Carlson reference.

"This one's a fucking gold mine, Charlie."

"Can you get her off?"

"Hey, who gives a shit?" Fox was positively gleeful. He managed to refrain from rubbing his hands together. "It's a youth case but she's seventeen and the Crown's gonna bump it up to adult court. Charlie, I fucking love you, you know that? The bump-up hearing, pre-trial prep, the preliminary, the trial, the appeal, the second appeal. Let me ask you one, Charlie: if I blow you right now will you be my friend forever? "

I held the envelope down below the tabletop and fanned a thick wad of bills, mostly twenties with a few fifties in there. I could picture it: Fox would have set an official retainer for his tax records and then talked in circles about spreading dough around to grease things until the client understood a stack of additional cash was necessary. The client would send a courier back later with a sealed package and leave it with the girl at the front reception. She'd lock it in a filing cabinet for a few days, then give it to one of Fox's secretaries who would leave it in her desk for a few days, unopened. Eventually the courier package would be opened, the envelope inside would vanish, the tracking sheet be burned, and the courier packaging torn to bits and carried home by another secretary, who was tasked with disposing of the bits. Fox had been burned before running bulk cash through his office, and the money-laundering laws had him in a greedy funk of creative paranoia.

There were twenty-five hundred dollars in the envelope. He laid his finger against the side of his nose. "What you got there? A free paper somebody left? I don't know how a guy can pay a half-a-buck for a paper, leaf through it, and just toss it. Give it to somebody, put it under the cat litter. Anything. A hundred and fifty bucks a year some guy pisses away. About six-, seven-hundred, if he buys all four papers. Go figure."

I slipped the envelope into my jacket pocket.

The greasy spoon had no wait staff. He called to the fry cook for two bacon and eggs, white toast, jam, and coffee. The cook drew two coffees and put the thick mugs on the counter. Fox crossed the small aisle and brought them to the table. His suit was immaculately draped. "Fuck, I'm starving. Worked late last night trying to see what I'm dealing with here. Up early this morning, had my first breakfast with the Crown. This's my second."

I poured creamer and sugar into my mug. "Who's the Crown?"

"Jefferson. Right now it's Jeffy, anyway. One of the punks'll do the youth hearing, then the turf war'll start and we'll see. Don't mind if it's Jeffy, though. He's a pal, you can talk to the guy."

"He say what they got?"

"Everything but a confession. They got tape from the

Queen's Park cameras, shows our little pal there, Corolla Carlson, and two buddies wandering on-screen like bit actors, Corolla's carrying a cardboard box, and they walk out of sight. That's camera one, the approach. Camera two picks 'em up walking up to the east steps; they stop and Corolla puts the box down. Buddy number one, a chick, Barbie Dembrowski, a bony little thing, lesbo, shaved head, sunglasses, takes some ski masks out of a knapsack, hands 'em around. She takes out rubber gloves, nice mauve colour, the kind you wash dishes in. Everybody dresses up for the felony ball. Buddy number two is a peckerhead named Peter Welsh, skinhead, face metal, mohawk, and tattoos. Distinctive guy. He points to where our Corolla is to place the box. They roll the ski masks down their faces—they don't seem to realize surveillance cameras are wide angle—and they snap on the gloves.

"Corolla places the box against the door at the top of the stairs and steps back. Peter starts laughing and approaches the box with his hands up like this ..." Fox put his elbows on the table, forearms straight up and palms facing him, fingers straight up. "Like it's, Dr. Bomb at your cervix, step into my orifice. Jeffy said it's pretty fucking funny and it'll give the jury a laugh. Dr. Peter leans in over the box and does something, arming it, I presume, steps back and walks away, hands up the same way. He bows like he's just finished a really tough heart transplant. Barbie—you can see her laughing through the hole in the mask—pats at his forehead like an operating room nurse, taking the sweat off a surgeon. There you go, Dr. Stud, blow job in the lounge after scrub-up."

The cook announced the eggs. Fox sprinkled a ton of salt on everything, including the toast. I poked a corner of toast into a yoke and chewed it. I ate a piece of crisped bacon with my fingers. "Where's Corolla Carlson in all this?"

"Well, we were just at camera two. Bunch of stuff happens now. On camera one we have young Corolla wandering into view, mask off. She's crying and using the mask to wipe her eyes. Back at camera two we have Queen's Park security having sport with the Doctor and Barbie. There's six or eight of them and they just *fall* out of the sky on the two of them, drag them right away out of the picture; we now see only the box. On camera one Corolla's in a headlock; she's flailing and twisting. She elbows a female guard in the groin. The guard is smart enough to know the viewing field of the camera and Corolla is wrestled out of view where an accident somehow befalls her, a black eye, I think." Fox built a little open-faced salt and egg and bacon sandwich on the toast, folded it like a pita, and began chewing, holding it like a hot dog. "They haven't had to show me anything yet, all this is by way of Jeffy. He said he'll make full disclosure over time. There's guards' logs, there's their statements, there's the bomb squad commander, there's the bomb squad guys, there's the bomb squad techie guy who'll testify the bomb was armed and he'll estimate the amount of damage to the building and anyone nearby. Ooooo, the horror of what might have been."

"Sounds like you're gonna have your hands full with this one."

He shrugged. "Full hands, full bank. If the Crown gets it to adult court, and I can't see how they can't, I'll get a deal. Get Corolla to sing, make the other two swing." He mopped up his plate and took a piece of my bacon and salted it. "Look, Charlie, you know the family, right?"

"El does. Old friends." I waved my hand airily. "You know: the races at Ascot, the tennis set. The club. I met the sister and her husband last night at a little cocktail thingie El put on."

"Okay, a few things. First is, I'm hiring Bobby Clarke's

crew to do the background work, the interviews, any surveillance. Clarkie's a little expensive, but he's the man for the job." This meant Bobby Clarke would kick back a portion of his inflated invoice to Fox in cash; it didn't really matter because tactically Clarke's crew were the best, ex-homicide and ex-intelligence detectives well connected throughout the city. They hired Elodie and me occasionally; in turn we sometimes referred them when it looked like the client was going to take somebody to court, or have to defend himself in the dock. "Second, I'll get Bobby to throw research to Elodie. She can send me a case of wine at Christmas, if she wants, no matter. But key to all this, absolutely key, is that we keep the client wet. We gotta keep her wet right up until the last minute, whichever way it goes. If you and Elodie get work out of this you're gonna have to sign away the children you don't have. I'm going to write a confidentiality agreement so tight that if Elodie tells you what she had for breakfast, I'm going to take you both to court for breach of contract and I'll own your swank condo and every fucking piece of flagstone on your cool terrace."

This was the Fox I knew and didn't love a whole lot. The twenty-five hundred wasn't just a finder's fee, it was a down payment. Keeping the client wet meant keeping her sweating. Fox would wring his hands at the evidence, would say even if God showed up in court to tell the jury he told the bombers to do it, the accused were going south. If the bomb turned out to be railway flares and a cheapo Timex digital watch, he'd say the Crown could prove they *thought* it was a bomb and therefore it *was* a bomb. Kill 'em with almost-hopelessness and make them pay, pay, pay. If he got a deal, say five years, they'd be grateful because for the last few months he'd been talking fifteen, twenty, twenty-five, eternity. At the end, when Fox had enough money, whichever way the case went, the client, if cooked right, would provide bones for soup the next day, trying to get themselves or their family or friends out of another batch of sticky stuff. A bad loss, and Fox would have laid enough track to say I told you it was hopeless but we did everything we could, don't blame yourself. A long-shot win, and there was Fox on the television, the tearful grateful good sister tucked under one expensively tailored armpit, and bad Corolla sister under the other, weeping. Fatherly old Fox saying something quotable like, "The only bomb in this courtroom today was the Crown's evidence and, ladies and gentlemen, it blew up in their faces."

"Let me talk to El," I told him. "We've got some stuff on the go. And it might be too close to home for her."

"Okay." He put some bills on the table and we stood up. "I like you, Charlie. You remind me of me when I was young and always hungry. We can serve justice and grow rich, if we play it right. This is exactly how God wants it."

7

Back at the condo I went directly to the underground, got the car out, and drove to the nondescript east-end building where Bobby Clarke's crew was based. It was a blasted old brick, two-storey, former autobody shop that had been gentrified and cut into eight expensive commercial complexes. Carrying my bag of shred I went to the second floor. I passed the entrance for Clarke's guys—the door had a sign reading R.B. Clarke, Associates—and went to the end of the hall, where I stopped at an unmarked locked door that didn't have a handle or a lock, but it did have a peephole. The door was fortified with something like sheet steel and likely violated fire codes. My dull thumps brought the sound of movement from inside. An inch of the front snout of a lens poked out from a neat hole drilled in the ceiling at the end of the hall. A shadow passed over the peep and several locks were deactivated.

The glue room was well lit with four drafting tables all facing each other in a square that took up most of the floor space. Pots of glue, glue sticks, staplers, a couple of microscopes, and various tape holders were littered on the desks. The walls were covered with cork; there were probably thousands of different coloured pins jammed into cork. Someone had arranged red thumb tacks into a happy-face smiling head. Much of the wall space was decorated with re-assembled long-shred, recreating all manner of documents. I recognized an almost complete Visa bill, several invoices, telephone bills, envelopes, handwritten letters, and receipts. Bright lights, the kind you see in laboratories, and several swivelling magnifying lenses were clamped to the edges of the desks. Against the far wall were plastic bags, both garbage and the clear kind used to dispose of leaves and yard waste, and all had identification tags stuck to them. On the opposite wall were shoeboxes, stacked floor to ceiling. Sheets of plain glass with partial reconstructions glued to them were stacked in the corners. The place had the same busy feel as a boiler room I had once worked in.

Four guys worked in the room: a sorter, a colour man, a paper man, and a jigsaw man. The colour man went through the shred, separating the various colours, including the vast range of what different paper producers called White. The paper man took the sorted colours and, using his swivel magnifier, sorted the paper into grades, weights, textures, and linens. Once sorted in colour, paper, grade, and linen, the shred was dumped into a shoebox and given to the jigsaw man who began meticulously putting individual documents back together again. The four men were all ex-cops, guys with pensions who could use the extra undocumented cash. They made between fifteen and twenty-five an hour.

Barry White waved me into the room and away from the door. He took my bag of shred and filled out a data traffic report. He asked after Elodie—all the old cops loved Elodie—and told me to treat her right. Without asking, he poured me a cup of coffee and we stood watching the jigsaw man.

Barry White was an old hero who'd once carried four children, all clinging to his gun belt and tunic collar, from a flaming building. He'd been shot at twice; he'd been stabbed twice. He'd never lost a fight and was proud to say he'd never hit a handcuffed prisoner. He vainly dyed his hair red, had a square Irish face, a cop's face that carried behind it a secret history, a history of bandits dumped into the lake, rapists tossed off buildings, and the small acts of indifferent kindness that completed a man. I had a lot of time for Barry and could spend hours listening to his long obscure stories that always ended in heartbreak for someone.

"Kid," he said, "you want a red on this?"

I said no. A red is a red circle that expedited the processing of the run. My client was in no hurry: he had lawyers and accountants building a case against the renegade former employee and when he was ready he'd go to court, *exparte*, and get an Anton Piller injunction. The Piller would allow his investigators and lawyers to raid, without warning, the renegade's new company in Oakville, and freeze all records relating to production of the software. The more money the ex-employee made from the pirated software, the more my client would be claiming in recovery and damages.

"Barry, you hearing about the bomb thing at the legislature?"

He stared at me a while. "You on that one?"

"Friend of the family's got an interest. Just informal."

"Haven't heard nothing about it, Charlie." We sipped coffee and watched the men work. "Somebody brought us a bag of dot-shred, looks like confetti. A regular client, he comes in and says, Hey I know it can't be done, but can you guys do it? So we're looking for people with ..." he made a hand miming very small detail work. "You should give Bobby a call, if you know someone."

I said, "Hire some rug makers. Go down to the Afghani or

Iranian social services, tell 'em what you want. A lot of them, when they were kids their hands were so small and their eyes so sharp, they wove Middle Eastern rugs." I told him how some tyrant, Hussein or someone, had grabbed the dot-shred from an American government facility in the Middle East and used thousands of rug makers to assemble a complete document during the Gulf War.

Barry stared at me. "Fuck, Charlie. You should've been a cop. I'll tell Bobby."

He took my coffee cup and tossed it into a wastebasket. "C'mon, I'll walk you out." He activated several locks and let us out. "I always feel like I'm working in an insurance company or something," he said, walking the carpeted, well-lit hallways. "Got to get out once in a while, hear some traffic."

At the outside exit he walked with me to my car. "That thing with the bomb, at the legislature, that's a weird one, I think." He shrugged. "Hey, I ever tell you the story, kid, about how we dressed Connie Lombardozzi up as a mafia don?"

I accepted one of his cigarettes and he lit us both. His eyes scanned the buildings around the parking lot and he seemed to be gathering his thoughts, looking for a way into the Lombardozzi story. He started with what was called the Old Farts' Lament: Back in the old days.

"Back in the old days, when we were trying to keep a special project running to work the Italians. Nothing we could do worked. We tried rats. We tried the clipinski, putting alligator clips on their phone lines to listen in. We tried, I'm of course ashamed to say and would never condone, tuning them up. After a couple of months, nothing. We were sitting around the office one night, worrying the province was going to pull our funding, and Connie Lombardozzi came in from a night out. Someone had the bright idea: let's dress Connie up and make him into one of the boys, put him in play. Nothing to lose, right? He speaks the southern dialect, he looks like a thug. We don't show a result we're going to lose our funding and all go back to real police work.

"So we got a Cadillac for the night from a dealer, we got New York Staties to get us a New York plate. We got a tailor to make Connie a swell double-breasted suit. The gold tie. Silk socks and patent leather shoes. The pocket puff. Cufflinks and a diamond tie stud we got on the arm from a jeweller. A black fedora from the hat man on Spadina, wide brim, light grey band. We took him to the cutter down at the King Eddie and had him trimmed and shaved. Remember, this was in the sixties and that's how the big New York guys looked. So we got a driver for Connie. We sent 'em up to St. Clair Avenue. All the boys hung out at a place called Ciro's, a coffee bar all day and a boozer all night. The Caddie pulls up, and out gets Don Connie. The driver holds the door to Ciro's open and stands back and in goes Connie. He stands in the doorway and lights a stogie, looking around. He looks around in disgust and walks out again, crosses the street to another joint and sits in the window having a little glass of something foul.

"Now the boys are wondering, wow, who the fuck's this guy? We get a buzz on the wires that they're going: is New York making a move? What the fuck?"

Barry was clearly enjoying his reminiscences but he was looking at me closely. He laughed. "Next day, same thing. Day after that, same. A week later Connie shows up—we got more wheels from the dealership, more rags from the tailor—with five guys and they all go into the joint across from Ciro's. Finally one of the boys crosses from Ciro's to find out what the fuck? He goes up to Connie and says, very respectfully, welcome, *compare*. Connie blows some smoke at him. The guy says: we are at your disposal, we're *amici*. Connie just stares through the smoke, gunning the guy. The other guys,

guys we'd costumed up to play the role, laugh at the Ciro's guy. The Ciro's guy asks if he can be of service. Connie says—I don't know if he rehearsed this or not, anyway he was shit-faced from drinking the foul Italian shit for hours on end. He says: mice eat the small grain and hide; the wild boar forages and endures.

"Now, the Ciro's guy is thinking, Holy fuck? See, we had bad guys from Italy here, we had some Americans. But here, no one was really in charge, they're pretty small potatoes, and the local cheeseboys wanted to make the big American connection.

"So here's Connie the *Capo* and this mutt from Ciro's. We'd heard some of the lingo on the clipinskis—*capo bastone, picciotti*, young men of honour, *capo giovane, capo decina*. So Connie goes: Roots planted deep yield fruit for all, forever. He's winging it. The Ciro's guy's got to be wondering if he's back on a mountainside in the old country, shitting in an outhouse, carrying a blunderbuss. But he nods his head, Truer wisdom, never spoken. That kind of thing. So Connie says he wants to put his roots deep, and he wants to put them here, to make a thing of true honour, whatever that means. Now we got a live wire going at Connie's table and we're down in the basement listening. We're pissing ourselves, we're as confused as the wop. Every time the Ciro's guy says something that Connie doesn't have a clue about, Connie makes this, you know, little hiss or smacks his lips with frustration at this local yokel.

"Long and short, Charlie, is Connie set up a whole Mafia family. They set about extorting the groceries, the cheese shops, tossing bombs in the bakeries. All for Don Connie. Every time they wanted to do something, they checked with the Don. He told them to go to it. Finally, we got 'em all." He looked at me, then looked around the parking lot.

"Funny story, eh? The thing about police work is, it never changes."

He walked back towards the building, laughing.

When I got back to the condo Elodie was sitting in the sunshine wearing sunglasses, miserably drinking from a pitcher of ice water. I knew better than to speak; instead I went into the bedroom and got out the suit coat I'd worn the day before. I took the envelope from the body job, added it to Fox's envelope, and spun open the small round wall-safe we'd had put into the back of the closet. There were more than a dozen envelopes in there, some fat, some thin. In the kitchen I opened a lunch beer and picked at the remains of a roast of beef the day-lady had covered with foil. The guest shower was running and steam leaked from under the door; faintly I could hear singing inside. It sounded like "Big Girls Don't Cry," and Janine, the good sister, was hitting all the high notes adequately. I thought about her there, in the shower, then decided I shouldn't maybe think about it any more.

I put together a platter of leftover meat, shrimp, and salads, opened another beer, tucked the remote phone under my arm, and went silently onto the terrace. Elodie was crunching ice. I put the platter and some napkins down on a round table near her, made a stack of beef and cold shrimp on the palm of my hand, and went silently to sit at the other end of the terrace. Looking her over, a pathologist would write: white female, undernourished, blunt-force trauma to the head, self-inflicted, liquid.

I punched in to the messages. The neutral and cool voice on the phone said we had six. Fox, from earlier, moot since we'd already met; the client of the Gone Wong engagement who asked for a final invoice and a final report, thanks and never mind pursing the matter any further; a woman called

Judith who thanked Elodie for a fine evening, a woman called Mary with a similar message; and the good sister's husband asking where the hell Janine was.

Janine Carlson-Appleby came onto the terrace, unaware I was at the opposite end watching her. She was fluffing her hair, with a white towel, and she wore a bleached, stiff-looking bathrobe Elodie had stolen from a hotel someplace. Her feet were bare and her toes were painted red. She stood looking down at Elodie and said something in a low voice. Elodie's head moved up and down in affirmation and pain. The phone rang in my hand, startling me out of a fairly erotic reverie involving the three of us and maybe the girl at the photo lab.

I watched Janine Carlson-Appleby look at me as I answered. Elodie didn't move. A client who'd been out of circulation for several months gave me information on eight investors he wanted checked out for an off-shore gaming investment. Off-shore gaming had, in the past year or so, become a major source of due diligence research. The very nature of off-shore Internet gambling was tailor-made for money launderers to wash criminal profits. I wrote the names, dates of birth, social insurance numbers, passport numbers, and business affiliations on a napkin, got a due date for the report and arranged a Phase One flat rate based on quantity. The client okayed the estimate.

I hung up as Janine Carlson-Appleby came down the terrace. She sat on a little marble stool across from me, careful to control the skirts of the bathrobe. She was a little punched around the eyes, but otherwise handled her hangover like a sailor. "Our friend's a hurting unit. I'm sorry I kept her up with my sister's ... situation."

I said it was no problem, I'd seen Elodie worse than this after much shorter parties.

"El said you could help. Can you?"

I told her it didn't look good. "Your sister's in juvenile court today. They're probably going to want her tried as an adult. She could be looking at a lot of time, if this thing goes through."

"You sound like that Mr. Fox. He as much as said it was hopeless. My grandfather said you recommended him. Is he good? He seemed a little ... opportunistic. Oily."

I thought about Fox. In spite of cleaning them out for as much dough as he could get, he was a pretty good lawyer, although he sometimes was more sizzle than steak. "Well, yes, I think so. He's very expensive, but I guess you know that. I don't know what his strategy is, but he knows a whole lot of people and if things look like they're unsalvageable he'll put together a deal, get her the shortest time in the best of places."

"Will you work on it, too?"

"That's up to Fox. He'll get all the facts, put them in the best light. He'll make the Crown prove everything. He'll put every witness through the wringer, try to make it so expensive they'll deal. But he's running your sister's defence and if he wants us in, we're in. But probably he's going with a bigger firm that your family can afford, guys who'll come to court and testify. We don't do that."

"What about other stuff, not the case itself? Could you and Elodie find out how Corolla got into this? About this black box stuff?"

"Black Bloc. If you want you can hire Elodie to work up a research engagement on the anarchists, the Bloc, like that." I wondered if she remembered Elodie's spacey offer the night before to work for free. "It's not too expensive, I'm sure El will put together a package for you, at a good rate."

Her eyes told me she did indeed remember the offer. I felt, maybe too sensitively, that my status in her life had altered slightly, and not necessarily for the better. I changed the subject and said her husband had called, looking for her. She stood up, careful again with the robe.

"I'll get some food, check on Elodie's condition, and you can interview me later about Corolla." She took the phone, dialling as she swayed away from me and began speaking softly as she went inside. A few seconds later I heard her speak in that even and level voice of anger rich people use to show how civilized they are in spite of the tribulations they're forced to endure.

An hour later Janine Carlson-Appleby was gone. Elodie and I sat inside while I tapped the new off-shore gaming engagement into the computer. Elodie was in somewhat better shape, for having a shower and some food. She was dressed in blue jeans with the knees gone and frayed, a silky t-shirt, and sandals. Elodie has a hundred pairs of shoes—shoes that she'll never wear out, much less need to re-sole. I sat in a swivel chair, she sat in her wheelchair. I lifted her feet up onto my lap.

"You quoted too low for this," she said.

I said, "Package rate. He's giving us eight pieces of work. He pays for six and gets two free. The cost of the last two is negligible and we have to make the same moves, make the same calls, anyway. And," I added, "it's more than the freebie you offered your pal there, last night."

"They're family friends, Charlie."

"They're rich, Elodie."

"She's nice."

"She's very nice. She wants a service and she's very rich. I'm very nice, and can deliver a service, and I'm poor. Somewhere in there I see a symbiosis."

She leaned forward and used her hands to lift her feet from my lap. She had a little mean fun with *symbiosis*. It scratched at me, someplace, and I asked her if she wanted to play around with *parsimonious*, *cheap*, *tight-ass*, and *freeloader*. And away we went. We managed to escalate into a bit of a fight, then into full combat. At one point as things showed signs of winding down, her needling about using big words like *symbiosis* came back at me. So I mentioned uptown inbred tightwad motherfuckers who squeezed nickels until the buffalo shit.

She hissed at me to just fuck off—not *Fee-a-zuk E-a-zoff*—and rolled herself down to the bedroom, her muscular but slim arms pumping away at the rims of her chair. I knew the word *symbiosis* mostly from reading about the Symbionese Liberation Army, the California crackpots who kidnapped Patricia Hearst back in the bad old days of Black Panthers, anti-war demonstrations, bank robberies, and armoured car heists. And that made me think of the Black Bloc. And, in turn, I thought of rebels and anarchists. Ergo, I thought of my twin daughters.

8

I went first to the Krak Bar, wandering in and shocking the customers to an immediate sudden silence that almost instantly degenerated into comments about bacon, pork, pigs, and the accompanying chorus of snorting and snuffling. Someone, in a surprisingly well-trained voice, sang, Put pork on your fork. The room was about the size of a coffin and the same shape. The walls and floor were all painted flat black with round fluorescent disk lights stuck into the purplish ceiling. An abandoned band stage was set up at the end of the room beside a fire bar that was wrapped in a thick chain. The furniture consisted of mismatched patio stuff, a couple of wooden chairs, and some off-balance square plank tables. A butcher knife pinned a performance poster to the wall above a jukebox that had been destroyed, it looked like, by axes and sledgehammers. The performance poster, a black and white photocopy from which the grey tones had been dropped, was for a band called the Raging Dootchbags. Allie was second from the left end of a row of five young women. She held a bass guitar straight up in the air with her left hand and gave the finger to the camera with the other.

The real Allie wasn't in the room. I went to a little Filipina working behind the bar. I'd met her before, a year or so ago, a compact, tough-bodied type who, I'd been told, had a job as a bricklayer for cash on construction sites in the area. She had metal in both ears and her nose, a hoop in her lower lip, but she wasn't about to let her hair go. It was thick and long, interesting shades of blues, but she clearly maintained it, keeping the crown of it under a red bandanna featuring a white peace symbol. In spite of all the metal and the faint sneer she sometimes wore, she couldn't get away from her beauty, or the warmth of her eyes. I sympathized: no matter what I wore, or how I scrubbed up, I couldn't get out from behind my own thuggishness.

I groped for her name. Before I could speak, recognition opened her face. "Allie's off today, Mr. Tate. They played all night." Her voice was soft and polite.

Behind me a voice called, "Hey, Pia, get a lawyer. You don't have to talk to him."

"He's Allie's dad."

"Oh." The voice was silent a moment. "Hey, cool dome."

"How about the Mouse?" I hadn't seen my kids in a couple of months, had no idea where they were living. For a long time, back after they split from their mother, they'd been living on the streets, in some underground status that rendered them invisible to me. A year after they vanished from Judith's home, they popped up, seventeen-year-olds in handcuffs after a running street battle with neo-Nazis. They were around for a while, then gone again, appearing again, this time as adults, in handcuffs after a riot at Queen's Park. I went down to the police division after Judith called. The desk sergeant had liked a piece I'd written on his foot patrol guys working in Lavender

Valley, the gay ghetto, and he let me have a few minutes with them in an office. I told them I could get them out, the cops'd find a JP to come down to bail them.

"What about the others, Dad?" Allie said. "There are eight of us. They're beating us in here. Help."

"Just you guys."

They were leathered out and there were faint holes where the cops had removed their metal, citing weaponry. Both looked exhausted, except for their eyes, which still had the spark of battle in them, and they looked like fighters for a fierce hill tribe in a country at war. Allie had some bruising to her face and picked at a visible splinter of wood that had buried itself in the back of her hand, wood from a picket sign, I guessed. The Mouse showed no wear and tear. Clearly, Allied'd got it worse.

The Mouse shook her head. "All or none, Dad."

Allie got the splinter out and stared at it. "He called me white trash, a race traitor. I called him a Nazi cocksucker." She glanced up at me, then down. "Sorry."

The Mouse laughed. "But he was cute, eh, Al? I thought you were asking him out for a date. Dinner, and then a night out burning synagogues. Then you kicked him in the nuts. Nice."

They were playing to me. They'd done it since they could talk, two schemers with their own secrets, telling me stuff by talking to me through each other, like children with talking puppets. You had to listen to what the puppets said, not the children. For a long time I thought I was a failure with them, then I thought they were a failure with me.

We'd sat talking. They wouldn't budge. I told them about going into the bucket, how they might end up getting a whole new perspective on sisterhood waiting for trial. Allie said that was a decision for later, right now the decision was for now. The desk sergeant stuck his head in the door and said the wagon was loading up. They'd be kept in the women's cells at 55 Division in the east end overnight.

I hugged them, amazed at how small and resilient they seemed. The leather jackets creaked in my ear, the faint residue of tear gas came to my eyes and nose. I said I'd see them at court the next morning. The Mouse asked if I was all right, as though I was the one going back to the cells. I said I was fine; she screamed, "Call Amnesty International, Dad. Torture. The water treatment. Cattle prods." She was still screaming and laughing at the same time as the desk sergeant pulled her out of the room.

He'd stuck his head back in a few minutes later and said, "Jesus Fucking Christ, Charlie."

Pia said the girls were living together in a third floor flat around the corner. She tried to explain where it was and finally came out from behind the bar, taking me by the hand. We walked to the corner and she pointed out a junk clothing store a half block away. "They think the Red Squad's on them, so pound on the door three times. If they don't come down do it again, three times. They won't talk inside their place, though, you'll have to go out to the park or something."

"You think there's really a Red Squad, Pia?"

She became dark and mysterious in a sad kind of way and squeezed my hand like I was an idiot who wondered if there was a blue sky and, if there was, which way I'd look to find it. I'd forgotten Pia's story and felt like an asshole. She said, "Goodbye, Mr. Tate," and I stood among the markets and stalls and baskets of who-knows-what fruits and vegetables. I stared after her as she walked away in the edge of the gutter, slightly pigeon-toed but well-balanced, avoiding the throngs on the sidewalk, indifferent to both the chaos of people and the crawling traffic beside her. She lived in a land of constant political battle, of constant avoidance of memory, like a guerrilla fighter who swam among the fishes and forgot there'd ever been pleasures in life.

I remembered the Mouse telling me about her. "Pia's from Manila. Her father was killed by the government, they cut her mother's hands off, not at the wrist, but just behind the knuckles with a machete. Pia screams at night, Dad, no one'll live in the same house as her. She keeps her hair long because she thinks it's her mother's hair, that it gave her the strength to make a noose of her hair with the heels of her hands and use it. Pia's going to live with us."

I said, "It's good of you to look after her, help her get strong."

The Mouse said, "Dad, she looks after us, she shows us how to be strong."

I banged at the door as Pia had told me to do, but there was no answer. A disappointment because although I love them both the same, the Mouse had a sly and bitter way of telling you things that made you examine them even as you heard them. It wasn't the same bitterness I'd wrestled with in my life, but a more quirky way of speaking her thoughts and feelings, of slyly telling you something without you knowing you were being told. Once, feeling dadly, I asked her if she'd had sex. She said, "You mean: today?"

I was standing there wondering what to do next, when Allie came up the street. We hugged. She said, "Let's walk." We wandered aimlessly, not speaking. She kept an eye on the cars on the street, glancing inside each of them. Everybody who passed seemed to know her, all the guys and girls in mohawk haircuts, metal accessories, and ripped clothing. They looked at me with curiosity, then back at her to make sure she was okay. We rounded the block, up the Chinese section of Spadina, and back into the throngs of Baldwin Street. I went to speak and she shushed me.

"Watch this, Dad." She stopped suddenly, her hand looped through my elbow like a debutante being escorted into a father-daughter charity ball. She wheeled me suddenly in a gentle circle. Now in front of us two men, who had been behind us, walking separately, seemed startled. One man handled it well, brushing by without making eye contact; the other, though, couldn't decide whether he should pop into a shop or cross the street. He made eye contact and his eyes widened slightly. Obviously an apprentice at his tasks, he actually bent to tie his shoelace.

We walked around him, back out onto Spadina. Allie stopped at a Chinese food stall and bought some black hairy fruits. We stood in a doorway and she pulled out a small Swiss Army knife and cut through the hairs and skin. The fruit inside was almost sweet and had a moist juiciness. I used a linen handkerchief to blot my lips and brushed the cloth against hers. She laughed a little and hugged me. She thought linen handkerchiefs were from another generation, a generation of horse-and-buggies, busting workers' unions, and running Indians off the best land.

She said, "C'mon, Dad," and we jogged across the yellow light to the east side of Spadina. Walking quickly she led me down to Dundas Street and into an almost impenetrable crowd of shoppers and wanderers. She said, "Here, Dad," and we darted into a Chinese bakery with booths in the back that seemed populated by ancient Chinese opium smokers in oversized worn-out winter overcoats.

She startled me by saying something to the waitress in Cantonese. When coffee and custard tarts were in front of us, she took a package of Marlboros out of her knapsack and lit us both. The Chinamen didn't care; the waitress brought a plastic ashtray.

"Jesus, Al, you some kind of spy?" I was confused by the

roundabout darting walk and dash. "Some kind of, like, agent?"

"You'd think they thought so. Pretty funny, huh?"

"You're pretty paranoid. You can talk on the street, for Christ's sake."

She looked good. Both she and the Mouse were vegetarians. They weighed about as much as Elodie. Allie was a little more far out, more politically active than the Mouse and had a myriad of tattoos over her body. When she first showed them to me I thought: someday I'll have to pay to have them removed. But now I wondered.

She said, "Once we figured out how they knew what we were doing, we went outside to talk, keep walking and keep talking. Cover our lips. Like we were some kind of gangsters. Still they showed up wherever we went, usually got there before us. We used to walk on Dundas Street and talk. But you know what they did? They got there right after rush hour and parked a dozen cars, each with a microphone in it. So as we passed we went from one microphone to another." She reached into the pocket of her leather vest and put a grilled microphone as thick as a double-A battery and as long as a cigarette filter onto the table. "This was in our flat. You know what this is, right?"

"How long has this been going on?"

"They've always taken a look at us, but about six months ago all of a sudden they were everywhere. The Red Squad."

"Allie, there is no Red Squad. There used to be, but the police commission disbanded it when they found them working up dossiers on commissioners, politicians, and the press. Maybe it's the Nazis."

She looked at me and thought about it. "No. They're some kind of cops. We know most of the undercover guys from demonstrations, but we also know they're the ones we're *supposed* to see, supposed to get used to, get to know so they can *bump into* us and *chat* and they can be our *friends*. This is all different, Dad, strange. People are kinda scared. It's the Red Squad, trust me."

I looked at her, trying to separate adolescent dramatics—although she and the Mouse were in their early twenties, twenty-two or twenty-three, I could never remember—from reality. She looks like me, not her mother, I thought. She didn't have Judith's visible and naked avarice, her greed for things she desired, things she thought were necessities of life. Like the Mouse, Allie had a direct stare that demanded honesty; in the absence of honesty, only silence sufficed.

"Elodie thinks you might be living some kind of movie life."

"How is Elodie?" She was genuinely fond of Elodie, was interested in her and had once said to me Elodie would be a great revolutionary if she'd been poor and crippled by a fascist, if she'd get pissed off, if she had to fight for accessibility and could bring herself to kill off her parents and learn to burn money.

I said Elodie was fine. A little hungover but basically on a pretty even keel, all things considered. I said, "Allie, the thing at Queen's Park? The bomb?"

"Ah, that. Pretty weird, huh?"

"You know them? Corolla and the other two?"

"Corolla. We called her the Hummingbird. She floated in, came to meetings, came to the bar, and just went from issue to issue. Poverty rights, she's there. Next week it's the Native land claims, she's there. After that it's free tuition at university and she's there. She couldn't settle on a cause, she didn't understand it's all one cause. She just wanted to belong. She cringed all the time, cried."

"She belong to the Black Bloc?"

"Dad, Dad, Dad." Allie shook her head and didn't add: *you poor dumb bastard.* "What do you think the Black Bloc is? Some global network, getting cheques from Fidel Castro? Think there's meetings to plan strategy? Democratically elected leaders who plan actions? Cadres of suicide demonstrators willing to give their lives to stop globalization?" She lit another cigarette.

I noticed there was no tax stamp on the package: bootlegs. I took a cigarette from the package. "So, what is it? Who's in it?"

"I'm the Black Bloc, Dad. The Mouse is the Black Bloc. You could be the Black Bloc; even Elodie could be. You just have to be pissed off. People we've never met, never even thought of, they're the Black Bloc. We're all the Black Bloc and none of us are. The Black Bloc is like ..." She thought a moment. "The Black Bloc is like jazz fans. It's like people who like movies, like people who like Chinese food or pizza or shopping at St. Lawrence Market. People who like the same tunes, the same food, the same shopping experience." She wrinkled her brow. "Like that Christian stuff: first believe that you believe, and then you'll believe. There is no Black Bloc, except there is, and if you want to belong, you belong. A hundred people all like a movie, say, and they all show up at the same time in the same place with their tickets to watch the opening. Is that a conspiracy? Is it an action? Or is it just people who might have the same idea of how things are or how things could be and they appear en masse? Who's the leader at the Cineplex on Friday night when the next Coen Brothers' movie opens? The guy at the head of the line, because he got there first, it was his idea? Someone, some sapper with a bomb stuck to his or her body, halfway down the line?"

"But there's no one with firebombs and ski masks at the movie lineup."

"The cocktails are like alarm clocks, waking up the media, waking up the citizens. Starbucks can afford new windows, if you look at what they pay for the coffee and what they sell it for. The masks are because it's the play that's important, not the players."

I looked at her. Elodie was wrong, Allie and the Mouse weren't living in some 1940s movie of German-occupied France; there was a parallel reality, one no one could touch from the outside, or even understand. Clearly Allie was a master propagandist. But, perversely, I didn't mind her lecturing me. If the Mouse were here instead of Allie, the information I got would be just as accurate but much funnier and a lot more entertaining and maybe more difficult to get a line on. We'd have had a few yuks; I would have gone away sorting knowledge and she would have gone away with the reinforced mindset that her dad was dizzy but not hopeless.

"Tell me about the Hummingbird, about Corolla."

"Tell me why you care." At least she didn't say: Tell me why *you* care.

I said, "When you disappeared into all this, I cared, Allie. I looked for you guys, I had the cops trying to keep track of where you were. When you slept in doorways or in abandoned squats, I knew where you were, some of the time, maybe not all the time, but some of it. No matter where you were or what you were doing, someone cared. Me. Judith. Later Elodie. Corolla Carlson has someone who cares, too. She's a friend of Elodie's family and the family just wants to know what happened, what went wrong. That's it. I'm not looking to put the hat on anyone who might have been involved in the bomb at the Park."

"So," she said, "you're not getting paid for this?"

"Well. I'm negotiating. Right now I just want to know. If you don't think you should tell me, then don't. But Corolla

Carlson's looking at a lot of prison time. If there's something there, something her lawyer can use to shorten that time, then I need to know it. It isn't a betrayal, Allie."

She looked over my shoulder, but she was actually looking somewhere else, remembering. I sipped my coffee and bit into my *daan* tart. Across the aisle, in a booth alone, a shivering old Chinese man took a plastic bag from his pocket and threw up into it. He tied it off, put it on the floor under his bench seat and went back to watching the door, some sick lover waiting for somebody with something. The waitress came by our table and filled up our coffee, spilling a handful of creamers onto the table.

I remembered talking to Judith when they were beginning school and saying I'd rather my kids have loyalty to each other than to us, the parents. We'd be gone one day and if they couldn't trust each other with their secrets and their desires, who would they have? Judith thought as parents we had a right to know everything, a duty to make decisions, the power to lead. Our discussion turned into argument. She finally slammed down her highball glass and told me: "That might be okay in the *rag-and-bone* world, but these kids aren't having those values. They'll be honest and proud and they'll rise above the *rag-and-bone* life, Charlie. They'll be the ones throwing out the junk, not the ones who grub through it."

Allie worked her way to her decision while stirring creamer into her coffee. As soon as I saw her face I knew I'd brought something down on her.

"Everything's a betrayal, isn't it, Dad? This coffee oppresses the pickers in South America. This creamer is from cows that are just slabs of steroid-filled meat that squirt juices, and then we finally eat them. We only raise them to kill them, otherwise would we give a fuck? That's their life." She rubbed her fingers on her leather vest, agitated. "This, death." She touched the gold ring on my finger: "This, slaves who work underground. If they get caught stealing they get whipped." She touched the stainless steel Rolex Elodie had given me on the first anniversary that we lived together. "You can look at the sun and tell when it is. What's so important that at, say, three o'clock you have to be someplace to do something? What's so fucking important that you read a piece of metal and some numbers and go, Oh gotta go? What if you didn't have a watch and the guy you're meeting didn't have a watch? Then what? Nobody'd be late, but you'd both get there sometime, right? That watch would feed a family for a year." She was crying openly but no one except me noticed. "I wish I could die sometimes, you know? Every time I turn around there's compromise, there's the edge, the rationalization. I feed my dog on the carcasses of horses. I play in my band but all they hear is the music so they can bang heads, they don't hear the words. They hear, but they don't listen. I look around me and I shame myself. It's all shit. It's all shit."

I moved around the table and put my arm around her shoulder. She was tense a moment, resisting, then slumped her head against me. A Chinaman now facing me in the forward booth gave me a look: why you make that pretty girl cry, huh? Why you do that thing, huh?

Buddy, I thought, I wish I knew.

I asked her how come she cared so much, too much?

"How do you do that, Dad? How can a person care too much? How do you love me too much? How do I hate these things too much? Tell me how to not do it and I'll not do it. Tell me how to be dumb and dead again."

"I dunno. Stupid thing to say, Al. Is it some patrimonial conspiracy, or can I say I love you? I mean, I don't want to be, you know, committing some social faux pas here, some patriarchal emotional genocide I'll be judged for later? At the tribunal?"

She laughed and sniffled. "You know, when Mom said you were an aimless goof, I thought that was a bad thing. But it isn't, is it? She must have hated you so much."

"Goofiness is underrated. And besides," I said, "how can you be too goofy?"

"Can I ask something? You won't get mad?"

"Shoot, kiddo, a free shot."

"How'd you feel when you found she was sleeping with your boss? How come you didn't kill them both?"

"I could take it. I didn't like it, but your mother was that kind of person. Conspiracies made her important, secrets made her interesting. I thought I could change her, like you think you can change the world."

"I'd hear you fighting. Was it about what she was doing?"

I thought back. It seemed so long ago but the answer came to me instantly. I could take the frailty, the weakness, the fear of commitment, and the lack of faithfulness. Hell, I was no saint myself. But what it was, what killed it, was when she always threw my old man into my face. She used to call me the rag-and-bone man of journalism, remaking the junk of other people's lives into something to be recycled. The rag-and-bone man of his own children, trying to tinker with them, make them work better. All I could do was shrug.

Allie got up, somehow energized. "We have to go. We've been in one place too long."

The Hummingbird came on the scene about a year earlier, she said. A pretty but sad-faced girl who slept with anyone who didn't ignore her and didn't make her cry. She was constantly grateful. She wasn't called the Hummingbird at first. The crowd at Allie's bar called her Ola. Allie didn't think much about her, one way or the other, but when she did think about her she thought she had a history of mental illness, maybe a self-cutter who hated the body she had to live inside.

We sat in the park on the grass, away from trees, away from the benches. While we were strolling through, she suddenly picked the spot. It was growing cool and I offered her my jacket. She declined.

"She tried to fit in. She showed up at all the actions, she sometimes showed up with money, lots of money. For posters. For gas masks. When we needed a drummer for the Dootchbags, she bought herself a drum set. She couldn't play, but it didn't matter. She got tattooed, she got drunk, and she got high. She came to the self-defence classes, the civil disobedience seminars. She said she was sixteen, but I thought she was, like, fourteen, maybe. Her age didn't matter, except to her. She was up for getting hurt if she had to. She talked about offing pigs, burning buildings, taking direct action. She wanted to organize a cadre and she wanted to fund it. I think she was insane. She didn't actually care what she did, as long as she could do it. When she found out how things were, how disorganized and fucked up, she drifted away. We didn't see her for a few months, but she left the drum set behind, which was okay. The Mouse played for us until we got a drummer. You ever hear the Mouse play?"

"No," I said. "A pleasure I somehow missed."

"She's pretty good. Must've been the ballet lessons." This sounded too much like the Mouse. The flat delivery, the wry conclusion. "Doesn't hurt her, either, when the sticks are swinging and she does a little jeté."

I laughed and remembered the ballet lessons that didn't take. Somehow Judith and I had thought we could have normal middle-class kids. Ballet Tuesdays and Thursdays, acting at the Young People's Theatre on Saturdays. Fill their time with culture, with important things, keep them too busy to think their own thoughts, to find their own way.

And, I wondered, how did Judith and I expect anything different than this grown-up kid, sitting on the grass worrying the benches were bugged?

Allie was going on about Corolla. "She was gone one day and we didn't see her. Then she was back. It was about six months ago, maybe more. She didn't come into the bar, but we saw her hanging around the new coffee place across the street. Some stoner skinhead ran it. Ola started showing up again at actions. She was very political, very much into anti-globalization. Her hair was butched and she'd put on some muscle tone, lost a lot of weight. She had, it seemed, even more dough. And she had a plan. She talked about direct actions against what she called *the very underpinnings of the power structure*. She had a boyfriend, an older guy, a stoner who ran the new coffee place, and they got pretty rad. Next thing is there's a whole bunch of them over there, including a bunch from our place. I went over a couple of times and it was like a cult. Very polite, very, you know, *interested*, but basically nobody at home. I thought it was like: you're cool enough but you're not, like, *cold* enough."

"So, she was in the bomber mode? She'd go and put one in the legislature?"

"Dad, everybody's sometimes in the bomber mode. I get some mad, sometimes. Music isn't going to save the world, and if it is, it probably isn't going to be my music. But that's my bomb. Songs for goofs too drunk to hear, headbangers who scramble their brains. But it's my way and I can live with it. The Hummingbird wants to change the entire world. I guess she almost did. I didn't think she had many moving parts. Who knew?"

"And the other two that were pinched?"

"Dunno their names yet. She had a bunch of guys, I think. Could be any of them."

I walked her back to her place. I was giving her a hug when the Mouse dashed out the door. She gave me a quick hug and a kiss on my cheek. Following after her was a tall guy with a red mohawk, what looked like silver staples in his eyebrows, and a beanpole pure white body. "Dad, this is Grunge. Grunge, my dad, Mr. Tate." Polite to a fault, as I'd taught her.

Grunge said, "Cool dome, Mr. Tate."

As they blew by, I heard him say, "Jeez, Emma, your old man's one scary fuck. You sure ..." I didn't hear the rest before they were gone up the block holding hands, she pulling him.

"He called her Emma." Allie had big eyes. "Hmmm. That's new."

"I don't even call her Emma, anymore. I think of her as the Mouse."

"She's been seeing him for a few months now. She didn't like him at first because he's got a job."

"What's he do?"

"He's a stockboy at the Office Depot. Goes to Geo Brown at night, cooking. He wants to open a restaurant some day."

I thought about the Mouse and relationships. "Come for dinner, you and the Mouse, soon, okay?"

"Can I try to rehabilitate Elodie, get her mind right?"

"Well, you can try. But: good fucking luck."

"I'll set it up with the Mouse. I'll call."

"Allie, one thing. If the revolution comes, you can't assassinate Elodie. Promise?"

"Don't worry, Dad. We'll just burn her money and she can find out who she is. Maybe she'll surprise you."

I said, "That'd be nice."

The coffee bar across from Allie's club was closed and for lease. The windows were smeared with dry white detergent and someone had written in magic marker: KILL THEM ALL. Someone had put an X through KILL and written in SAVE. Someone using a black grease pencil had X'd out SAVE and written in LOVE. I passed by slowly, glancing into the Krak Bar. Pia was leaning on the bar. I stuck my head in. "Pia, you okay?"

She nodded distractedly. For no reason I said, "Thank you."

I turned away and saw a dirty old bum sitting in the doorway of the building next to the closed coffee bar where Corolla Carlson the Hummingbird had finally found a home. In his surprise the bum made an amateur mistake: he looked directly at me. I wondered if he was trying to remember that he'd seen me before, talking with Jerry Hamer in front of the hotel downtown where a fat Russian was hustling Western bucks.

9

Elodie was printing downloads off the Internet, filing each into eight folders with tabs bearing the names of the eight subjects in the offshore file. Her anger had made for her an efficient afternoon. A task sheet with the client's name at the top was waiting for me. It listed the eight, their dates of birth and addresses. My job tomorrow would be to run loans-and-liens, civil court indexes, corporate documents, and land title searches. All the open source information that was the foundation of everything we might have to do if we went into Phase Two. I liked the client, so I'd do criminal record checks, gratis, and report to him verbally if I came up with anything.

I took a beer from the fridge and thought about dinner, wandering through the place, not wanting to speak first. In the past we'd gone two days without speaking after big blow-ups, but that was rare. I couldn't read the play, so I waited and wandered.

She'd been industrious: the bed was made, her clothes were put away, the terrace was cleaned up, and there was no sign of the gruesome all-nighter she'd pulled with Janine Carlson-Appleby. An unmistakable sign of a burning anger.

I was halfway through my beer, but Elodie still hadn't acknowledged I was home. In the bedroom I changed into workout clothes and dug out a towel and some lightweight khaki shorts I used as bathing trunks. The condo building had a swimming pool and gym on the third floor, sauna, and efficient shower pressure. The gym didn't have free weights, but some of the machines were interesting and space-age. The pool was always immaculate and very quiet. It was seldom used except on weekends and on the hottest of summer nights. I let myself out silently and took the stairs.

I stayed in the gym as long as I could, looking down on the traffic outside the window. A snake-like stream of demonstrators in black masks or Palestinian neck scarves wound their way between cars below. There was a heavy police presence on bicycles and motorcycles. I kept an eye out for the twins while I worked the weights, jerkily at first, then with a rhythm that came with my body calming itself. The stair machine was a truly stupid thing, but I hopped on that to give my upper body a cool-down, then went back to the weight machine. A squat, smiling Chinese guy was working the other machine; he nodded and matched my rhythms perfectly. He was clearly competitive and I wondered if he'd left a pissed-off woman up in his apartment. He was wearing a sleeveless Olympics sweatshirt and tennis shorts, and while he was solid and a little chunky, I didn't think he had the bulk muscle to keep up with me. We both had the machines singing, neither of us looking at each other, pacing ourselves by the other's breathing and the thump-thump of the fixed weights. It grew dark outside; cars turned on headlights and made little streaks against the windows of the gym. There was a point when I was sure I was going to collapse and die; then I heard him grunting instead of breathing and that gave me a kick. But then it was me grunting. My jaw hurt from grinning to show it didn't hurt. I folded and he did two more of whatever we'd been doing and collapsed.

When my heart was under control and I could breathe without sucking, I went through to the showers, wet myself down and on into the pool. The water was still, as though no one had penetrated it for years. I did laps, praying the Chinaman didn't come in and go all gold-medal on me. When I stopped and stretched between laps of an uncoordinated Australian crawl, I heard the shower going and a surprisingly deep voice singing. I backstroked myself into a relaxing cool-down, then floated around like a kid in a pond thinking about my day's conversations. I laughed out loud thinking about Connie Lombardozzi and how Barry looked acting out the roles of the mutts and the cops. Old cops and their old stories, oral history that no one gave a shit about. I wondered if he'd actually expected me to believe all that guff. Cops love to string old stories, testing your credibility, seeing how gullible you might be. I wondered, too, about the guy that the Mouse dragged through Kensington Market. Would Allie get so depressed that the world wasn't changeable that she'd harm herself? The kid was pretty tightly wound and seemed to be approaching some kind of crossroads; I wondered what devil would meet her there, and what he'd offer. The bum across from the Krak Bar was a bit of a puzzle; he'd looked as surprised to see me as I was to see him. Maybe there *was* a Red Squad and he was seconded from the Sisters for some national security reason. There were globalization meetings coming up and maybe this was some surveillance prior to nasty preventive detention. I replayed the sad urban tale of Corolla, the Hummingbird, another rich orphan like Elodie, maybe crippled up in her own way, a way that didn't give her that hour of rest on the roadway when she lay busted and cried with amazement at the proliferation of stars and the sudden shrinkage of her own self.

The bomb had been a good excuse to see my daughters, but I didn't have a client paying me to go any further. I was as stubborn as Elodie and I'd gargle glass before jumping into the Carlsons' shit for free. If Fox wanted to hire us, fine: ultimately the money would come from the Carlsons' bank, whether they knew it or not, and there'd be a hefty markup when Fox translated our invoice into his. I thought of the paternal, silver-haired Fox sitting in his office of muted mahogany, verbally stroking the crushed good sister, warning her in his fatherly whispering baritone of the almost-hopelessness of the situation. But not too hopeless, otherwise there'd be no point in her hiring him. Keep 'em wet, he said.

I showered to rinse the chlorine off. The clock in the weight room said I'd been down there for hours. The Chinaman was outside the sliding doors on the balcony, smoking a cigarette in the invisibly light rain. I went into the pool room and racked the balls, playing for position, not pockets. When I came out an hour later the Chinaman was in the weight room doing tai chi. His movements were fluid and imperceptible, as though he were underwater and didn't want to disturb the surface. Watching him made me feel calm and centred.

I went upstairs to deal with Elodie.

The next morning I awoke upside down in the bed, Elodie's head on my chest and strands of her hair across my lips. Faintly I could hear the traffic of rush hour. We'd left the window open. I moved carefully so as not to disturb her: no matter how fine the night Elodie had been, the morning Elodie was another matter entirely. I showered and went through my morning ritual of coffee on the terrace. There wouldn't be many more mornings of this left: the city was fighting off autumn and while it looked like it had a chance of winning, the weather was like a bout between mismatched middleweights. The fix was in.

We'd gone to bed fairly early and fairly sober. Both of us knew booze wasn't our friend, especially when we ourselves were being enemies. When I'd come up from the gym Elodie had been on the floor beside her wheelchair, pumping up and down on a bicycle pump with her hands, firming up her wheels. I threw my workout clothes in the washer in the hallway closet, opened a beer and finished it quickly. My stomach growled.

"Good workout, stud?" I knew then it was over, the battle or whatever it had been had ended.

"The popsies were down there," I lied. The popsies were three absolutely stunning young women who lived somewhere high above us. They had some game they played, an erotic splashing and tussling in the shallow end of the pool. The first time Elodie and I went swimming the popsies were in full popsy bikini mode, giving each other little massages, wringing the water out of each other's hair. The popsies had been seen in the company of men; the popsies had been seen in the company of women. Best of all, I thought, was the popsies holding hands and strolling across the downstairs lobby in thin summer frocks. Never, however, had I seen a popsy alone. It was a cult of pleasure, I believed.

I rotated my neck and shoulders and worked to get a spasm from my hamstring. "Geez, I think they might've hurt me this time, El."

"You like them, don't you, Charlie?"

"Truly, I do, Elodie. I like them fine."

"They wouldn't give you a hard time, would they? They wouldn't, you know, challenge you or anything, right? You guys'd have a ... like, *symbiosis*?"

"Well, Elodie, I suspect they'd be pretty obedient and not overly demanding."

She shook her chair by the armrests, tested the firmness of the wheels and, quick as an acrobat, flipped herself up onto the cushion. She wheeled past me into the kitchen and took a bottle of wine from the fridge. She poured a glass, glanced at my empty, and got me another. "Do you think, Charlie, you'd find them boring, you know, after a while?"

I affected to consider that possible turn of events. She was staring at me, her eyebrows raised in a caricature of intense interest. I said, "Maybe. Maybe after a couple of years, El. Maybe, maybe three, at most."

"And then, Charlie, what would you end up with?"

"I think, Elodie, I think I might need hospitalization. For sure a vacation, anyway."

"But they wouldn't go with you, would they, Charlie? You'd be an old fucked-out guy too tired to look after himself."

I was enjoying this immensely. This was, to me, the real Elodie, the real game. "But," I said, "what's my alternative, Elodie? I'm a lonely guy."

"Well, Charlie, maybe we should examine that, don't you think? Before you make a decision that causes you further grave injury." She turned and wheeled into the bedroom, the crystal wineglass balanced on her wheelchair cushion beside her thigh.

Later, at some point, we took a break and she asked me if we couldn't perhaps give the Carlsons a discount, maybe look around a bit on the cuff, and then negotiate a fair wage. I knew I was being played and she wasn't subtle about it. I told her I already had, that I'd spent the day poking around the Black Bloc.

"You think there's something there?"

I tangled my hands in her hair. "Yeah, I think so. I don't know what, but, yeah, there's some weirdness there."

We lay still a few minutes. Then she said, "The popsies. The three of them, together, on their best day, couldn't love you more than me, Charlie."

I couldn't think of anything to say to that, not even to comment on the syntax.

It was a motorcycle day, clear and crisp and cool enough that the bike's engine ran optimum, clean. I could have walked down to the government office buildings but I took the beast out, running the long way around and over to the government offices on University Avenue, then over to the land titles office at the Atrium. I spent the morning running back the eight targets in the investment scam. It took a few hours and I compiled a fat stack of computer printouts, land titles, deeds and mortgages, loans, liens, corporate filings, and several civil lawsuits that didn't really go anywhere.

I called the detective office at 52 Division and asked for Carl Hanson. We arranged to meet for an early lunch far enough from his office that he wasn't likely to run into anyone who knew him. Hanson arrived at a coffee shop an hour later, parking his company car illegally with the red light on the dash. We sat outside on the patio in the rear of the place, unseen by passing pedestrians or passing traffic. Hanson was paranoid enough to be smart, and smart enough to be paranoid. He'd worked a special task force—Project Four—looking into municipal and provincial corruption, and had been too successful.

In the backrooms of police headquarters, City Hall, and at the legislature, he'd found bribes, payoffs, and kickbacks were hidden in the very culture of bureaucracy and policy. There were strange and fluid ways in which things were done.

Everybody involved knew exactly what they were doing and, to the naked eye, they appeared to be doing nothing except practising public protection or political governance.

In bidding for government contracts, Hanson found, the bids weren't rigged, but the bidders were, each taking a turn at filing a bid for, say, building playgrounds, a bridge, a waterfront cleanup project. The bidders decided among themselves who would enter a bid and who would purposely fail to meet the specifics of the call for tenders, or come in too high. No one went out of turn. If someone won, say, a construction project last year, this year he'd put in a bid that would never be considered, or he didn't bid at all. Some crumbs might fall to him, maybe the leasing of his equipment, a couple of dump trucks to carry away construction waste. Anyone who went out of turn was excluded from participating in the next round; indeed, in extreme cases labour peace might be fractured or a mysterious combustion might strike.

Hanson thought someone wanted to actually clean things up and he went to work. Quickly, he found the weak link, a second-term city councillor who had the bad old ward-heeler's habit of wanting his payoff in cash-in-a-bag, instead of future favours or appointments to powerful commissions and committees. He'd pick up a bag, take a little out—his end—and pass the bag on, a little lighter, to the next guy, who would do the same, until the bag had swung on the merry-go-round through a complete cycle and came back empty, only to be filled again. A bad drinker with a poor memory, the bagman had a check-off list that identified which envelope went to which politicians.

The ease with which Hanson uncovered the circumstance only showed the arrogance of the players and the petri dish in which corruption multiplied upon itself. "I was surprised that no one had looked before," he'd told me several years ago when I was working a story for Kent. "It was like, when I came up and pointed it out, they all went, Hey, it's above board; if it's crooked, why isn't it hidden? Well it wasn't hidden, dumb-fuck, because no one gave a shit as long as they got their end and no one complained."

As he filed his reports his inspector got more and more nervous, but no further action was demanded and the investigation seemed mired. Hanson told the inspector the potential for it to be a major case was huge and he needed some bodies and some funding. In turn the inspector warned the superintendent he had a crusader on his hands, and the superintendent told the brass that the patsy they'd put onto the corruption allegations was getting all Christian. It didn't take long for Hanson to feel the heat, the kind of heat that could put him on the courthouse pickups and deliveries, not a good circumstance for a guy who wanted to retire with a strong pension.

Hanson got his break when the young councillor stopped off to have a couple of pops on his way to do a drop. Hanson followed him to the bar. Before going in he disconnected the brake lights on his own Cadillac. Inside the bar he sat beside the councillor at the bar, started a conversation. The two of them got shit-faced. Except Hanson didn't.

"See, what I wanted to do was get into his car in a way that would generate some official paperwork, and get it all out in the public," he said. "The Project Four guys were just going through the motions; all the reports I was filing didn't seem to have any purpose or result. I was getting pissed and they were getting pissed at me."

At closing time, Hanson invited his new pal to an all-night boozecan. "I told him to follow me closely, I didn't want him to get lost."

A few hundred yards from the club Hanson buried his

brakes and the councillor, too drunk and following too close, ran about halfway into Hanson's back seat. Hanson, who'd taken precautions before the impact, jumped out of his ruined Cadillac, checked on the unconscious councillor. He grabbed the keys and popped the trunk. He found a gym bag containing a dozen envelopes full of cash, numbered from one to twelve, and a check-off list. He took the list and left the trunk open. The traffic officer who first arrived at the scene adjudged the councillor at fault, him being the second man into the play, searched his car, and found a bagful of money.

Hanson told the cop, "I don't know you, buddy, and you can do what you want. But here." Hanson handed him the superintendent's business card.

"When the traffic guy made the call and turned that bag in, I was golden forever. Everyone knew there was a list, but where was it?" said Hanson, years later, never tiring of the details of the story. "I ended up with a new Caddie. I got detective-sergeant and the traffic guy was assigned to drive the chief around. The bag of money disappeared. The councillor is now on the police services board and is proud to be a friend of the police. The Big Chu became the first Chinese chief. Win-win-win, right?

"That moment, that moment when they paid me off I knew they were a bunch of fuckers who didn't give a shit about the bandits looting the town, as long as the councillor knew which way to vote on the police budget. That was all they wanted me for, to find a dirty councillor, measure his head for them, and put the hat on him. Now, I can whip out my dick and jerk off on the Big Chu; he'll say, a great piece of police work, Carl, go ahead and come in my mouth, I dig it with fat white guys. Every once in a while they'll cruise me for the list."

Now on the patio he looked to be a happy man. He was

one of those guys who actually thought of himself as a peace officer when he signed up. He was disappointed maybe that he had to play the sharp games at Headquarters, to corrupt himself so he could be incorruptible. I liked him and enjoyed his company, so much so that when we found ourselves together we could talk all manner of things that had nothing to do with policing or corruption. Too, he was crazy about Elodie and at the first retirement dinner I'd taken her to he'd been the first one across the floor to ask her to dance.

"How's El? She walking yet?" He was rummaging in his inside jacket pocket.

"She says not. If she is, then I'm the dumbest doughnut in the day-old basket."

He pulled some photocopies from the mess in his pocket. "Give these to her." He handed over news stories about breakthroughs in spinal cord research from newspapers across the country, South Africa, the UK, and the US. He shrugged: "I'm sure she knows all this stuff, but in case she missed any."

I carefully refolded them and put them in my pocket. "I got some guys, you up for it?"

"Gimme. Anything here that's going to bite me in the ass?"

The danger Hanson faced was that one day I'd give him names that were silent hits that would flash an alarm at some special squad. Silent hits were put out when cops wanted to keep an eye open for someone's location or movements. Even the cop punching the names into the computer wouldn't know the suspects were hot, but within hours he'd get a call from the squad that filed the hits wanting to know the wheres and whens and whys of the computer search.

"Business guys. Due diligence."

We talked about various subjects, a little gossip, a few jokes. I mentioned the bomb at the Park and he stared at me. "You in there, someplace?"

I explained Corolla Carlson and her connection to Elodie's family. "The Big Chu isn't on this particular bus. I'd think he'd be riding it into an emergency budget. But the Chu is gone."

"I don't know much about it. We got the call from Queen's Park security the other night. The witches went in." The witches were the bomb squad. Their logo was a black silhouette of a witch in a pointed hat, holding a cartoon bomb. "I sent a couple of guys up there, the staff-sergeant had his whole shift up there. We brought the mad bombers back to the station and kept 'em separate. Then the Shiv called, saying no one was to interview the suspects until his guys arrived, all paperwork to be routed to his office. Burn before reading, that kind of shit."

The Shiv was the head of the intelligence bureau. He'd been the superintendent running the Project Four corruption investigation that turned out to be bogus. The Big Chu's first appointment when he became chief was handing intelligence over to the Shiv.

"What's it all mean, Carl?"

"Who knows? But that isn't the interesting part."

I waited. The waitress came by and we ordered some more beer. I couldn't wait him out. I asked. "What's more interesting than that?"

"The bomb guy."

"Which bomb guy?"

Something was tickling at my mind. When Magda the K had taken over media relations at the Swamp she had convinced the chief that the best way to get positive media coverage was to find a hero in every success and make him available at press conferences and for one-on-one interviews. I didn't remember seeing the defuser on the television or in the papers.

"The guy who went in and defused it." He drank off half his beer, glanced at his watch, and pushed the mug away. "You'd think he'd be a media star by now, right?"

I put down some money and we got up. "You'd think."

"Funny," Hanson said. "They sent him on a training course in England the next day. He's gonna head up the child porn task force when he gets back."

"What child porn task force?"

"Beats shit out of me."

10

A block from the condo, I passed a taxi dawdling a left-hand turn, on the outside, cutting pretty close to his front fender. I spotted Elodie wheeling down Bay Street, a bag of groceries hung over the armrest of her wheelchair. She was intent on the cracks and undulations of the sidewalk immediately in front of her. She seemed tiny and, with her head down, a little sad. It's moments when someone you love doesn't know you're watching that you see their true face. I eased the bike into a driveway a half a block ahead and waited as she approached the apartment building. It amazed me how many people looked at her in either pity or curiosity. There's a slight decline just north of the building and here she gave a mighty crank on the wheels and sailed, hands-free, her hair blowing back, her body hunched a little like a downhill skier. She spotted me idling and glided up beside me; we rode down the parking garage ramp with her holding the back of my seat.

In the elevator I showed her the whack of paper I'd accumulated and said we were running a criminal record check on the eight targets. It was a favour she likely thought I shouldn't have spent, but the mutual meanness of the day before kept us both in check. The cleaning lady had been through the apartment and it smelled faintly of a lemony furniture polish. While Elodie unpacked her groceries I picked up messages. Two hang-ups that came after a second or two of statically dead air, then Janine Carlson-Appleby asking Elodie to call back, and then Fox asking me to call back.

While Elodie began filing the data into a report, I called Fox back. His secretary said he was unavailable but when I identified myself she said he was at Renato Billiards on St. Clair and would be there for another couple of hours. I should feel free, if it was convenient, to head on up there. I told Elodie I was going back out and that Janine Carlson-Appleby had called.

"There's no way we can do this for her on a family-friend basis, Charlie?"

"I'd feel demeaned and so would she, deep down. I don't think she'd appreciate us giving her charity."

"Nice one, Charlie." She shrugged. "I got pork chops for dinner."

"Do you know what to do with them, Elodie? You don't, do you?"

"I don't, Charlie. But I know a guy who does, don't I?"

"Indeed you do. We finally alone tonight?"

"We be."

"Let's go for a swim. I'll show you how I snorkle."

"Something the popsies taught you, no doubt."

"No doubt."

In Little Italy I found secure parking for the motorcycle a couple of blocks from the Renato. I wandered my way to the pool hall, stopping several times to buy imported pasta, some thin slices of prosciutto, a hunk of Parmesan, anise cookies, olive oil, and a half dozen cannolli. My knapsack was bulging when I paused in front of the looker. I told him I was meeting someone named Volpe, which is Italian for Fox. He smiled, said to wait, and hit the speed dial on his cell phone. He spoke, then said, "Okay," and stepped aside. "You can go up but the bags stay. I'll keep an eye on them."

The Renato is one of those places that changed names and locations so often its mention in intelligence reports is cross-referenced for convenience. An afternoon game of baccarat was constantly in play, often with as much as $60,000 passing over the tables in a day. Management of the Renato was fluid. The previous owner, Romano Volpe, had floated up in the lake, his body in pieces without enough ballast to keep him on the bottom. Seamlessly, the games at the pool hall came under the governorship of Enio Palma.

I'd met Enio several years ago when Kent's Portuguese cleaning lady was going to be deported for overstaying her visa. He assigned me to write a long piece about immigration, comparing how his cleaning lady was kicked out, but not a warlord who had claimed he was a political refugee in order to avoid being returned to Somalia to face trial. The cleaning lady had claimed she had been religiously persecuted in Portugal for being a Jehovah's Witness; however when she held the Bible in her hand to testify, she broke down in tears and couldn't make herself lie while touching the black book. She was gone from the country two weeks later. The warlord remained. During a break in the two hearings I noticed a deportation appeal for Enio Palma. For several afternoons I dropped into the Palma hearing—the government wanted him out for organized crime activities; his position was he had done nothing of the sort. His lawyer had shredded the government's case, which was weak at best. My presence taking notes in the hearing room didn't escape notice. As I left the building I found myself in the elevator with Enio, his placid, big-eyed young wife, and their lawyer.

"Congratulations, Mr. Palma," I said. "You got a winner."

He was morose. "Yeah."

When we reached the main lobby, he took me aside. He was hesitant. "Look, you gotta write this?"

"Well, yeah, it's my living. You're going to come out okay. You won. The court says you're not a gangster."

"Ah," he said, drawing it out. "My kids, though. All that crap in there, sure it isn't true, but they're learning English at school from the papers. They'll all read it, those lies, all those kids, friends of my kids. You ever think sometimes there's money in not doing something, sometimes?" At his elbow his lawyer said warningly, "Enio ..." Enio said, "It's all right, Warren, relax. Nobody's muscling anybody here, right? Just talking."

We talked about generalities and I wished him and his lawyer a Merry Christmas. I went into the coffee shop next door to meet the government lawyer. He was already there, despondent over a cup of coffee, a bag of Christmas presents in a shopping bag beside his chair.

"It was a great fucking stinking piece of shit, the whole thing. We had nothing. Fuck, I'm going to look like a dunce when this gets out."

We talked and I told him about my conversation with Enio Palma.

"You thinking about not doing it?"

It was coming up to Christmas week. I said fuck it. And on Christmas Eve afternoon a case of red wine appeared at my apartment. It seemed I'd made as much of an impression on Enio Palma as he'd made on me.

I thought about the case of wine and sad little Mrs. Palma

as I went up the hallway stairs at the Renato. The second-floor looker took a signal from the guy at the bottom of the stairs and let me in. There were twelve pool tables, each covered with a sheet of plywood with green baize tacked to it. Each table had men around it, playing cards, firing money into the pot. The dealers, most of them paying off overdue loans, looked bored. A dice game was underway someplace out of sight and someone, it sounded like Fox in his outraged courthouse voice, yelled, "Motherfuck whore of a Madonna," to rough laughter. I recognized the biker-looking guy behind the bar but couldn't place him. The courthouse, maybe, or some strip club near the airport. I stuck my head into the backroom until Fox saw me, then went to have a beer.

When Fox came out he was sweating. His shirt sleeves were rolled up and his suspenders hung loose. The shock of white fatherly hair stood atop a beet-red face as though he'd just done a marathon in a whorehouse. I realized at that moment he was a degenerate.

"Charlie, come sit. We gotta talk."

We went across the room and sat near the windows. I saw Enio Palma take some drinks from the bartender and carry them over to us.

"Calogero," he said to me as I stood up. "Long time. These are on the house, as usual." He looked at Fox. "It's just one of those days we all have, Mr. Fox. Next time I'm sure you'll own part of this place."

"Next time," Fox said, remaining seated, "I bring my own dice."

"My friend, agreed. Of course." His voice was jovial but his face took on a bland hardness, like cement. "You'll have to spit them from your mouth because your hands will be flavouring the sausages at Tio Nino's trattoria."

I could see Fox had been angry and now he looked a little slapped down.

"Please enjoy the place, Calogero, join in the social amenities if you'd like. I'll tell my nephew at table five to give you unlimited credit."

"I have enough misery in my life to suit me, Mr. Palma. But thanks for the offer."

"Ah, misery." His face became bland. "And how is your young lady? Elsa, is it?"

I studied him. "Elaine."

"A jewel. When you are to be wed, let me know. We have a fine banquet hall and for the lady it will be my wedding present." He turned to Fox and his face changed. "Mr. Fox, a pleasure."

Fox said, "No doubt." When Enio Palma walked away, he said, "Greasy wop fucking cocksucker. You know how many times I saved his ass? Gonna put my hands in the sausage mill, is he, the fucker? I'll put his ass in jail." I could see he was a little drunk and patted the air between us to hush him down.

"Why we meeting, Cornelius?"

"You working for the good sister, Charlie? You showing her a little sunshine in this time of inclement weather?"

"Nope."

"That'll be news to her, then. We bailed the bad sister today. Close loving family recently undergone a tragedy, yak yak yak. Tons of bucks and not shy about spending it. She, bad sister Corolla, goes into therapy, behaviour modification, anger management. Not to associate ... curfew ... report daily ... surrender passport. So after we sign her out we're dotting the tees and crossing the eyes and she, the good Janine sister, says, Mr. Fox, I want you to know that I've asked Charlie Tate and Elodie Gray to look into things for you. Any assistance they can give, you ask them and they'll be glad to provide." Fox stared at me in a glare. "Are you fucking stupid, Charlie? What, pray tell, the fuck is that about? You realize there's a fucking ski chalet in Collingwood here for me? Over time I can move out that fucking pile uptown and get something decent out in the Hills? You fucking me, Charlie? After I gave you that ..." He stopped and looked around; the pool hall wasn't the best place to run at the mouth so he rubbed his thumb and forefinger together, " ... newspaper I was done with."

"Cornelius, becalm yourself. I'm sorry Enio's mechanics trimmed you a new haircut back there, but take it easy. We have no client. Elodie's talking to the good sister, that's all. They're friends. Mostly moral support, a little liquid nourishment. No money has changed hands, no work has been done. You can run up a tasty bill with Bobby's crew, making a living."

He wasn't satisfied and seemed to grow redder. I saw something of the serpent there, a yellow venom in the sagging pouches under his eyes. I don't think he even heard me. He spoke as if I hadn't said anything. "Because, I love you, you baldheaded cocksucker, but I'm telling you, if that bitch of yours ..."

Now we had a game. My hand was across the table at his neck and my fingers were into his throat. I stood up and I took him up with me. He was a few inches shorter than me, so when I still had a way to go to becoming fully upright, he had reached his toes and was still ascending. The biker at the back bar said something loudly, it sounded like, "Boss, dust-up." I heard a voice, Enio's I think, say something back, sharply, and it sounded like, "Amaretto straight up, just pour the fucking thing." A few sets of feet began leaving the poolroom and I heard them clatter down the stairs. I only heard all this because I was seeing red mist. Without volition my hand squeezed and my arm brought him across the table close to me.

There's a mental place I used to go, back in the days when I was a bad boozer who boxed. Sometimes I could go there merely by lifting insane weights to prove I was strong and still a young man. I could lift into the mist and come out the other side, a little frightened, maybe a little reborn. I hadn't been there in a while. As I said, Elodie might be the rag-and-bone man of me. Cornelius Fox in a few seconds had dialled me back to an age that never really was gone. The fragility of the new Elodie-me surprised me.

The first time I slammed Cornelius Fox against the front window it didn't even crack. The second time there was a sharp cracking. His arm swung over mine like that of an awkward girl throwing a baseball; the loose fist hit me on the side of the nose, but he wasn't really fighting back, he was flailing. I tasted blood. I heard Enio say, "Go, Aaron, go, go now."

The heaviest part of Cornelius Fox was his head and I was swiping him like a rag through the air so his head was contacting repeatedly with the window.

Aaron had bare arms under a leather vest with conches where buttons would be. He had been drinking what smelled like cherry brandy. His arm was thick with bulk muscle but he knew enough to use his forearm bone on my Adam's apple to jack me. It felt like an iron bar and was hard and locked. I had to put Cornelius Fox down to get my fingers between his forearm and my throat. His other hand came around and locked under my chin and he was taking me away.

"Not him, you dumb fuck, the other fucking guy."

Like a trained attack dog being given conflicting signals, Aaron barely paused to reorient himself, then went for Fox, immediately going to work on his lower torso with a slow but powerful combination of jabs. As Fox's hands went down to his abdomen, Aaron worked his ribs and upper chest. When Fox's hands went up, Aaron hooked him a long slow looper in the groin and it got very messy on the floor.

"Okay, okay, go back to the bar, Aaron."

Patiently, Enio Palma watched as Cornelius Fox massaged his groin. He bent over Fox and, squatting just out of the vomit, spoke to him softly. The roaring in my ears was subsiding and to me Fox looked like a pretty good target there, on the floor. Either I shifted my feet or Enio was a mind reader; he turned his head slightly to me and said, "Don't. It's over." He called to Aaron, "Make this guy a drink." He went back to talking softly to Fox.

At the bar Aaron asked what I wanted, smirking pleasantly and saying, "We're out of Jew's blood, but I expect a shipment any minute." He had SS zigzags on his left forearm and an AN on his right: Aryan Nations.

"Beer." I coughed a little harder than I had to; Aaron looked like a guy who needed praise and liked making friends. "You got a good arm bar there."

"When I met my old lady she asked how I got the muscles. I said I pump black assholes, bench press, free weights." He held out his hand, crusted with cheap silver rings. "Aaron Bower. Aaron like Aryan, Bower like Power. Don't let the hebe name fool you."

It was something he shouldn't have said. That, with the Jew's blood comment and the black assholes, was a little too *I've-done-time*. He wanted to be my pal and suddenly I knew exactly who he was, where I'd seen him before. The last time he'd been in a uniform, doing a paid-duty assignment at a Chinese banquet. I could tell he didn't recognize me at all.

When I didn't give my name he apologized for going for me. I nodded and took my beer down the room. The players had gone back to losing money. Enio Palma was reaching out to slowly tap Cornelius Fox's face in a humiliating, casual rhythm. Fox got up, trying to block Enio's lazy slaps. He didn't look at me, probably didn't even know I was there, and made his way to the looker at the top of the stairs. He went past him and I heard his slow feet making their way out.

"Hebe cocksucker." Enio was wiping his hands on his suit pants as if to clean away soil. "My kid is in law school. Another couple of years and we won't need these greedy fucks picking our pockets, double-talking us into taking pleas. You okay, Calo-ger-o?"

I said I was fine and apologized for the dust-up. He said Fox was going to go into the shit anyway, better with me than with Tony on the door. "You got muscles, kid, but Tony's tough."

He walked me to the stairs and down past the lookers. In front of the place we stood a moment, watching traffic, me slinging my bag of groceries over my shoulder, Enio with his hands in his pockets.

"You know, Calogero, I know her name's Elodie. It's okay that I know that."

I looked at him, feeling vaguely ashamed. "Mr. Palma, you should lose the bartender."

"Aaron? Aaron's coming along. Why?"

I stared into his eyes. I could imagine those eyes watching Romano Volpe being chopped into nine pieces of meat. I could imagine Palma watching the pieces being stuffed into plastic leaf bags. I could imagine him, cold and predatory, studying the ripples in the lake dissipating before nodding his head and telling the guy operating the boat to head for shore.

"Mr. Palma," I said, "you should lose the bartender, okay?"

I went looking for my bike.

11

At the apartment Elodie was sitting in the sun, reading the newspaper. The bomb story was still on the front page. The headline read: More Terror To Come, Sources Say. I got two beers from the fridge and took them onto the balcony. I crossed to look down at the traffic below and when I turned around she saw my face.

"Charlie, what did you do?" She was panicky and breathless. "What did you do? You've got blood on your face."

"Nothing. I was doing some work."

She took my hand. "Tell me."

I said, "Let me get the pork chops started and then we'll go for a swim."

"Is anybody hurt? Did you hurt somebody?"

"Well, I think we've lost Cornelius Fox as a client."

I took the chops from the fridge, patted them dry with a paper towel, and made pockets inside them with a boning knife. I was extremely calm and very centred inside myself. I felt like I'd visited a friend doing time and had been allowed to take him out for a walk around the prison grounds but now he was back in his cell. Elodie put on music as I julienned some prosciutto, shaved some Parmesan, and cut pieces of cold butter. Whitney Houston came on loud and quickly, a disco version of some movie soundtrack hit, where the bodyguard falls in love with the woman. The Whit's lyrics were slow and the music was fast; her voice was modified by echoes and wowed by a technician. I was doing my half-shuffled dance of little steps by the countertop. When the chops were stuffed I used long toothpicks to seal them shut, coated each chop in flour, then egg, then bread crumbs. I put them out of reach on a rack on top of the refrigerator to dry, should the neighbour's cat come mooching. I put some olive oil in a fry pan and rubbed through it with a clove of garlic and left the stove on the lowest of heat.

I licked my fingers and thought about Enio. Enio was a crook who knew he was a crook. He almost never went outside his circle for victims; they came to him. Borrow money, ask a favour. Arrange a patio licence with the bent city councillor he owned, push through permits. Enio and I had met occasionally at some boxing matches, back when I was finding the missing debtors for Cornelius Fox. Enio had run into Elodie and me at an Italian joint one night and had been courtly and polite to her and cancelled my awkward ordering of a cheap Chianti and sent over a bottle of Donnafugata, although he had little use for anything Sicilian. He made sure the bill never saw our table. Like most of the men of *mala vita*, the evil life, Enio maintained two distinct and opposite faces: the visage he wore when he was working and honour or profit were involved, and the gentleman's mask he maintained socially. I remembered him gently and slowly shaking Elodie's strong little hand, and I could also imagine him taking a hacksaw from a cheese boy, showing him how to saw through a man's elbow joint without running into much more than tendon and flesh. He knew her name was Elodie, not Elsa or Elaine or Edith. It might have bothered me, but it bothered me more that Cornelius Fox knew Elodie. Enio was a gangster, but Fox was a lawyer. I might have to be careful with him.

You make the biggest mistakes in the littlest of ways, in the smallest of things. Once, for a client who felt he'd been cheated in a business deal, Elodie and I took a stock down on the market simply by making little comments in the right places, having lunch with a few newspaper folk. It was the little things, sometimes, that had the biggest reactions. I wondered why I was thinking about this. Then I realized what was bothering me. I took the phone out onto the balcony and called Carl Hanson at 52 Division. He thought I was calling about the eight targets and said he'd done six and would do the other two when the opportunity arose. The six were clean. I told him I was calling about something else and said I'd heard around that there was an undercover working the bar at the Renato. He thanked me and hung up.

The pool was still green and calm and vacant. No popsies lurked or frolicked. We came out of the changing rooms and I carried Elodie down the steps into the shallow end and let her float away. Her legs were like floating sticks and I remembered the first time I saw her from underwater at one of the family cottages. It was as close as I'd ever seen her to standing, those skinny things with knobs for knees and atrophied flesh, dangling in front of me. She had a great little torso, but it was mostly bones with some flesh packed around them. Her breasts had shrunk since the accident—although her brother always told me he had a bigger set—but they had shape. She had a lot of junkyard dog scars: a faint white one from the surgery on her back, a nasty tear up her left leg where she'd got a bone infection from a pressure sore and hadn't noticed it in time to catch it, some burn marks that looked like scuffs from when she fell asleep in bed smoking and set herself on fire, the smell of the bedding burning alerting her.

She began doing lengths of the pool, using her arms in a measured breaststroke. I frolicked, swimming under her and popping up like a big walrus until I pissed her off enough that she told me to go away, she was counting. I sat on the steps, half in the water, and thought about the missing witch, the defuser who suddenly got a big lift in his career.

While I cooked the chops Elodie set up a table on the terrace. I boiled some pasta, strained a few spoonfuls of the fat from the pan, chopped some parsley and opened a bottle of Riesling. The air was chilling a little outside. I put on a jean jacket and got a wrap for Elodie. The candle flame was steady and there was no wind.

We chatted about our respective days. She'd finished her portion of the report on the eight and was holding it for the criminal record checks. No red flags, she said, although one guy had declared bankruptcy a few years earlier. She told me Janine Carlson-Appleby had called and said Corolla was out of custody. Janine Carlson-Appleby also said Fox had told her it would all be a little more expensive than he'd originally thought: the Crown's case, he'd said, looked iron-clad and, he said he'd heard, one of the other two accused was going to flip on her, which would made a tough case even tougher. It appeared to me Fox had taken a financial hit at the Renato and was looking to lay off the damage. Neither of the other accused had been granted bail yet. Elodie had also banged off a quick engagement that was pure profit: an investment group that had been scouring the town for backers had worked their way down to one of her clients. Elodie had already done the group's personal and financial background twice for other clients and she rewrote those reports. No matter how she wrote it, though, it always came out money laundering. The investment group included in its structure a paroled drug trafficker, who, while he had been caught and convicted fifteen years earlier, had managed to hide away millions of dollars in profits. She said she was going to hold the report a day or two to make it look like it was worth what she was charging.

By the time she was done bringing me up on the day, we'd finished the meal and were working our way through the heel of the Riesling. Suddenly it grew cooler and the sky seemed to darken into the chaotic portents of autumn. A breeze came up and quickly developed into a wind. We cleaned up and went inside and Elodie poured amaretto and nibbled on an anise cookie.

The telephone rang, the stuttering bleeps that indicated it was the concierge. As I went to answer it, Elodie said there was a saved message for me; she didn't know who it was but his voice sounded familiar.

Jerome, the concierge, said there was a package for me. It was heavy and he could bring it up in a half-hour or so. Jerome was the hundred-dollar guy—the other concierge got fifty bucks at Christmas, but Jerome was studying to be a pathologist and somehow managed to work at two jobs. Elodie was kind of in love with him. She made him stutter much of the time, and she loved to make him blush, telling him, "You need a body to practise your homework on, Jerome, just buzz me, okay? I've got all the parts and half of them don't work but the ones that do, work fine. Plus, if you make a mistake in the right place, just stick on a Band-Aid."

I went down and found a case of Alsatian wine with a bright bow around it and a card sticky-taped to the top. The card read: "Charlie, Charlie, Charlie. We can do great things together. Forgive, forget. Let's make some dough!" It was signed From the Law Offices of Cornelius J. Fox. I asked Jerome if he liked white wine. He said he did and I said, "Take it away."

Upstairs, on the closed circuit, Elodie was watching Jerome stash the carton of wine behind the concierge table. I had to tell her the wine was a very good one but it was from Fox and that Fox and I had had a parting of ways. Professional differences, I said.

"Professional wrestling, more like it," she said. "You looked like you were in detonate mode. You hit him?"

"A tussle. Remember Enio Palma? We were at his place. Fox was gambling like a drooling fool. He figures if he hangs out with the boys, loses a bit of money, the boys'll steer some more of their more complex business his way. He lost his shirt. Afterwards we had a bit of an argument and the bouncer had to break it up."

"A hey-rube." She was proud of her obscure carnie slang. "A buster."

"Indeed," I said, smiling, "an actual hey-rube."

Elodie said she didn't like Fox but she hoped I hadn't hurt him. "But if you did, well, I hope you got him good." She poured some more amaretto. I went into the freezer and poured some grappa. "You give him a good slam in the snot-locker?" She concentrated a bit. "You bust his chops? Powder his jaw?"

"I cut him a new asshole."

"Cool."

"He's wearing his ass for a hat."

"Yikes."

"I hit him so hard his mother's in hospital."

"Nice, very nice." She smiled at me. "Okay, your turn. How was your day, otherwise?"

I told her about seeing my kids, and their paranoia about the Red Squad, about seeing the bum in the Market, the same one I'd seen after finishing the body job. I told her the Mouse had a gawky boyfriend named Condom or something. She laughed when I related the story about Connie Lombardozzi and the Fall of the Mafia. The strange low-key press conference at headquarters, I said, was a bit of a puzzler, as well as the absent Big Chu. She was as curious as I was about the missing witch who'd defused the bomb but never got his five minutes in the sunshine, and had been sent off on a plum training assignment.

"Curious stuff, stud. What do you make of it all?"

"Dunno. Nothing there that'll help Corolla Carlson, but it's kind of interesting. After the problem with the Fox today—bear in mind it started when Janine Carlson-Appleby told him we were doing something for her, which is news to me, eh?—I doubt there'll be much need for us to be involved. Anyway, Fox is hiring Bobby and the crew. They're not going to miss much."

"Why does he care if Janine has us look around?"

"Fox is after two things. Big money, and lots of it. He wants to keep the Carlsons sweating so he can not only do this case for them, but any other work that might need doing. What he doesn't want is someone poking around, finding out stuff that might take some of the fear out of the clients. He'll let Janine know that if we can be of use, he'll do the hiring."

The phone rang and she went to get it. I heard her say, "Janine ... Yes ... Yes ... No, of course not ... Anything we can do to help ..." She hung up and reminded me there was still a saved message waiting for me.

"Janine just met with Fox. He told her that if he had any chance of making the defence work, he had to have absolute control. He told her he can't have any elements in play, that he's in delicate discussions with the Crown. He told her we were good people, but we don't have the infrastructure required to finesse a case this complex."

"That would be us, elements in play."

"Seems so."

"So she wants us to fuck off?"

"Looks like."

"Thank God."

She handed me the phone and wheeled into the kitchen to pour more amaretto and grappa. I picked up the saved message. It was from Barry White at Bobby Clarke's glue room. He didn't identify himself, one of the golden rules of intelligence being not to say anything on a telephone you wouldn't stand downtown at rush hour and shout out loud. "Hey, kid. I forgot to tell you the best part of the story. One night our guy, Connie, misunderstood some complaint about a guy who might've been dicking someone's wife. The guy, the dicking guy, I mean, was going to Italy for some family business. Connie listened, he's still, or again, completely shit-faced, and said, Hey, if he's gotta go, he's gotta go. Connie says he meant if the dicking guy had to go to Italy, he had to go to Italy, we'll deal with it later. But the guy he was talking to thought he meant, like, he's gotta, you know, go. We found the dicking guy in his car near the airport, his ticket to Italy in his pocket and his dick in his mouth." I heard him laughing. "The best thing about things is they never, ever change, huh?" He added a note to Elodie. "And, sweetie, if it's you picking up this message, 'scuse my language." Then, strangely, he added: "And, kid, I hope you got all that."

Late nights, when we watched old movies, Elodie could tell by looking at the time when things were winding down. When we watched old noir mystery movies, she'd get impatient, knowing the end was near and whoever was in the final few scenes was going to wear the hat for the mysterious murder. "It'd be nice, stud, if our engagements were like that. No loose ends, ending in time to catch an hour of old reruns and then a quick roll in the hay."

The Corolla Carlson case wasn't on anybody's clock. Sure, it had a beginning, a middle, and an end, and probably ran on some vague timeline governed by the inner workings of the Crown attorney's office, and maybe to a degree by Fox's avarice. But it had nothing to do with us anymore.

And that was it. Then Corolla Carlson went off our radar and we got on with our lives.

The autumn seemed to just appear one October morning. Elodie and I liked the time of year, me mostly because I could start planning a winter getaway, Elodie because it meant Christmas was coming, and she was a meticulous planner and wrapper of gifts. I stopped shaving and Elodie stopped buzzing me. I took to wearing hats, toques, and baseball caps, as the stubble on my skull grew out and took some shape. We took long walks out of the apartment and up through Queen's Park, Elodie's wheels crunching the bright dead leaves, or through the throngs of Chinatown, half the time wheeling on the road to avoid the indifferent crowds. We roamed various parts of town and I found a Sri Lankan restaurant where the owner couldn't get a liquor licence and was suffering for it. He kept some wine and beer out of sight and, once we became regular customers, would bring us drinks in big thick coffee mugs. One night he said he was being slaughtered by not having a licence.

"When'd you apply, Sab?" Elodie couldn't pronounce either his first or last name.

"Eight months ago, when I bought."

"What do they say when you call?"

"Oh, miss, I don't call. If I'm to have it, they will give it and I shall. If not, this country is great and there are many opportunities." Sab was the gentlest of men and Elodie enjoyed the place, even though she'd accidentally ordered a meal containing goat and, in spite of herself, had liked it.

The next day Elodie called one of the Gray family lawyers and he went down to the Sri Lankan's and got him his licence. I said it was a nice thing to do. She said, "Sure, Charlie. And now we'll never get a seat."

I found a fighting club in Chinatown and went a couple of times a week, an informal place where you went in and, if there were no partners lolling about, you could work on a heavy bag or lift a little. Each time you walked in, the owner, who looked like the vacant opium guys at the bakery upstairs, took ten bucks off you and put it into his pocket. There were no showers and he sold bottled water at a dollar a pop. You brought your own headgear and gloves, if you had any. One memorable afternoon a fourteen-year-old black kid repeatedly kicked me in the head with flicking roundhouses, not hitting too hard, but laughing as I became more frustrated. If you liked what someone else in the room was doing, you could idle over and copy his moves. I did tai chi alongside a man who never spoke to me; he silently and firmly corrected a few of my awkward moves but never said a single word and then one day he was gone.

There were fresh engagements, but nothing too taxing, mostly due diligence that required a couple of hours of legwork, bouncing around government offices and standing in long lineups, reading newspapers, and edging forward an inch at a time. The garbage runs on the software file ended when our client reached a settlement with his renegade employee. Towards November things fell off a bit and I did some fry work for a trendy new coffee shop in the financial district, scraping the grill smooth as a whetstone in my spare minutes. Cornelius Fox came in one day and sat at a rear table with a well-dressed guy I sort of recognized from TV and I thought might be from the Crown's office; the waitress was busy with a table of six so I delivered the food to Fox's table. He didn't notice me. The Big Chu came in once with Magda the K and some of the PR staff. Buddy the people's buddy came in to check the place out and look for eligible voters among the immigrant staff. After he posed for a photograph with the owner, the owner ushered him out and paid me my week's wages in cash.

Aside from Fox coming into the restaurant that one time, the only time Corolla Carlson broke surface was when Elodie received a very nice note from the elder Carlsons, thanking us for our thoughtfulness and attention to the family's time of trouble. *As you know*, the note read, *we retained Mr. Fox to act for us in this matter and we're pleased to tell you and your friend, Charles, the matter is successfully concluded to our satisfaction. If our family may be of service to you or yours, please don't hesitate to let us know.*

When November came on full, Elodie and I were sailing smoothly. The investigative research business was providing for our daily expenses. I didn't have to touch my envelopes of cash in the round safe. The fry cookery was letting me buy decent wine and interesting foods. We had a laugh when the client who'd been scammed by the Gone Wong turned up as a target in another engagement. The original client and the Gone Wong had gone into business and were running an advance-fee scheme together.

An editor called me up and asked for a three-thousand-word profile at a buck a word on an actress passing through town; her latest movie, he said, had Oscar written all over it. I used the word *comely* to describe her in the article and he was ecstatic and asked if I'd fucked her. I said no, but he immediately gave me another assignment, profiling a photographer who had bridged the bitterly fought distance between traditional photography and digital. I did a comparison of Henri Cartier-Bresson discovering the Leica and Paula Maloney discovering the Apple computer, heretics both. The first cheque came in and cleared before Christmas so I took myself to Birks and bought Elodie a necklace of diamonds.

Elodie weeded out the Christmas parties we'd attend. She took me to a fashionable men's store where the Gray men had their suits made. The distraught tailor at one point said to Elodie, "Ms Lady, the tuxedo it is perfect, but the … the …"

"You can't make a new face, can you, Marc?" Elodie said. "Do your best, he's all I've got."

My daughters came for Christmas and we all got suitably wasted, Elodie at first looking askance at the eight-paper joints the Mouse had contrived to fashion with an off-hand ease that hinted she'd rolled them before. They stayed the night, then stayed a second, using the pool and the gym, and having long tearful talks with Elodie, talks I thought might have to do with my ex-wife, me, and my father the rag-and-bone man.

Between Christmas and New Year's Day the second cheque came in in time for Elodie and me to head south. We chose Rio and lazed around in one of the family compounds. After we came back north I went back to fry cooking. Looking back, I realized I'd stayed under the radar, hadn't even thought about the Carlsons and their problem or how Fox had solved it, or why he'd put it down so quickly, rather than running for the long dough. In the Tobermory Bar one night I looked up to see Cornelius Fox sitting a few tables away, staring at me. I nodded and saw a look of hateful triumph on his face before he hid it away and nodded back pleasantly.

My life seemed to be straightening out and except for lifting too much weight and drinking too much wine and beer, it felt endless and fine and it suited me and it fit me. Between odd bits of writing, fry cooking, and doing Elodie's legwork, I found my days were full and I even read my way through Somerset Maugham and Graham Greene. I was afraid to mess with George Orwell, or I'd wind up back in Rangoon, a cheap photocopied edition of *Burmese Days* under my arm, wandering Book Street and Plumbing Street and Electrical Street, playing innocent games with military intelligence before going to the Strand Hotel for carrot curry soup, wishing I actually lived there, a footloose 1920s remittance man with no home to return to.

At the first real hint of spring and when the days allowed for it, we unbagged the trees and shrubs on the terrace, checked the new bulbs, and scrubbed down the stone and iron furniture. We planned a massive indoor-outdoor party for two months hence. In the still-wintery evenings we sat in the living room, pretending the gas fireplace was a real one, Elodie contentedly smiling at me while she learned to crochet; me poring over an atlas planning a trip to either Sicily or Asia. Sicily was my choice, money-wise, but ideas more exotic had been planted by Maugham and Greene. I was envious of Judith and Kent. Kent had suddenly up and sold the magazines to a media giant and had left his wife, taking Judith for a year in Spain, shuttling between Malaga and North Africa.

I dusted off the Leica and one morning went shopping for a darkroom I could set up in the spare bathroom. I found the film I'd shot the previous year and managed to make some smoky mysterious prints that had eggshell whites and eggplant purples. Elodie bought frames and matting and I hung them in the front foyer.

In mid-April there were fresh demonstrations at the legislature, very early events, considering the still-variable weather. The cops busted heads, the demonstrators harassed and assaulted the police horses. Acrid smoke from Molotovs drifted over the park and the clack-clack-clack of police batons on police shields echoed through the neighbourhood. Then a week-long cold snap came and we had to do replanting and the demonstrators and the cops took a break. The day the snap ended there was a riot we couldn't see but could hear over on Yonge Street where the Black Bloc trashed a couple of dozen stores and coffee outlets because, I think, Third World debt hadn't been dealt with. The neighbour's cat squeezed through gaps at the end of the terrace and we took to putting minced bits of shrimp and meats out. Up the street, at police headquarters, the Big Chu, his round shaven head bobbing on his round body, held a press conference and warned of a summer of violence to come—a season of wanton anarchistic destruction, he said—if he didn't get the funds to hire more cops on the street.

Buddy the mayor stepped up, said he feared that unless other levels of government kicked in some dough, the whole town was going to a fiery hell. He said the cost of putting down a revolution would bankrupt the city.

The popsies returned from wintering somewhere hot and sunny and only looked all the better in their tiny bikinis by the pool.

Springtime, shyly at first, was upon us.

PART TWO

12

In late April we had our seasonal party, an event that crammed the terrace dangerously and spilled inside throughout the apartment. Colin and Martha Gray were in London attending a wedding, but had arranged for some cases of wine and a wooden box of port, from one of Colin Gray's enterprises in Portugal, to be delivered. Martha Gray had centrepieces made for the food tables, and a crew from a catering firm she had invested in years ago arrived early to arrange food stations in each room, and one at each end of the terrace.

Elodie's brother, David, and his wife, Sharon, came early and we four sat out on the terrace, getting a start on Colin's port. David talked knowledgeably about the history of port while Sharon sat beside him saying little, mostly nodding and smiling at Elodie and me. Sharon was, I thought, a tragic figure. That she was once attractive was undeniable but she seemed to suffer a lack of human nourishment from living in the Gray shadow. Elodie had told me she was the fireball of their school years, the sparkplug who fired up charity drives, effortlessly headed committees, was a persistent social seducer who could reach out and get any speaker for any event, from the prime minister to the current hot author. Now she looked in terrific shape from her days at the club, and I always felt she was wearing a bland mask of acquiescent disappointment, behind which she might entertain interesting deep thoughts and probably some puzzled regrets. I knew a Vietnamese taxi driver who was a surgeon in Saigon, an accepting fellow who got lost in the shadows of bureaucracy and language of his new country and its medical boards. "I feed my family, I work, I save. There is no good life and there is no bad life; there's only life and life is enough." He wore the same mask.

Looking for something to say, Sharon asked about my daughters.

"They're coming tonight, maybe you'll meet them."

She asked when Elodie and I were getting married. David stared at her. I got the impression this had been a subject of some interest in the Gray clans.

Elodie said, "I keep proposing but he always says no."

In any case, they left and my daughters didn't arrive. Neither, it turned out, did Janine Carlson-Appleby and her husband, who had RSVP'd an enthusiastic Yes weeks earlier. Someone that night on the terrace mentioned that the Carlsons, young and old, were in the south of France, having stopped on the way to visit Corolla the mad bomber at a clinic in Switzerland. There was idle gossip and chatter about folks I knew nothing about; in fact I couldn't keep the family trees and bloodlines in order. But I nodded at the right times and made comments that spurred conversations further and, I had to admit, I had a pretty okay time.

At four-thirty the old and the weak had left and a dozen of us were left standing outside, toasting each other, springtime, and the coming dawn, with the diminishing bottles of port.

Elodie was as good as unconscious in her chair and I was drunk and flirting with the young wife of a stock jockey who'd almost put his tongue in my ear tipping me off to a gold company that was making an acquisition the following week. This, I thought, is how they do it. They catch the big fat greasy chicken, but they don't tell you. They carve off the best parts and eat them, and they only tell you about it afterward. Then the skeleton is used to make a salty soup stock and they let you have your fill. This guy was offering me a chance to get intimate with the chicken while it was still feathered.

Several police cars, emergency task force vans, unmarked cruisers, and ambulances screamed along the street below us, their racks strobing red and their sirens wailing in magnified echoes. I turned away from the young lady and looked over the balcony wall. The convoy was headed west. I looked for smoke in the sky in that direction and saw nothing. The sirens stopped somewhere west of us. Then another wave of whooping sirens, flashing reds went past. Two news vans blew by, then a cranky old yellow Citroen I recognized as Michael Bailey's, from the *Post*, then two more news vans.

"Even with the noise, I envy you and Elodie living downtown," the young wife said, leaning against my back and looking down to the street over my shoulder. "Bart got us a place in Caledon and when I say we should move back in town, he just buys me a new toy and keeps adding rooms onto the place. You could get lost in there, and sometimes I do. Some nights, when I'm in town for an opening or something, I stay at the King Eddie and don't care if I never see the country again."

I was drunk enough to actually entertain taking this somewhere. Her husband had walked another guest, a young black actress, down to her car and hadn't returned. It had been about an hour.

At five-thirty everyone was gone, except for the young wife who was crying herself to sleep on the sofa. I picked a sleeping Elodie up in my arms and carried her into the bedroom, then brought in the wheelchair and parked it beside the bed. I called the cleanup crew and left a message on their machine to come later in the day, after lunchtime at least. I took a last beer outside and watched the sun gild the towers down Bay Street.

There were seagulls screaming over the city. Someone once told me that when seagulls come inland it's because the closest body of water is too polluted to sustain their diet. I finished the beer and went inside, securing the doors behind me. The young wife was flung on the couch, staring at the ceiling, crying. I got a duvet from the closet and covered her. I felt sorry for her, trapped by everything she wanted, and leaned to kiss her a peck goodnight. Her tongue was in my mouth and we played that way for a few minutes. She was a frenzy. Sometimes I told Elodie she snored; she denied it aggressively and now I heard her through the open door. I thumbed tears from the young wife's cheeks, our faces still vapour-locked together. I ran my hand over her silky full blouse. We were fumbling, then. Desperation, loneliness, port, dawn, desire, pity, and heat. The seven dwarfs getting together to relax after a hard day. Put them all together in one room and they spell, like any seven clowns I ever met in the circus, chaos.

Outside a seagull screeched; it sounded like it had found the detritus of our all-nighter. I thought of the young wife as a seagull. The body of water and the beach she wanted to inhabit was polluted and didn't nourish her, didn't sustain her appetites or her diet. She'd moved inland.

For better or worse, the telephone rang then and it was the cops.

I took a long, sobering shower. Carl Hanson said to wait until after eight o'clock, there was nothing to do until then, until the whole thing had some semblance of order to it. "They went in the middle of the night. They even coordinated calling the troops to a DOD office for a briefing so no one would leak. All my guys, both staffs, four sergeants, and all area foot guys were called in. They're milling around, half asleep. I got the call an hour ago and just got here. It's bedlam. The cells are packed. When I went down there I thought I'd better get you down here."

My first thought was about Corolla Carlson, the bombing debutante, who I'd forgotten was overseas being expensively gentled back to reality. "It's Carlson, right? They got her again?"

"Call me when you're in the area and don't say nothing on the phone." He hung up.

My hair was still wet under my helmet when I jammed my motorcycle between two television station wagons parked in the handicapped spaces out back of the station. Media vehicles were parked half on the sidewalk on the side streets on both sides of the building. On the wide pedestrian walkway in front a huge truck was telescoping up the live eye, and techies wearing headgear and microphones were chattering back and forth with their producers. In front of the Dundas Street doors a throng of reporters was gabbing and comparing notes. Some film crews had their gear stacked up along the sidewalk; some of the cameramen dozed. Others were shooting footage of the building, the media, and uniformed cops going in and out. Messy, hip-looking people were being interviewed by print people, members of the Black Bar who'd been called when the word started to get out that lawyers were needed.

Michael Bailey was speaking with a compact blonde I recognized from morning television. As they spoke neither had still eyes, watching what went on everywhere, looking at anybody who moved with direction or purpose. I paused in front of them a moment until I was sure he saw me, then walked east towards a doughnut shop. A few minutes later he came in and helped himself to one of my doughnuts.

He asked what I was doing out so early. I said I'd been up all night, in fact had seen his yellow lemon go by my place a few hours earlier. I asked him what was up.

"Something, for sure, Charlie. I got a wakeup call from a friend at the radio station and they said the scanners were going nuts, a bunch of guys yelling into the radios, other guys coming on and telling them to shut the fuck up and get off the air. Some old doll called from her bedroom and said there were ambulances and sirens all around her house, is it a fire? Am I safe? Are people dead? She said there were men carrying shotguns outside her place. Cops are grabbing each other, the uniforms haven't got a clue who they're grabbing, but they got guns and they're getting grabbed. Lucky no one was shot."

"And?"

"And? And, of course it was a secret operation run on laser beams from Planet Chu. It was the ETF guys told to go on a back-up and they'd get instructions at the scene, but didn't. It was some intelligence guys no one ever heard of. It was, I'm told, the Funny People from CSIS. Some guys from national defence. The bomb squad." His cell phone chirped; he listened and jumped up and ran out to where the morning television girl was frantically waving at him, holding her cell phone to her ear. Buddy the Mayor showed up in the Limousine Powered by Dead Voters and the media charged him immediately. Buddy went into windmill mode, knocking into a couple of video-camera snouts and several microphones before he was swallowed up in the scrum. I saw his handler, a tall, balding, muscular guy I knew, whose only job was to hold the mayor's mouth closed. The bald muscular guy too vanished into the scrum.

I used the pay phone to call Hanson's office. A woman answered and said, "Fifty-second division," and I hung up. She wasn't a cop: a cop would have said *fifty-two*, *detective office*. I tried Hanson's cell phone and was told by a mechanical voice the subscriber wasn't available. After another doughnut, watching Buddy be Buddy, I called Hanson's cell again, got the same message. When I hung up it rang immediately.

"Hey, you down here someplace?" Hanson sounded hollow, as though he was in a basement or an elevator.

"Having a sinker, watching the Bud go ape for the media."

He wanted to tell me where to meet him and it became a little complicated with "that place where the guy was who ..." and "the liquor licence guy whose wife's got the big tits ..." and a few more obscure hints and finally I said I knew where he meant. As I left the doughnut hole I saw Magda the K's spiffy little Mercedes, the kind Elodie craved, pull up behind the limousine and the elegant Magda parade herself out, a series of arousing, long-limbed linkages. I paused and greeted her.

She gave me a bare nod, not surprised to see me there, for some reason. "Charlie." Crisp, simple, and very arctic. It was unlike Magda, a very tall blonde with a wide Slavic forehead above wide-set blue eyes, lips that looked collagened, and efficiently cut hair just sweeping her shoulders. She wore an immaculate business suit of what looked like tan silk. Magda was friends with everybody: in her field she could never tell who might be a client one day, who might be useful for whatever client it was. The second-oldest profession, her old business card had said.

"Busy day for you guys."

"I shouldn't be talking to you, Charlie. I'd like to but ...

not here, okay? Call me." As she walked away I watched her long, narrow stride, a slim woman with a slim briefcase dangling at the end of her long slim fingers. It was said the Big Chu was involved with her in some nasty way. I believe there's someone for everyone—witness Elodie and me—but I couldn't conjure up the image of her shaving that lumpy and bulbous Chu skull.

I took some little precautions on my way to meet Hanson, wandering in and out of shops, backtracking a little. The place we met was an Asian mob joint and the owner had been engaged for the past several years rehabilitating himself, to mixed success. Harry Quan funded numerous charities, brought cultural troupes from Hong Kong to Canada, donated food to the needy, not just in Chinatown, and had for years bagged the votes for whichever mayoral or city councillor candidate he thought had a chance of winning. But life clearly wasn't all food banks, kung fu midgets, and participating in the democratic system. A machine-gunning at a Scarborough restaurant this past winter had elevated Harry Quan from third man in the organization he said he no longer belonged to, to number two. Number one, it was said, was weighing his options and was looking at real estate in Shanghai. I liked Harry and whenever I took someone to his restaurant for dinner, I always introduced them as journalists. This guaranteed fast service and good free food, but meant we had to endure Harry's photo albums: happy Harry with a string of mayors; smiling Harry with the prime minister; sombre Harry with the past two police chiefs, but not the current one; grinning Harry surrounded by cheering homeless. Missing was one photograph I was positive I'd seen several years ago: short toothy Harry in the middle between two of the city's first Chinese-Canadian graduates of police college, one of whom I'm positive was the Big Chu.

The Closed sign was still out but the door was unlocked. Hanson was in the farthest reach of the restaurant at the unlucky seat, a half-a-round plywood table with two legs on the floor and the cut part of the table screwed into a bracket on the wall. Billy Chi, on the lam from Boston, had foolishly used this table at lunchtime several years ago, unmindful of the fact that when the kitchen double doors were opened by waiters carrying trays of treats, the left-hand door caused the diner to briefly lose sight of the front entrance. The day Billy Chi was snacking, one of the waiters, a new guy with a just-off-the-boat haircut, held the left-hand door open to allow several dim sum carts to emerge. When the cart traffic had passed, the left-hand door swung away, revealing to Billy Chi two Vietnamese guys, also from Boston, there standing to spray him down with short machine guns they dropped immediately after unloading into him. You could see, behind Hanson's shoulders and above his head, dimples in the old plaster walls where the fill material didn't have the same smoothness and the paint had been imperfectly mixed, unable to match the patina of age. Billy Chi's ghost might prohibit canny diners from sitting there, but if you wanted to have a private chat, it was perfect.

When Hanson stood to shake my hand and clasp his other onto my shoulder, I knew it wasn't about Corolla Carlson. Hanson was the wise-ass, corner-of-the-mouth, deadpan kind of cop who could stand over an eyeless, carved, and burned murder victim and comment, "Yikes, that's gotta hurt." He was famous for naming murder cases. A dead panhandler in a Dumpster became Bum in a Drum; a crabby wife dumped on the side of Hwy. 404 became Bitch in a Ditch. Years ago, it was said, Hanson shut his public heart when he worked on child abuse cases and his partner found him in his car in the parking lot of the old police headquarters licking the front sight of his service revolver.

Right away, still standing, he said, very quickly, "The small one's okay, the big one's in St. Mike's, she took some wood in the head but it's just stitches. Keeping her for a day. The small one, it seems, did more damage than any of 'em. Two of the guys, I guess they thought she was a midget or something, got lazy and she nailed one in the nuts, the other she took a chew of." He saw I wasn't understanding what he was saying or what he was talking about. "Your small girl? Blue hair?"

"My daughter?" I sat down. He might as well have been talking about my refrigerator, the one with the white door. I couldn't process enough information to picture it.

"Her."

"Emma. The Mouse."

"She's in the cells, they're still adding up charges for her. The big one ..."

"Allie."

"Right, her. She's in St. Mike's, but she's okay, Charlie. She got caught in a back swing, that's all: low power out, maximum power back."

I stood up. "I want to see them. The Mouse anyway."

"Nobody's seeing anybody, Charlie. Sit down, you'll want to hear all this, and you'll want to call somebody, Cornelius Fox, maybe. 'Cause I'll tell you, you're gonna need him."

13

Elodie woke while I was closing the safe door, clutching my pathetic wad of fat white and buff-coloured business envelopes, leaving the round box empty except for a .40 Glock I'd received as a gift several years earlier from a biker I'd interviewed. He'd sworn it was clean and lacked any pedigree but it made me nervous, thinking where it might have been, what it might have done in passion or greed; I suspected the Glock had bodies on it. My passport was in there too, and another one in a different name but with my photo as well as inoculation documents, and my birth certificate.

Elodie greeted me with, "The fuck?" as she rolled herself over, burrowing in the pillows and sheets. Her voice was thick with sleep and she sounded irritable. I tried to remember back when we began, if this monster had emerged at every wakening and morphed into something a human being would want to live with, spend days and nights with.

"The Mouse and Allie got busted last night."

She sat herself up with her arms and looked across the

bedroom at me. She stared at me and I realized I was holding the Glock in one hand and the clutch of envelopes in the other. "Don't do anything, don't go out. Ten minutes, okay?"

I put the Glock back, went into the kitchen and started coffee. The young wife had fled sometime in the morning, her coverlet neatly folded on the sofa, a single gold earring flashing on the floor. I sat down to count out my stash, it was $17,000 even. The safe contained my exit strategy. Travel documents, loose cash, the Glock for some reason. Half my life I'd expected things to go south for me some day, and I was always ready to make a run from it, whatever it was. Some nights when Elodie and I were in battle I'd go to sleep on the floor and, as when I was in foster care, fantasize about hitting the road and reinventing myself into something with no past. Washing myself up on some faraway shore with enough money to get something going. I wasn't sure where the Glock fit into it all.

When the coffee was ready I poured two cups and brought them and the fixings out onto the terrace. The mess seemed to have been left by a party I'd attended years earlier. I left the envelopes on the table inside. Elodie came out, her hair still wet, wearing terry-towel shorts and one of my T-shirts with Chinese characters and a red dragon emblazoned on it.

She sipped her coffee, put her hand on mine and smiled. "Charlie, they said life was going to be more interesting with you in it. They, whoever they are, don't lie."

It was, I told her, as Hanson had said, a Chinese fire drill. I told her, as the Big Chu told the reporters, a year-long investigation. Putting together what I overheard at the scrum in front of 52 Division—I stood beside Michael Bailey—and what Hanson told me, it appeared the cops had learned that an elite cadre of the Black Bloc, frustrated with the heretofore ineffective moderate actions carried out against the city, the citizens, and indeed the very country itself, had conspired to commit a reign of political terror that included bombings and attacks, up to and including assassinations.

"We were able to infiltrate this group and determined the threat was very real," the lumpy-headed little bastard told the cameras and microphones. "We uncovered a full-blown terrorist network with infrastructure, financing, and a series of safe houses. Within the intelligence bureau—but separate, at a satellite location, for security purposes—we set up a special unit, the K Squad. This unit ran on two tracks: continued infiltration and intelligence gathering, and a tactical strike force that has been on standby for several months. The Canadian Security and Intelligence Service provided expertise and intelligence analysis, and the Department of National Defence provided expertise and coordination. The likely threat of explosives being used was identified early in the Project Kensington operation, and the DOD provided advanced training to our bomb squad.

"In the early hours of this morning the K Squad, backed up by heavily armed Emergency Task Forces officers, the intelligence bureau, DOD bomb experts and security officers, CSIS, the RCMP, the Ontario Provincial Police, and other special squads, conducted a series of raids in the Kensington Market area." Here he was handed a sheet of paper by Magda the K. He read from it. "Nineteen people were arrested, bomb-making materials, weapons, and documents were seized. The documents are being analyzed. I don't have a complete list of charges yet, but they'll be made available as the suspects are processed. Six suspects are being sought. One dog, a pitbull, was turned loose on the raiding party; its owner urged it to, quote, Kill the Pigs, unquote. The dog had to be put down. Two members of the raiding party were injured effecting the arrest of one of the ringleaders of the group. Both officers required hospitalization; I don't have their status but their injuries aren't life-threatening. One target was injured while being subdued. Those injuries are minor.

"This investigation is an example of what can occur when all levels of government work together in a coordinated effort. I wish to thank ..." Here, the Chu went through the list of agencies, both obscure and well-known, that participated in the task force. He ended by saying the investigation was continuing, more bodies were being sought, and more charges would be laid.

Beside him Buddy the Buddy impatiently awaited his turn. The vibrating little fool thanked the Chu, thanked the various agencies and levels of government, and used up his time pleading for funding for the city, saying he didn't in any way support the violence planned by the Kensington group, but noted the lack of federal money for social, health, and housing policies was responsible for the underlying discontent in the city. "Don't take from that that I have any sympathy or understanding for these goons, these thugs, these damn terrorists, but we can't keep sending our officers into dangerous situations caused, in part, by a federal government that's letting the cities go to hell, just to hell."

Beside me Michael snickered. "Going ..."

Buddy started to foam and strain and his handler crowded him back a little. Buddy shook him off. "No," he said loudly, his mouth ratcheting and his brow dampening and turning red. "It's, it's, it's ..."

Michael said, " ... going ..."

"... It's goddamn time the people learned just how bad our situation is. Our streets are overrun by these damn terrorists, young thugs who, I don't know where their parents are, are making bombs and placing the citizens of the city in extreme deadly danger, Black Bloc anarchy, attacking police horses—horses, for Chrissakes, what'd the horses ever do? Federal government, why don't these damn anarchists get on a goddamn bus or something and I'll pay for the goddamn tickets and they can go, Starbucks, a good corporate citizen making jobs for students who just want to get ahead, broken windows, coffee, some damn complaint plantations, and let those ... those bastards in Ottawa look out their windows and see the Parliament lawns ... see ..."

Michael, laughing, barely moving his lips, said, "Liftoff, he's *outta* here."

"... little bastards bombing and and and and *defecating* on the grass, health hazard, there'll be bodies in the street, ripped apart, citizens just shopping and going about their business, and these little c..."

The mayor's handler had a smooth move used by store security to subtly control shoplifters without causing disturbance. He inserted two fingers in the cuff of Buddy's suit jacket, twisted his fingers and made an effective, low-keyed come-along, broke the mayor's balance and took him away from the cameras and microphones. Magda the K was behind the Big Chu, trying not to laugh. The Big Chu looked sympathetic. Michael was laughing with abandon and the cameramen were laughing too.

Buddy's last words, "little *cocksuckers* ..." floated out as a hoarse scream as he was manhandled towards the dead voters' limousine. "I'll take your questions now ..." He was gone.

Smoothly, Magda the K said the Big Chu would take questions. And Michael called out, "How many cocksuckers did you say were in custody?"

Magda the K laughed and nodded to the blonde television girl. Next question.

"They call it the Cadre," I told Elodie, wrapping it up. "The bomb attempt last year at the legislature was part of the Autumn Offensive, and it was only by the grace of God, and the excellent work, the Chu said, of Queen's Park security that a bloody massacre was averted. The Chu said the almost-detonation meant more funding and manpower would be dedicated to the Kensington Project. Michael asked if there were any international terrorist connections—he was joking, really—and the Chu said he couldn't talk about those at this time. Someone asked if it was true the Cadre had received *killer karate* training and if in fact it had been used on the arrest teams. The Chu said it was clear some of the Cadre were highly skilled in the martial arts, noting one suspect took out two of his team, they themselves highly trained men of good size. Michael asked if it was true that some accused had poison available when they were arrested and had vowed never to be taken alive. The Big Chu said he had information, as yet unconfirmed, that suicide by rat poison was an option for some key players in the Cadre. However, he said, the Cadre was taken by overwhelming force before they could ingest it.

Elodie asked, "Rat poison? They seize any?"

I said, "You been in Kensington Market lately? Everybody's got rat poison."

"What did your friend, Hanson, say?"

Hanson couldn't help laughing when he talked about the Mouse taking down two of the arrest team. "They came in and shot her dog. One of the guys with the shotguns took one look at it and just rounded off. He was the Central Command drug guy who was bit a few years ago doing a door-kick on some bikers. Scared shitless of dogs. But he shouldn't have been worried about her dog. Next Christmas, if your kid's not in the joint, I'm sending her that sign, you know the one? FORGET THE FUCKING DOG; BEWARE OF THE MIDGET. He's holding a smoking shotgun and she just turns around, doesn't even call him a fucker, just hoofs him square in the nuts. Bang, he's down. The other guy raiding the place can't believe this. Some karate technique she used, it woulda made a Jap clap. By the time the other guy realizes they're being hammered by a dwarf, he's got her teeth in his hand doing what the dog wasn't going to do in the first place, only they didn't give him enough time not to do it. Personally, if I'd'a been there, I'd'a taken out your kid with the alley-sweeper, rubbed the dog's belly. I wouldn't be walking funny the next day and I'd have a new pal."

He was making me laugh. They'd tried to take Allie, Hanson said, on the street, lugging her bass guitar a few doors from the Krak Bar. They'd waited until the throng inside the club thinned out, I told Elodie, grabbing a few suspects on the street a few blocks away. Allie came out with another girl, he said, a Filipina who took one look at the shotguns and the flak vests and flashing red rack lights and started running in circles, screaming for her mother. "Your kid went to help her, but the Flip kid was toast." That took the heat off Allie and she dropped the guitar case and was in the wind. She knew Kensington too well: she was down alleyways, through unlicensed after-hours joints, through a card game in the kitchen of a restaurant screaming something in Chinese.

"Whatever it was, *immigration* and *run*, probably," Hanson said, "it was fucking *raining* Chinamen when the guys after her ran in."

She was wise enough not to go to her place; instead to a friend's flat where she climbed over the roof and through a back window, thereby missing the emergency vehicles on the street out front. A bit of a hey-rube had ensued in the kitchen of the flat and the back-swing of a baton caught her above the eye. Fifteen stitches, St. Mike's. Police guard.

About two dozen cops and agents were involved in the raids, Hanson said. Six cops were overpowered and arrested by other cops, who hadn't been clued-in on what was going on. Two cops held each other at gunpoint, each screaming for backup. An old lady who called 911 suffered a near-fatal heart attack.

"All in all, except for the dead dog, your kid being in St. Mike's, the other one in the cells, two cops getting aced by a midget, all the cops all arresting each other, and the old lady nearly going tits up, I gotta say it was a successful pre-dawn operation," Hanson said, I told Elodie.

Her laughter made me feel better. I turned on the television news and worked my way through the million-channel universe. Elodie made some telephone calls, rattling through my envelopes, making notes on the backs of them, absent a scratch pad. She wheeled up beside me as I was watching Buddy's meltdown; the tape editor ran some quotes, then cut away at about the time Buddy went off the dial. The reporter did a voice-over while the camera showed a pan of 52 Division and the media horde. The mayor, the woman's voice said, was distraught at the thought his city almost went up in flames. He urged, she said, the federal government to review its funding to the cities, particularly this one. Another channel, one that obviously monitored scanners all night, had footage of gun-and-run teams, trotting along Baldwin Street with shotguns and vests. There was a lot of shouting. Two men were having a fist fight in the middle of the street; both looked like cops although neither was wearing a raid jacket. The television showed the Mouse being wrestled out of her place, a cop on each arm and leg and one holding a handful of her hair as she snapped at him like the dog she didn't own anymore. She looked deranged when she saw the camera. The immaculately planned pre-dawn lightning takedown had made no provision for smooth transport of arrestees and, while waiting for a paddy wagon, the cameraman was able to get a long piece of footage in which the Mouse made a statement. Once the bleeps were added, she didn't seem to have much that the station thought the public would be interested in. Swearing removed, it seemed like she was now laughing and saying, "Take me to Starbucks, you guys. Double decaf latte. I surrender."

Elodie said, "Ferocious little thing, isn't she?"

"No mouse, is my Mouse." I was actually feeling pretty good. We held hands as I flipped the channels, but no one had anything better than the Mouse getting arrested. Some ambulance pictures of an old lady in an oxygen mask on a gurney, being loaded; some other ambulance screaming out of the Market, one of them no doubt containing two surprised cops and my other little terrorist. I asked Elodie, "Who'd you call?"

"How come you got the envelopes out? That's the money for the Harley and the sidecar."

"I'm gonna have to get a lawyer. Eat shit and call Fox."

"David."

"David?"

"I called David. Colin and Martha are away."

"I got this covered, El." With most of the family, all of it in fact, I felt like I was a sufferance, a time bomb ready to explode Elodie and the clan into all forms of trouble or heartache. Except for his moments when we both drank too much, David clearly didn't have me in mind as first choice for his little sister, crippled or not. "How's David liking all this?"

"He told me to call the family firm." She squeezed my

hand. "And he told me to tell them to get off their expensive asses." She had tears in her eyes. "To tell them my stepdaughters have been arrested and to get them the fuck out of jail."

14

Elodie opened a file—Kensingoofs—and sent me out for blank videocassettes so she could record all the newscasts. When I came back she was busily writing notes to herself. She opened the tape boxes and meticulously labelled each one. While we chatted, Hanson called and we wrestled with the obscure verbal moves required to arrange a meeting, settling on the underground parking lot of the condo in fifteen minutes.

I was standing by Elodie's car, polishing the chrome on my motorcycle when he walked down the ramp behind a resident's inbound car. He waited until the resident had parked, taken groceries from her car, and gone to the elevators. He said he didn't have much but wanted to keep me up to date.

"All paperwork goes to the K Squad, the Special K Squad, we're calling it, for cereal terrorists," he said. "Your big kid's being kept in St. Mike's until tomorrow. They're just checking for concussion. Both cops are out. The midget won't tell them if she's HIV positive. She says, Tell me if your guy's gonna give me trichinosis. The matron called her a little lesbian and your kid told her, Suck my dick. The guy she bit's an okay guy, Charlie. He's shitting, his wife's pregnant. Can you help him out?"

"I'll have to see the Mouse."

"No can do. I can get my cell phone in there, and even that's dodgy. The Special K's have taken over the station. The guys say they're monitoring phone calls in and out. How about it?"

We arranged that I'd be at the upstairs phone in fifteen minutes.

Hanson said the Funny People were crawling all over the station, grabbing up phones when they rang, poking through paperwork, monitoring the radio freqs, forbidding interviews with the accused. They were coordinating the booking procedures themselves. The Black Bar was going nuts at the front desk, demanding to see their clients. A support rally was teeing up and Black Bloc actions were promised at various locations, including headquarters, the division, the courthouse, Queen's Park, all Starbucks, Gaps, and Banana Republics, the US Consulate, for some reason, and St. Mike's. The Chu was everywhere, seemingly on every channel at the same time. Magda the K had clearly forbidden him to shave, change his suit, tie, or shirt, wanting the image of a weary battle commander under siege but keeping his troops going around the clock to keep the city safe. Buddy had vanished, it was said, into a Valium holiday; he'd fired his handler, then rehired him, having to promise a raise. The old lady had died at hospital.

Hanson left, back up the ramp, and I went upstairs to sit by the phone. A half-hour later it rang and it was the Mouse.

"*Help*, Dad. They're beating us in here." In the background I heard Hanson say, C'mon, tell him, quit fucking around.

"They really beating you, Mouse?"

"Well," she said, laughing, "They'd *like* to."

"I have to know, you're not HIV positive, right?"

"Am I going to get trichinosis, biting that guy? Can I bite this fat guy here? Is it safe, if I put pork on my fork?"

I heard Hanson going, C'mon, c'mon.

"Emma, it's important. That guy's a good friend of mine, and he's a friend of the guy you bit. I'm doing everything I can here, Em, but I need this."

"What happened to Aunt Mary? Can you get her and bury her?" Now her voice was choking. Her emotions were wacky, she sounded both high and low. But adrenaline rinses out quickly. "Take care of Mary, okay? We'll bury her like we used to do with the kittens and hamsters. On the beach."

"I'll get her. You'll be out in a day or two and we'll do the right thing." I paused. "Em?"

"I'm not, Dad. Tell your friend I'm not."

"For sure?"

"No, for sure, okay?"

"Ah, kid. Tell him. Tell ... tell the fat guy." I heard her say something to Hanson.

I heard him say, "Okay, but be quick."

Emma's voice came back over the phone, sadly. "Dad?"

I said, "Yes."

She started laughing and screamed: "Help me Dad they're beating us sticks electric shocks oooooh *I like that, big boy.*" As she wrestled to keep the phone she screamed, "*Starbucks*, take me to *Starbucks*. Triple fucking espresso with a twist ... and just ten bags of sugar, *I'm on a diet so I fit into my prom dress ...*" She was gone.

The line was dead and a few minutes later Hanson called back. "Thanks, Charlie. I know this is a hard time for you, but can I ask you a question? A personal question?"

I said, "Go ahead."

"Would it bug you if I married this midget? I know that'd make me older than my father-in-law, but, Jesus," he laughed, "good thing she didn't tell me to suck her dick, I would've."

We spent the rest of the day getting the details on the charges against Allie and the Mouse. Elodie put her files in order; we had a quick meal of leftovers from the fridge, watching for news updates. A reporter standing in front of police headquarters said a press conference had been called to update the media on the Kensington investigation. I unearthed an old press card and walked over to headquarters. At the duty desk a cadet gave me a set of majors, a list of recent arrests, and incidents of import. The Kensington operation was a separate handout, fifteen pages of general information, lists of accused and charges, and it ended by noting the investigation was continuing, more charges were pending, the accused would appear in court the following morning, and that other individuals were being sought.

The elegant Magda the K, now in pale blue smooth cotton, ran the presser, reading for the cameras what the release said. She stuck closely to the text. I read on ahead of her and found Emma Tate, 23, and Allison Tate, 23, both of no fixed address, charged with several counts of conspiracy to detonate an explosive device, conspiracy to commit murder, attempted murder, assault police, assault causing bodily harm, possession of noxious substance, and resisting arrest. The Mouse was also charged with a count relating to inciting a dog to attack a peace officer. Sherelle "Pia" Filipina, 25, of no fixed address, faced several conspiracy charges and one of resisting arrest. I didn't recognize any other names.

Michael Bailey came into the conference room as things were winding down. He was surprised to see me and said so.

"You're working something here, right, Charlie?"

"Off the record?"

"C'mon."

"Off the record and I'll tell. I might have something for you, in a day or two."

He thought about it briefly, then agreed, and I told him numbers one and two on the list were my kids.

"The Tates, right? Cops say they're among the ringmasters in this circus."

"What are they saying about the bomb stuff seized?"

"Still being examined by forensics. They say it's enough, if assembled, to level the entire Market. But they say that wasn't the aim." He leaned in. "They were going to blow up headquarters. Get the Chu during a police services board meeting, take out Buddy as collateral damage." He took my elbow and steered me away from the media. "Look, Charlie, what chances your kids'll talk to me? You can set the ground rules, just get me five minutes. They want to go into background, no names, that's okay."

"I'll ask 'em, that's all I can do. They'll have lawyers in court tomorrow and the lawyers'll have to make the decision."

"You got my numbers, right? If they won't talk to me, then at least make sure they don't talk to anybody else. I'll let you know what I hear, deal?"

I spent the evening after dinner walking through the Market. Carpenters were rehanging doors, glaziers puttied glass into window frames. Camera crews were on the corners; in front of one video camera an otherwise sane-looking young reporter wore a glass mask hanging loosely on her chest. No one stopped to talk to anyone from the outside world. The place was eerily silent: no music, no bustle, no shouts. There was a brief rain of stones and bottles from the rooftops. I glanced up and saw four people in black anarchist T-shirts and ski masks screaming obscenities. The scampered like monkeys out of sight.

I went to the Mouse's flat and found the downstairs door hanging from one hinge. At the top of the stairs the inner door was lying flat on the floor.

She lived a strangely barren lifestyle. Stacks of tattered, second- or third-hand books were arranged along the baseboards in the bedroom. There was no television. A mattress had been slit open and stuffing puffed out. In the refrigerator were containers of yoghurt with Middle Eastern writing on the packaging, and bottles of various organic drinks

Aunt Mary was crumpled against the wall under the window with a massive smear of blood around her. Shotgun pellets made little holes in the plaster. A shotgun shell casing had landed on a glass-topped wicker table.

I took the sheet and blanket from the bed and wrapped up the pit bull. Around her neck was a thick chain and a silver identification tag in the shape of a heart. "Her name is Aunt Mary. She won't bite. But if you're reading this, you already know it. Or she's dead. Please return to Emma Mouse Tate, Kensington Market."

I took a cab home, and put Aunt Mary into the trunk of the Intrepid. I stopped at Canadian Tire and bought a shovel and drove down to the lake. I buried her on Cherry Beach, the place where, a lifetime ago, I'd lied to my kids and told them I'd put their dead pets to rest.

Michael was waiting for me the next morning inside the security barrier at Old City Hall. It took a while for me to get through; after going past the metal detectors, each entrant was wanded down. Each time the doors opened behind me I could hear chants through a bullhorn. About thirty or thirty-five demonstrators were crowding around the Cenotaph, about half of them wearing black balaclavas and black clothing. Intelligence guys were monitoring the crowd from a few feet away, shooting video and snapping pictures. At one point while I was watching, two cops in plainclothes charged into the small crowd and pulled out an unmasked demonstrator, a young woman who apparently matched one of several photographs the intelligence guys kept referring to.

A bum sitting on the edge of the demonstration caught my attention. It took me a minute to remember him: from the Russian body job at the hotel, and later, across the street from the Krak Bar. Today he looked the same as he had then, only worse. His hair was matted, he'd grown a straggling beard, and he kept shivering and hugging himself.

Inside, Michael and I went downstairs to the coffee stand and had stand-up breakfast. Michael was my pal now. A second security post was set up in front of the courtroom reserved for those arrested in the Kensington raids. Identification was checked; a trim looking black man in a Free Mumia T-shirt sat holding a knapsack and he seemed careful to keep it moving slowly, panning the corridor outside the courtroom. I assumed he had a videocamera inside the bag. An ETF officer with a German shepherd on a leash wandered around the area, the dog stopping often to sniff at pant cuffs and briefcases. Through the small glass window I could see another dog team going up and down the spectators' rows; four big men, one at each corner of the room, waited for court to start. Carl Hanson started walking towards me, saw Michael's press card, and slipped past us. At nine-thirty the doors opened and we went in.

The room was full when the judge came in, a sleek-looking number with grey wavy hair, pince nez on his nose, and a glistening shave. Spectators and the lawyers and Crown attorneys in the well of the court stopped their bustle and everyone stood up. The judge said, "Bring in the first bunch of desperadoes."

Allie, the Mouse, and Pia were in the first half dozen brought into the prisoners' dock. Allie had some stitches across her forehead, up near her hairline, and looked tired and angry. The Mouse looked bored with it all; Pia was pale, very still, catatonic. The girls seemed less interested in the proceedings than in Pia's comfort. They stayed close to her and patted her. Pia didn't respond.

The duty counsel identified himself and said he had been advised numbers four and five had counsel on the way who should arrive in the next few minutes. The doors behind us opened and a few seconds of noise filled the room.

The duty counsel glanced at the back of the room and said, "They're here now."

I turned and saw three immaculate lawyers in full pinstripes and power ties make their way up the aisle carrying corporate briefcases. They looked impressive and out of place among the other tired lawyers and the fidgety families and friends of the accused. The judge said he'd deal with the others in the dock first. One lawyer looked around the room and came over to me. I recognized him from Colin Gray's Christmas party a few years earlier. As he approached I saw Cornelius Fox at the end of a back row. He nodded and looked at me sympathetically.

The lawyer crouched beside me, careful with the creases in his pants. "Allison Tate and Emma Tate, right?"

"And Pia—Sherelle Filipina—there, the Asian girl."

He wrote her name on a piece of paper. "They're not coming out today, nobody is, everybody's being held. These are heavy charges, but we'll go for a bail hearing."

I said I had seventeen thousand dollars with me.

He smiled. "Good," he said, putting his hand on my shoulder, "that'll just about buy us all lunch. How's that Elodie of mine?"

While we'd been in the courtroom there'd been a confrontation outside the building. After all the accused had been remanded into custody, I left, leaving Michael Bailey taking his voluminous notes. Cornelius Fox didn't look up as I passed. When I came out there were tattered signs littering the pavement in front and lengths of gauze blew in the breeze. There were no demonstrators but there were a lot of uniformed cops and two remaining ambulances. The old bum from the Russian body job and Kensington Market from the year before stood apart with his nose running. A reporter was trying to do a stand-up, waiting for the bell tower to stop tolling. When he finally spoke I heard him say three police officers were injured and nine demonstrators hospitalized. He said police had come under a hail of rocks, bottles, and clumps of earth torn from the ground around the Cenotaph. A leader of the Black Bloc, he said, the young man who had exhorted the crowd into attacking the police, was being sought after escaping from a police car en route to 52 Division.

I walked over to the bum who was now leaning against the grey blocks that constructed the base of Old City Hall, trying to keep warm in a patch of sunshine. He stared at me a moment, then walked away with a half-smile on his face.

Carl Hanson passed me, going down the steps. I waited a few seconds, struggling in the increasing breeze to light a cigarette. When he was a hundred metres away, travelling south on Bay Street, I headed after him. We went into the caverns under Bay Street, a world of fast food, constant foot traffic, and anonymity. I found him lined up at a bagel joint and sat where he'd see me. I watched for the bum.

"Hard," Hanson said as he sat, "to escape a police car." He had blood on the cuff of his shirt and someone had scratched his left cheek. He looked pretty happy though.

"You okay, Carl?"

"Oh, yeah," he said dipping a napkin into a paper cup of cold water and working at the blood on his cuff. But he wasn't fine. "I'm fucking fine, Charlie. I had to grab a ninety-pound girl by the hair and pull her off one of the uniformed guys. Best part, though, Charlie, was watching him punch her accidentally in the tits a couple of times. A fucked-up day, but not a bad day, Charlie, you know why?"

"Why?"

"Today's magic day. I'm bulletproof. I hit twenty-five today, a quarter century watching fucks like the Chu and Buddy and the rest of them, or guys like them, operate. The operators. Watching them fuck up everything they touch, everything they couldn't steal for themselves. Watching them treat cops like dummies, watching them play budget roulette on the backs of working cops. They can send some goon squad into my station and piss all over the place, grabbing up phones, whispering to each other because, as we all know, cops can't be trusted, right? But today, Charlie, they might have made a mistake. Some mistakes, anyway." In spite of his now placid face, his voice was getting wound up.

"Be careful, Carl. Maybe you want to go for thirty, retire with an inspector's pension."

"I'm getting plenty, Charlie. I'm okay. I'm forty-five years old. I'm single again; I decided years ago that when the wife weighed more than me, she was outta there. I got commendations up the wazoo. I got the payoff list they'd blow goats to get their hands on. I got a nice steady pension. I got, you know, prospects. Bobby Clarke's been calling me. I lose a little of this," he rubbed his stomach, "I'm still a young man, in spite of the bagels. Not likely I'll get a shot at your midget there, but that's okay, she's a little too tough for me."

"You, ah, want to tell me, this mistake?"

"Why not? It's two things, really. It's hard to escape from a police car, even if it wasn't a real police car, but some fleet lease they use up at Intelligence. You handcuff the guy, which I saw they did, in back, you put him in the back seat, which I saw they did. You put a guy beside him, also they did. So, how come you drive, what, three traffic lights, maybe five minutes, and somehow he gets loose? Gets out and away? Show me a guy I can't, even with this gut, chase down on a city street, his hands cuffed behind his back, even if I somehow don't club him to death when he goes for the door of the car."

"This is the ringleader guy the reporter was talking about?"

"Yep. This is the guy, mister black mask, comes charging out of the crowd just when things get quiet. He fires what looked like a piece of brick at the uniforms guarding the stairs. He throws wide, like a girl, I guess, it hits the building way up high, but it's enough. On come the other demonstrators, on come the other bottles and rocks and clods. And here come the uniforms. Two plainclothes guys I've never seen before, they're on him before the uniforms even get there, almost like they were waiting for him to go off. Nice arrest. They struggle with him, and a third guy I never seen before, waves off the uniforms: we got him. Away he goes. At that point I had my hands full, stopping my guy from punching the little girl's tits right off her chest. He's a nice guy, I went to his stag when he got married, I went to his divorce party, when his wife left him. Shaves his head every year for the cancer fund drive. Once he slept on my couch. Plays ball with one of the beer companies, proceeds to charity. So I know him, I don't know him well, but what I do know is that he was a good cop and he could've been a great cop." He rubbed his face. "Fuck, what they did to him. Same as Gerry Adams. We all get fucked, eventually, you stay around long enough."

"Gerry Adams?"

"Yeah. You don't know Gerry? You should, you know. He's the guy who defused the bomb last year at the legislature. They sent him off to London to learn kiddie porn computer tracking systems for a squad that didn't exist. That guy." He glanced away at a pair of uniformed cops patrolling the food court. When they were out of sight, he looked back at me. "Spends rush hours driving in from Pickering in the morning, back out in the afternoon. That's not a cop, Charlie, that's a commuter." He examined the bloodstain on his shirt cuff. "Gerry. With a G."

I gave him a moment and went for another cup of coffee. When I came back, he waited a moment before continuing. "A great cop. What a thing, Charlie, to be. When I was doing the corruption thing, there, I thought, wow is this ever dirty, this goes right to the top. But that was okay, it wasn't us doing it. It was them. The operators. Cops expect that, that everybody's stealing but them. You go out and do whatever you're told to do, then you go back to your own kind of people and laugh about it.

"But this, today, oh, I've got to wonder. Seeing that guy like that, beating down a little girl." He seemed to be wrestling with something, then seemed to make up his mind. "You can't escape from a cop car, Charlie. Two guys up front, one guy in back with the prisoner, handcuffed in back. It was a two-door car. How'd you do that? Well, you don't. You just can't."

"Well, when you find him you can ask him," I said, just to say something.

"Finding him. That's interesting. There's a guy I saw once, maybe a couple of times, was always here, then there, then gone again. We all thought he was Internal Affairs, some trainee stooge they groomed and turned loose around town, looking at each division for something to chew on. Kind of a weird friendly guy, looked about seventeen years old. About a year ago someone said, Hey you remember that ratty kid, Gregory Johnson, always sniffing around? Well, he got fired. Sleeping on the job, maybe, taking sandwiches on the arm. Anyway, they got him and he's gone. I said, Jeez, too bad, and never thought about him again until this morning, for some reason." He looked at me. "You there yet?"

"Thanks, Carl."

"Just a little piece, Charlie." He stood up, drank off his water, and started stuffing the napkins into the empty cup.

"What's the second thing, Carl? You said there were two things."

He stood and thought for a moment. "Oh, yeah, second thing is whole different, nothing to do with today's stuff. You ever talk to Barry White, old ex, used to be intelligence, the wops?"

"Sure, with Bobby's crew now."

"Well, we were out last night, a retirement for Buster Brewer. I was telling him about your kids, about the thing in Kensington. I said it's all kind of weird. Barry said, Well, one guy who won't find it weird is Charlie Tate. He said, I gave it all to Charlie Tate last year, if he didn't get his kids out, well, bless him but fuck him; I did what I could."

I shook my head, remembering. "No, that's not right. He said he didn't know nothing about the bomb. Told me a story about a guy, set up a Mafia family, that was it."

"Connie Lombardozzi? He told you about that?"

"Yeah. Funny story."

Hanson shook his head. "Fuck, Charlie. What's the matter with you? You didn't listen right."

15

By the time I walked home, Elodie was out. A luncheon of Old Girls had been planned several months earlier, a dozen or so women who got together twice a year, once for lunch and once at a dinner from which I'd have to extract an Elodie who wasn't in the same condition as the one I dropped off at whatever restaurant they held it at that year. At these luncheons and dinners everybody caught up with each other and I had to, the next day, hear how each of the ladies was doing, who she was married to, and what swank boutique she now ran, where she'd wintered or summered most recently. It all got very rowdy and, invariably when I arrived to get Elodie, the Old Girls were always beautifully lit and flirtatious. Elodie, drunken, would be at the head of the table where the legs wouldn't interfere with parking her wheelchair, waving her arms and yelling, That's my man, that one there, my thug, come to get me, you brute. I always felt sorry for the waiters who had to wait on the women; grab-ass ensued as the evening progressed and one was always voted the Most Do-able, receiving a fatter tip.

I made a lettuce and tomato sandwich and found a frosted beer. I liked the apartment when I was alone it, particularly during the day. We'd had to dump most of the furniture from the old house and between us had made an eclectic mess of the new place. My pickings-up from Asia and Italy, Elodie's prizes from weekend forages at flea markets and antique shops. The dalliance chair was my favourite, a long dark teak chaise lounge type of thing with wide arm rests that winged out. The purpose of the chair was to allow a plantation owner in years gone by to sit reclined, his chilly gin and tonic on one arm while the object of his pleasure placed him- or herself on the other arm from whence he or she could be positioned for maximum penetration and minimum spillage. I brought the phone to the chair and set myself up with notebook, sandwich, beer, and television remote.

Michael Bailey must've been thinking of me because I was thinking of him. The phone rang and he asked where I'd got to. I told him I was trying to get a handle on what was going on. He told me all the Kensington accused were held in, and that the Crown on the case was going to be Jefferson. He asked if I'd talked to my kids yet.

"I'm going to see them later today or tomorrow. The lawyers are with them."

"You must have bucks I don't know about, Charlie. Those guys were Green Green and Gold. Everybody else had Going Going and Gone. I thought the judge was going to shit when they walked in. Jefferson came by afterwards and said he'd have to take another look at their clients, especially the Chinese girl. That kind of money, they must have some heavy backers, this little cadre, maybe overseas."

"Filipina, Michael, she's Filipina."

"Whatever she is, she's not handling it well. One of the court security guys told me she's on suicide watch."

I thought about Pia polishing glasses in the shadows behind the rail at the Krak Bar, her soft eyes calm and restful. "How you playing this, Michael?"

"Straight up. Yak, yak, appeared in court yesterday, yak yak, remanded into custody, yak. Riot out front, a dozen cops and protesters to hospital. One suspect escaped custody. Rehash the chief's avowing to protect the citizenry. I might do a greatest hits on Buddy's meltdown." He paused. "Why, you got something else?"

"It's complicated, Michael." I played him a little. "I just wish I knew you better, you had someone who could vouch."

"Hey, Charlie, you can ask anybody. Anybody'll vouch." He paused a second, working up a way to make me laugh. "If you can't trust a newspaper reporter, Charlie, then who can you trust?"

I gave him his laugh. "I've got some work to do. Tell you what, you make a couple of moves for me, I'll keep you keyed in."

"And the interview?"

"Let me talk to the kids and the lawyers." I asked him to contact Jefferson and find out what happened in last autumn's bombing attempt at the legislature. "That case is done, but Cornelius Fox was in court this morning and I wonder why he was there."

"Youth stuff's hard to get, Charlie. Give me a hint, a taste."

I thought about how things might go if I went back and reread all the signals I'd ignored because the Carlsons wouldn't pony up some dough. There might be a pretty good story at the end of it, but I'd probably have to promise to bury it to make things work out for the Mouse and Allie. "We'll go slow, I think. You might want to get whatever footage or photographs you can of the dust-up this morning. Make big blow-ups of the faces. Then we'll talk."

"What am I looking for in the faces?"

"I have to do it this way. Just hang in."

"I'll call the picture desk."

I rinsed my plate and put the beer bottle into recycling.

This time I did it right. I went to where the people were and I let them tell me what they didn't know they knew and I didn't know I needed to know.

I walked over to Kensington and noted the exact address of the place across from the Krak Bar. The place was now a surprisingly clean vegetarian food outlet named Lucy's Juicery. I crossed the street and went into the Krak. A surly kid with a half-dozen earrings in each ear slammed me a draft. There were few customers. I asked the bar kid his name. He said, "The Big Chu. Want a blow job?"

I told him I wasn't a cop, that I was Allie's father, and he calmed down a little. I asked him about the place across the road, if he knew what it was called last year.

"Tibby Kay's."

It was that simple and that stupid. A little bit of hubris, a nasty little bit of warpish humour I could imagine the Big Chu's unsound little crew coming up with the name, an inside joke they could snicker over. Nudge and yuck yuck. Let's call it Tibby Kay's. The jury'll get a laugh, too.

"You ever go over there?"

"Once or twice. Too weird. We're into music and stuff, some political stuff. But over there they were like ... that Manson, or something. The serial killer guy, not Marilyn."

"You meet the folks running it?"

"Sure you're not a cop?"

"Allie's dad. And the Mouse. Pia knows me."

"Pia's busted."

"I know. I saw them all at court this morning."

This sparked interest more overpowering than his surliness. "How's she? She okay? How's she look? She coming out?"

"We're working on it. This week, maybe."

"Pia won't make it in there. You know about her mom? Killing herself?"

"She told me. We'll get Pia out." I looked out the open door at the vegetarian store. "You know those folks in there, now?"

"Some. I think they're starting a franchise or something. Older lady owns it, but she's got some Market kids running it. She drives a fancy car, like a Corvette, parks it a couple of blocks away and walks. Place still feels creepy."

I paid for the beer and he gave the money back. "Get Pia out, you get free beers."

Tibby Kay's. TIB KS. Toronto Intelligence Bureau, K Squad.

Stupid.

It was mechanical after that, mostly, and it was work for Elodie to do. I went home and wrote a list of names. I went on the terrace and began doing long slow curls, half an eye on the clock, waiting for Elodie to return. I listened to thoughts and echoes. Funny how things don't change, eh, kid? Connie Lombardozzi, king of the Dons, makes his own Mafia, for Christsakes. Nobody escapes from a police car, handcuffed back, three cops in it, two-door model. How do you do that? If Cornelius Fox can't get Corolla Carlson off, then he'll cut a deal, make it look harder than it actually was, run up the meter. What's the best deal to make? New bodies for old. The rags and bones of the justice system. Nice guys, the witches who defuse bombs, but they're industrial arts kinds of guy, make a fully functioning pop-up toaster out of paper clips, a light bulb, and a sheet of tinfoil; not the kinds of guys to get a working vacation in London, come back to run an imaginary child porn task force.

I put the weights away and grabbed a quick shower. When I was towelling off I heard Elodie, outside the door. "I detect a naked man." She wheeled into the bathroom and ran cold water on her wrists. She said she'd had a glass or two of wine, that the ladies exhibited little mean moods bitching each other up with the opulence of their lives, the successes of their husbands. "You gonna make us a million, Charlie?"

As I dressed I told her about my trip to court and to Kensington. I said the girls looked good, and that I'd added little Pia to the charity list. Elodie said, Whatever.

She was having spasms that nearly jerked her out of the chair, so she took some Valium and we lay down on the bed and I massaged her lower back, below where she had feeling. She smelled of wine. I used to sit at her feet and bicycle her legs, an exercise I believed then and still believe could rebuild her tattered muscles. The only muscles getting exercised, stud, are your arms, she'd tell me.

We dozed until faint horns of building rush-hour traffic woke me up, and then the telephone rang and woke her up, too.

Even though Pia had full use of both hands, the knot she made out of her pants wasn't as immediately effective as the one her mother apparently made, one that held while she slipped herself from a tabletop in a Manila jail cell, snapping her neck cleanly. Even if Pia lived, the young Gray family lawyer told me over drinks at the King Eddie, she'd have brain damage. Not enough oxygen for too long a time, a slow strangulation. Her suicide watch notice had got lost in the massive paperwork generated by the Kensington case. I told the lawyer I wanted to see my kids, right away. He said he'd get me in the next day, there were special security procedures in place, but hopefully he'd get them out reasonably soon. I went to the lobby and called Carl Hanson at home. No answer. I tried the division and they said he was out, and asked for my name. I hung up and stood banging my head against the wall. I called Michael Bailey and caught him writing to deadline. He said he didn't know anyone who could get me in. His contact at the guards' union was at a conference. He said he was meeting Jefferson for breakfast the next day.

The Renato was in the telephone book. Enio finally came on the line; when I identified myself in a roundabout way he said to call him back with a phone number. I went into the lounge and borrowed the lawyer's cell. He gave me the number and I went back to the pay phone and called the Renato.

Enio picked up right away. He sounded serious. "Now listen careful, okay? Think about other ears, eh? You're gonna give me the number but you're not going to, okay? Listen. The game has a number. You know the number? Don't say, but you know, eh?"

It was, of course, nine, the baccarat nine. "Yes."

"Now add to your number enough numbers to make the game. If it's the zero, just say zero. That's okay. Then you wait for a call. Because of the ears, and there might be a smart one there, but maybe not too fast, this smart one. Eh?"

I did the arithmetic, gave him a number, and went back into the lounge. Enio would need a few moments to find a safe phone, likely in one of the shops along St. Clair. When the cell phone chirped, I grabbed it up.

"Calo-ger-o. How is Edna?" He laughed and sounded jovial. "The one pouring my drinks turned out to be bad. He didn't come to work that next day, after. You were right, and for this I thank you. It could have been a very unfortunate thing, having this man at my place. You know they hate us because we're *Italiano*, eh?"

I told him I had to get into the special holding facility in the west end where they were holding the Kensington group. "My daughters are in there."

"Ah, the *anarchisti.*" He laughed again. "When?"

"When? Just like that?"

"Calo-ger-o, getting in is easy, most want to get out. Just say when. Maybe one number less than the best number?"

"Fine, perfect." Eight o'clock.

"Okay, see? Easy. At that time you'll present yourself at the front entrance. You still have that baldo head?"

I described myself.

He said, "Mmmm. Have you met my niece? Aieee. My love to Elaina, Cal-o-ger-o."

A tall Mediterranean-looking man in a guard's uniform met me near the entrance. He said my name, signed me in for a visitor's pass under a name I couldn't read, and he didn't say anything else as we wound our way quickly through the building. We stopped at an office with medical equipment in it, an IV rack, two wooden chairs, and a leatherette examination table covered with paper. He asked which one I wanted first, I could only see one at a time. And to keep it short. Don't take nothing from nobody, don't give nothing to nobody. His manner was unfriendly and clearly he'd been told to do something he didn't want to do by someone who could make him do it.

He left and a few minutes later the door opened and Allie, in street clothes, came in, looking around. I hugged her and sat her down on a hardwood chair, pulling mine beside her. She looked haggard, as if she'd been crying since the day she was born.

She asked: "You know about Pia? They just said she died in the hospital."

"Ah, kid. If she could've hung on, just another day or two."

"They separated us. The Mouse is someplace else, they put Pia someplace else, too. If they'd've left us together, she'd have been alright. They knew she was fucked up, but they didn't care." She her lip trembled. "Poor Pia."

"How are you holding up? Can you go another day or two, even without the Mouse?"

"I'll be fine. How's Elodie?"

I said she was fine. There were good lawyers on the case and she shouldn't worry.

"We didn't do nothing, you know. The Mouse was with her guy, and I was going to open a club. We haven't done any actions in a year. Since Corolla got busted, nobody was doing nothing."

"Well," I said, "I think someone was doing something."

We hugged each other. She promised to hold herself together, to cooperate with the lawyers. "Did anyone tell Little Petey?" She said he was running the bar while she was locked up. I said I'd head over there when I left the jail. She walked to the door and tapped on it twice. It opened invisibly again, and she was gone.

It took ten minutes before the Mouse came in, and in those ten minutes I felt the defeat of Allie's life.

The guard stuck his head in and held up his fingers: two minutes. The Mouse crossed the floor quickly. She was wearing an orange jumpsuit, the sleeves and cuffs rolled up. She looked tiny. She hugged me.

"Did you hear about Pia?"

She nodded. "Oh those cocksuckers."

"I just wanted to drop in, see if you guys are holding up. They separated you, eh?"

"Divide and conquer. I burned my clothes and they gave me this. Cool, eh?"

"So, you're okay then, without Allie?"

"No problemo, Dad, don't worry, I'll look after her. You know all this is just bullshit? The Red Squad."

I said I thought she might be right. I asked if she remembered the names of anyone running the bar across from the Krak. She thought, then shook her head. "There were three or four of them. One guy, I think his name was Gary, or Gordie, Craig or something. A guy they named the place after, Tibby. Said he was involved in actions in Germany, he was on the run. I think he was the owner. The others came and went, but Gordie or Gary and Tibby were there all the time."

The guard opened the door and I waited while the Mouse was returned to her cell. He came back, gestured, and I followed him down another set of hallways and found myself going out a side entrance as he held the door back.

"You call and tell them it was okay, okay?"

"Yes. Thanks, I appreciate it."

"Fuck you." The door swung closed. He had a look that reminded me of Cornelius Fox, a greedy loser's look, the degenerate sadness of someone too far gone to remember how he got there.

16

Little Petey was in front of the Krak when I stopped my bike on the street. He'd heard from somewhere about Pia. Two girls in slut gear, short black miniskirts, seamed fishnets, and Doc Martens were comforting him. The girls had black lipstick on and thick black eyeshadow, the kind Allie and the Mouse used to wear.

"Petey, you heard? I'm sorry, man."

One girl said, "Fuck off, piggy."

I asked him if he was okay.

The other girl spat on the bike and said, "Fucking kill pig."

I slipped the bike into first. I heard him say, "That's Allie's dad."

One girl said, "They're all fucking pigs."

As I wound my way through the Market I spotted some unmarked cars, two men in each, smoking cigarettes with the windows open. They made no effort to be obscure or subtle. Intimidation was in the air like ozone. When I turned up Kensington, rounded the block, and came back out to

Spadina, I saw a paddy wagon backed up between two houses.

Elodie had taken extra medication to escape the spasms. She was asleep on the bed, her knees up by her collarbone. It was a popular position, I used to joke, that the girls in Bangkok attained without being crippled. I covered her up, found my swimming trunks, and turned out the light. The popsies were having themselves a late frolic. One put her bikini top back on when I came out of the changing area, the other two didn't bother. Mostly, they ignored me, keeping to the edge of the pool, talking low, while I tired myself out with laps. When I stopped they were gone. I heard them in the sauna room, squealing. I resisted looking in through the thick window. Upstairs I was too tired to shower off the chlorine. I lay down beside Elodie on the bed, forming myself to her back, and let my mind freewheel.

I could see what had happened, how the cheap politics Carl Hanson saw destroy his police force had whirled itself into a conspiracy. There would be a lot of cops like Hanson, embittered not by the work, but by the job.

Before now, when it was just to get my kids out of the shit, it looked like fun, some hard work requiring a lot of luck, but fun at the end of it all. But now I could picture the painstaking mechanics of Pia fashioning her noose, of the meticulous mechanics, thinking about her mother, of being alone and isolated from friends. Of the shock of not dying instantly with a clean snap as was supposed to happen, but by strangling slowly as shit ran down your naked legs and your tongue hung out, as fat as a running shoe.

In the morning I remembered I hadn't checked messages before turning in. There were eight. One new client who didn't have a reference, so we wouldn't take him on. Then a hangup. The next two were from Elodie's pals saying what a great luncheon it was. Then a hangup. Then Michael Bailey saying it was nine o'clock, he was leaving the office but was on his cell, and had I heard one of the Kensington 19 had died? Geez, Charlie, I pray it wasn't one of yours. Let me know; I'll call after I meet with Jeffy. Then another hangup and another hangup.

Pia's suicide was listed among Other Developments on the 24-hour news channel—she'd been under strict discipline and had vowed, the reporter said his sources said, not to be taken alive, and may have killed herself in fear of revealing information about other conspirators still at large. Comic book stuff.

The other developments were the detonation of a loud but ineffectual explosive device under an unoccupied police car in the Market overnight, the arrest of a young man and two young women for bombarding a police wagon with rocks from a rooftop in the Market. The miscreants weren't found, but as a precaution against escalating anarchist violence, police had flooded into the area and conducted several raids.

A follow-up item, live, from police headquarters, said Buddy and the Big Chu were appealing for federal and provincial money to fund an ongoing and permanent anti-terrorist task force. Video came up of Buddy, his eyeballs bugging and his shoulders jumping, commenting on the night's events, especially the bombing of the police vehicle and the stoning from the rooftops.

"Even in spite of the success of the K Project things are still escalating," he said. "Obviously the investigators haven't managed to root all these, these, these … these animals from their holes, yet, but lemme tell you we're gonna get every goddamn one of them, and when we do …" A thick hand appeared on Buddy's left shoulder and visibly squeezed; he took a deep breath, slowed himself down, and his eyes regained focus. "And when we do we'll let the due process of law deal with them."

A reporter was heard to ask if the city was in a state of insurrection. "Is the city out of control? Out of your control?"

Michael Bailey, off camera, evilly threw in, "Are we in a state of war here, Mr. Mayor? Do we need, like, troops? Should people fear for their lives?"

I thought, Michael, you crazy prick.

The mayor clearly hadn't thought about the army coming in, but his handler saw it coming and that was it. I could see the thick hand try to unbalance the mayor, but he was clearly a tough little fellow and twisted away: "Well, of course, for Christ's sakes. You see what happened at Old City Hall? Policemen being carried away on stretchers, not a two-minute walk from this building. You've got these little bastards stoning policemen, bombing police cars ... It's only a matter of time before some old lady is blown to bits down there trying to buy her goddamn vegetables. What did she ever do except work hard so she could buy good vegetables in one of the city's landmark neighbourhoods? No, we're exploring bringing in armed soldiers, but I can't talk about it right now. I ... I ... I wanna, I wanna ..." He shrugged off the thick hand entirely. "I wanna address the punks and creeps behind this wave of terror activity. You guys ready?" He looked directly into the camera, composed himself, and started speaking evenly: "Okay. I don't know *who* you are but I know *what* you are. You're a bunch of little bastards who never had to work for a living. Smoking dope, defecating in public, smashing windows ... Starbucks windows, for God's sake. What'd Starbucks ever do except make jobs for youth and make a great cup of coffee? Well, lemme tell you, we're coming for you, we're coming and we're not stopping until your asses are in jail, deep inside the jail where you'll wish you had a cup of Starbucks coffee, but you won't. What you'll be doing is grabbing your ankles while some big ..." He was gone.

I laughed.

Then I remembered Pia.

Later, when Elodie was up and around, we ate leftovers from the fridge. I told her what I'd come up with, what the stuff I'd written down meant. She was still a little spacey and sulky, "Yeah, yeah, go do something, okay?"

The Crown's office was a couple of minutes away on foot. I tried Michael's cell and it went to message. I went downstairs and outside. The morning outside was almost summery, a light breeze of promise, soft sounds of traffic. A bum was in an earnest discussion with the day man outside the building. It wasn't the grubby guy from the Funny People, just some guy cashing in on the people walking to work, walking to shop. I grabbed a coffee and a newspaper at the café by the entrance and sat at an outside table in the sun to watch the day man push the bum away, only to have him come back. Tactically, there was no reason for the guy to insist on my doorway: a block or two north he could hit both east-west and north-south foot traffic from the same spot. His buddies, a bunch of Natives in the parkette across the street, shouted encouragement. When the day man gave him a buck, he finally went away. The day guy took off his blazer and fanned his armpits.

"They're out early this year, Mr. Gray," he said, seeing me. The condo was in Elodie's name and to the staff I was Mr. Gray, except for Jerome, whom Elodie had made a point of telling I wasn't her husband. "My boy-popsy," she'd wickedly told the blushing, stuttering concierge, "but I'm wearing him out, Jerome. You ever work on, like, live bodies?"

I told the day man that giving the bum money would only bring his friends on.

"It's an epidemic, Mr. Gray. Jerome had to move one off last night," he said. "He kept hanging around and hanging around. Jerome gave him money, but he just sat across the street there, keeping away from the other bums, waiting for something. Funny bum, though. Jerome said it looked like he had a cell phone and he kept making calls." He laughed. "A bum with a cell phone, probably calling his broker. Put six dimes into Nortel."

I smiled. "Probably how he became a bum in the first place."

I tried Michael from the pay phone. Still busy. There were several, if not dozens, of restaurants and cafés in the area, and I began idly making the rounds. In front of a Greek takeout I saw, first, Jefferson come out and stride across the street towards his office. I remembered him as the guy with Fox at the restaurant when I was fry cooking. A few seconds later, Michael Bailey came out and stood on the sidewalk. As I came up behind him, he was punching numbers into his cell phone. I touched his shoulder.

"You calling me?"

"Hey, Charlie." He clicked off and put the phone into his briefcase. "You been sitting on me?"

I said I lived nearby and was just out for a walk. He said he was all coffee'd out and we went up to the parkette across from the condo. When the Indians moved on us, Michael was relaxed and friendly, and gave them each a buck and a smoke. When a big swarthy one wearing black jeans, a leather vest with no shirt, and moccasins, said he wanted another cigarette, Michael told him to fuck off and he went away muttering, "Tough fuckin' white man."

We sat on the grass and he lit a cigarette. "You know," he said, "when I graduated J-school I was working up in Ottawa and I got stopped by an Indian looking for a couple of bucks. I was a hotshot reporter, you know: everybody's a story, no matter who. I stopped to chat, gave him a buck, asked the Indian where he was from and he said from his mother. I walked away and thought, rude prick. Later I asked a guy who did Native policing about it and he said the guy wasn't being rude. They call the earth their mother; he came from the earth. Mother earth. Therefore he came from his mother."

He had a look of wonder about him as he spoke. I could see the younger Michael Bailey, eager to find out, eager to know, then eager to understand. All big eyes that were going to eat the world, grow those expectations, attain them. He had an almost religious air about him, not a born-again fanaticism, but the actual Christian aspect, in the best sense of the word.

I bummed a smoke from him. "What did Jefferson have to say?"

He laughed. "Well, Jeffy. Now there's a guy, when he dies they'll have to screw him into the ground. I finally caught up to him on the phone yesterday. Yeah, Mikey, glad to help you out with this. How 'bout coffee, Mikey, the Greek's on Bay Street, tomorrow, okay? You know the kind of thing, don't want to keep you waiting, help out with this big story. You're out in front on this thing, Mikey, and I'd like to keep you there.

"So, we meet. And I ask him about last year's bomb, about what went on with the case. He says he can't talk about that, even a year later. Youth Act. But he said he could say there were negotiations, a plea agreement. Off the record. The girl, Corolla, took psychiatric help because Fox said she'd been brainwashed. She got sentenced to no time, but she went into a loony bin for treatment. This, of course, is off the record, Jeffy said. The other two accused got out and they're long gone, didn't even report in, just seemed to walk out of 311 Jarvis with relatives, went to the relatives' homes, and both snuck out in the night."

"You're coffee'd out, hearing that? That was what, five minutes, a half a cup?"

"Well, that's what he had to answer to my questions about last year. Then we got down to it, and this time he was asking the questions. How come I'm asking about last year's bombing? Well, I said, because of the bombing stuff this week, I wondered if there's a tie-in. Why'd you think there might be a tie-in, Mikey? Well, jeez, Jeffy, I'm stupid maybe, but I'm not totally brain-dead: anarchists, the Black Bloc, bombs, Kensington Market. What else would I think? Well, he says, I saw you talking to that biker guy at court yesterday, big guy, beard. That guy, I said, that guy's a guy I see around the courthouse, don't even know his name. His name, Jeffy tells me, is Charlie Tate, and he's the old man of the two chicks ringleading this thing. Oh, I says, I wondered about him. Stay away from him, Mikey, he says, I can't tell you why, but we think that guy's part of it. Off the record. So I said, that guy? The biker guy? No, he's just a guy. And he says the guy, you, might be the international connection, you've been documented travelling in strange places. And your kids get Green Green and Gold to defend them and the other bozos get Pay Pray and Penitentiary. You the terrorist back end, Charlie?"

"Not lately. You mention Fox being in court?"

"Oh, yeah, I forgot. I said how come Fox is there, he acting for one of the 19? How come he wasn't up front? Should I be talking to him, too, Jeffy?

"Don't worry about Fox, he said. Fox has an interest, Fox is okay. I'll ask Fox, he said, if he'll give you the scoop down the road, Mikey." Michael flipped his cigarette away. "*Mikey*. How come, we're pals, you don't call me *Mikey*, Charlie?"

"To me you're a Michael, Michael. A *Mikey* is a hanger-on, a go-get-the-condoms. A dufus. But if you want, I'll call you *Mikey*."

"Don't. I hate Mikey. You'd think Jeffy, ace interrogator that he is, would have realized that. Only cunts call me Mikey."

The Natives came back, a little hesitantly. Michael said to me, "Watch this, Charlie. That mother earth thing." When the big one, shuffling, asked for cigarettes, Michael gave them each another one. He said to the biggest guy, a tall, solid, swarthy man with long black hair, high cheekbones, and no front teeth, "Hey, bud, where you from?"

The big guy looked at him. "Macedonia, bud." Mathedonia.

We got to our feet and walked south, laughing. I said: "Mathedonia, bud. Jesus, Michael, you're a real street guy. Math-a-doooooonia."

"Well, fuck," he laughed. " I ... Ah, fuck me." He took some photographs from his briefcase and we stepped into a coffee shop, bought some bottled water and sat in the back.

I went through the photographs. They were your usual demonstration pictures, most of them taken after the cops had made a barricade of their legs to prevent the recording of the condition of the guy on the ground. One frame showed most of the face of a young man, ski mask being ripped from his face, glaring up at the plainclothes guys. His mouth was open as though he was shouting. A photograph showed him being bundled into a two-door Pontiac. Another picture showed a uniformed cop wrestling with a teenaged girl; in the background, in mid-stride, his mouth open and his hands out, was Hanson. Laughing off to the side was the bum.

I liked Michael more, both for his telling of the Jeffy

interview and that he could laugh at his interaction with the Macedonian. I drank my water and looked over his shoulder at the street.

"Michael, I gotta admit to you, when we made the deal I thought I was gonna have to fuck you on this. My goal, then, was to get my kids out, whatever I had to do. I hope you understand that. When Pia, the Filipino girl, committed suicide, that kind of changed. I'm not sure what I'm going to do, but I think I'm going to burn down the tent. I can't promise I won't fuck you, but I can tell you if things work out, you'll get a great story and my kids'll be free, both."

"I'm going to need to get something out of this, Charlie."

"I know. I'll ask my kids if they'll talk to you. My guess is: they won't. I won't pretend. You got kids?"

"No, I'm gay."

"Well, you got someone you care about, right?"

He nodded.

"You care about them like I care about my kids. I've got to get them clear of this. I think, if I do it right, I can. And I think in the process I can give you everything you want. More, probably, than you think. If I can."

"So, I got to trust you?"

"Yeah, I guess."

"Well," he said, "as long as you're not Macedonian."

I told him I needed two of the pictures and he should print extra copies for himself. I promised that as I made each step, I'd try to keep him posted. I said Elodie was doing some work and he should be ready to go places and speak to people, as the information developed. She'd give him the information but he'd have to track it the same way she did, or at least confirm it in his own way.

"You got anything for me, now, for tomorrow? Something? Anything?"

I told him the story of Pia's mother, of Pia working as a bricklayer, of Pia being separated from her friends in jail, how the suicide watch went wrong, of how she hung herself just like her mother did, and how the mother did it. I told him to go to the Krak Bar. "The kid you want to talk to is behind the counter, Petey. Petey. He was pretty much in love with Pia, if I read him right. If he's not there, he's in custody or in hospital. Last time I saw him he was with a couple of girls and none of them was taking the news very well. There was some brick-throwing on cop cars last night, it might have been them. But probably I think it wasn't, that it was someone else entirely. If you strike out, call me and I'll ask Green Green and Gold what she told them about her background."

"Her mother had no hands? And she hung herself?" He looked near tears.

"Will that keep you busy for a while?"

"She really must have wanted to die," he whispered to speak a horrible thought.

I didn't know if he meant Pia or her mother. In either case, he was right.

Elodie wore a telephone headset, sitting back in her wheelchair, and I listened to her pretend to be somebody else, asking technical questions in a decent British accent about someone's financial information. The fax machine was printing out bankruptcy information. A tape recorder was set up on the floor by her wheels and she'd filled several pages of hand notes.

Hanson, I thought, was angry enough to be careless, and with Michael Bailey mentioning Jeffy taking time to dirty me up, I didn't want to bug him about the missing witch. I found a cellular phone we kept paid up to date but almost never used. I called the headquarters general number and asked for Gerry Adams, kiddie porn. He was out and I left no message.

Elodie pulled off the headset and tossed it on her desk. "Ah, the devil's work is done." She saw me with the cellular phone on my lap. "Things must be going good. You haven't used a ratfuck phone in weeks."

"Just looking busy while you toil, my dearie." We went out onto the terrace. I looked at the office windows facing us. Among other towers, there was clear line of sight down to the Crown's office; a parking garage off to the left was the height of our terrace and windshields of cars were arranged in a long straight line. Far away the Park was quiet. I went inside and brought out the bedside radio, plugged it in, and set it on the terrace wall. I found an Italian radio station and Elodie and I sat face to face, speaking under the noise.

Speaking quietly, she went through her notes.

Tibby Kay's was a doing-business-as company, not incorporated, but a partnership of two people: Terry Keller and John Gregory doing business as Tibby Kay's. The mailing address for the partnership was up on Yonge Street, in York Region. Elodie had determined it was one of those postal mail-drops where a suite number was actually a post office box. Keller and Gregory had set up their partnership a year-and-half ago, about six months before the Queen's Park bomb was discovered and Corolla Carlson was arrested. The building Tibby Kay's was housed in was owned by a Chinese man named Lui. Posing as a credit officer, Elodie had called Mr. Lui's real estate office and found Keller and Gregory had initially leased the place for a year, but had, after six months, closed the café, let it sit vacant for a while, then someone started up a juice and health food business in the storefront.

Elodie had run Lucy's Juicery and it came back as a dob company registered to Brenda Harris Partners, Brenda Harris and Lucy Harris. The address given was another mailbox-suite number at the same postal outlet on Yonge Street, north of the city. Elodie had run all Harrises, Kellers, and Gregorys within a mile or two of the postal outlet and found none with listed telephones or on voters' lists. She had a searcher checking tax rolls for the area. All the names were too common to raid on the motor vehicle database without dates of birth or addresses.

I told her about my meeting with Michael Bailey, how Jefferson the Crown was interested in my activities, how Indians refer to the earth as mother. And how Macedonians look an awful lot like Indians, sometimes. She laughed at the story. I told her I'd given Pia's story to Michael, and that we were going to use him.

"We going to fuck him, Charlie? Make him our stooge?" She sighed. "Poor Michael."

"We might have to, but I'd rather not. Let's see if we can meet his needs, and meet ours."

"But our objective is still to get the girls off, right?"

I thought about that. "I don't think so, El. Before Pia's death it would have been enough. We know what those fuckers did and we know what they're doing. It's just a matter of time until we have enough leverage to get the girls out from under. But why stop there?" I gave her the sheet of paper with Gerry Adams' scant information on it and said we'd need a home address.

17

We went out for lunch, having tube steaks on University Avenue in front of the courthouse at 361. The vendor was an immigrant from Lebanon I often spoke to. He ran the stand all day and worked evenings and nights at a variety store in the east end. He'd told me his dream was to become a Canadian millionaire. "Next," he'd said, "an American millionaire." Today, he was ecstatic. "Halfway there, Mr. and Mrs." He charged us for the hot dogs but gave us free drinks.

We took our dogs to the cement flower-beds in front of the courthouse.

"That's how the Grays started, Charlie. Small. Sweat it out around the clock. What a country. A chance for everybody."

"Hot dog stands? The Grays?"

She gave me a wide smile. "Gold, actually. We started with five shitty little mines turning out about five million a year, each. Hard times, those times, me bucko. It wasn't always bubbly champagne and foie gras for the Grays. Lots of years in there, getting by hand to mouth." She said, proudly: "I come from some shit, Charlie."

Cops and Crowns and lawyers and clerks and jurors went in and out of the building. The hot dog guy was moving product like nobody's business. I asked Elodie, "Hey, can you put a word in with Colin, let that guy keep some of the money for a while before he has to give it back?"

She sponged mustard from my lip with her napkin. "You're soft, Charlie. You'll never be a Gray." She looked at the hot dog guy. "I wonder if the Grays were ever that happy. Look at him, he's almost dancing. That's the time to live, Charlie, in the minutes or days leading up to being rich, when the promise is better than the reality. Look at his shoes."

I glanced at his feet and saw he walked on the inside of his feet, wedging the heels of the old black brogues. As I studied them, a pair of moccasins went by, moccasins and the cuffs of black jeans. He was lurching, my Macedonian, less balanced than he had been when he bummed Michael Bailey for cigarettes that morning. I told Elodie to eat up, we had to get back. We stopped at an office supply store on the way and Elodie bought red wrapping paper and I hunted up two twenty-four-by-thirty-six bulletin boards.

In the afternoon Elodie worked up her Kensingoof file, noting further avenues she could take. I watched the 24-hour news for updates and found little we didn't already know, except that a demonstration was forming up for that evening at the detention centre, a candle-lit memorial for Pia. Pia was now being described as a suicidal terrorist who, despondent at having been taken alive, had ultimately carried through on her intentions. The anchor said there were live developments at police headquarters and a camera jumped to a conference room crowded with reporters. The podium was vacant.

The blonde anchor I'd seen with Michael Bailey was having trouble with her earpiece, but she finally took the throw and said, "Thanks, Maria, I'm here at police headquarters where police are expected to release information on outstanding suspects in the Kensington 19 case, as well as to update us on the escape of a Black Bloc anarchist who broke free from a police vehicle after yesterday's violent demonstration at Old City Hall.

"Sources tell me the four wanted people still outstanding are all armed and dangerous and they may have fled the country, perhaps even to the Middle East. No one here will confirm reports there is an international connection to the K-19, as it's being called, but one of the wanted men is reportedly also wanted for terrorist activities in Germany.

"Police also won't confirm that a local man who has travelled widely in recent years is also under investigation as a possible financial mastermind behind the Black Bloc." She rehashed events of the past few days; I saw Michael Bailey sipping coffee beside the podium. I used my cellular phone to call his and watched, over her shoulder, as he put his hand to his belt, glanced around and punched a button.

"Bailey. Make it quick."

"Michael. If you get a chance ask about reports that a suspect already in custody has ratted and has been put into the witness protection program."

"Ah?"

"They've flipped Corolla Carlson." I kind of lied, but maybe not, and said, "A guy from the *Star* called up a friend of mine at headquarters, asking about her. He said she's gone over, gave them the whole thing and he wanted confirmation."

"Ah. Did he confirm it?"

"Well, I don't know this guy well, but he hasn't lied to me in the past."

The camera panned the room and I lost sight of him as he hung up. There was a jerking motion on the television screen and the operator jump-focused on a door behind the podium. The Big Chu, Magda the K, the Shiv—Superintendent Ben Izzard, commander of the intelligence bureau—and several low-level press aides paraded onto the stage. The aides moved through the reporters handing out press releases.

No photographs were available of the escapee, they said, because he'd got away before getting printed and photographed, nor were any available of the other outstanding suspects. Interpol had been notified. Descriptions were included in the press release. Odd, I thought, that they took them to court undocumented.

In questioning, the Chu also said the outstanding suspects were considered armed and dangerous. "You have to be desperate to break away from a police vehicle," he said with a straight face. "The others, we believe, are the technical component of both the Autumn Offensive and a planned bombing attack on police headquarters. I can't reveal details of their scheme, but I can tell you it was to be orchestrated to cause maximum damage and loss of life."

When the Big Chu took questions, Michael asked if it were possible more devices were somewhere in the city. Magda the K leaned in to consult with the Big Chu, then directed the question to the Shiv, who stood beside him with a face like a closed door and a squat massive body like a brick building. The Shiv said, "Under investigation. We don't believe the danger has passed, but with the arrests we've made we believe we have this terrorist network, this Black Bloc, on the run."

Michael asked if the financial component, the financiers of the network, had been discovered. Again, the K leaned in to consult with Chu, and the question again went to the Shiv. He said, "Under investigation. But I can tell you—and I won't take any questions on this—we've found a possible connection between the suspects and a local man with ties in Europe and Southeast Asia; we believe he may be arranging some support for the accused."

Michael yelled out, "Any truth to the rumour, Chief, that a Black Bloc member arrested a year ago has turned informant and helped out on this case?"

The Big Chu nodded to the Shiv, who looked grim. "No comment, Michael."

Michael loaded it up: "Well, okay. How about: did the task force have any difficulty with the fact that she was a young offender? Did this mean getting her into the witness program any more complicated?"

"I don't know where you're getting this, Michael, but it's news to me."

"Or that she was mentally ill? How about when she gives evidence? You foresee any problems down the road?"

The Shiv shook his head and clamped his mouth shut. When an off-camera voice asked why the K Squad was set up separately from the intelligence bureau and headquarters, Magda nodded at the Shiv. He said, "We felt we needed a dedicated unit to work on this project. The other special units are already over their heads with ongoing criminal investigations." The Shiv was an old-style copper and he clearly suspected what was going on: too many questions were coming at him and not enough at the Big Chu. "Let me add, the credit for this investigation, from its inception to our results-to-date, can fairly be claimed by Chief Chu. He's the one who, once we received the initial information, conceived the satellite squad, he liaised with the city, the Ontario Provincial Police, DND, CSIS, and all the other partners who participated. He arranged the funding needed—and I can tell you we're talking a significant sum—and he brought the best people in."

Magda didn't react, but from the look on Chu's face, he immediately heard the wood being sawed and the nails going in.

18

Barry White had a couple of days off from the glue room at Bobby Clarke's place. I tracked him down at home and asked if he was available for some freelance work the following day. He said he was conflicted on the Carlson case because of work he'd done for Cornelius Fox. But if it was something else, sure. I gave him the address of the postal outlet up Yonge Street and set him up for before rush hour the following morning. If he had another body, I said, he could take him, too, but it would require a second vehicle. I said there were two red packages being picked up at the outlet sometime in the next two days and I needed to know who took them, what they drove, and where they went: one, two, three. No analysis, no intelligence, just those three things. We settled on a price.

"And, Barry, on another subject?"

"Sure kid, what?"

"Thanks for the heads-up last year. I dropped it."

"Good luck with your kids, kid."

I rode the bike uptown, not hurrying, enjoying the constant decisions you have to make in heavy traffic, the constant speeding up and gearing down, cutting corners, watching for clues in drivers' faces in side mirrors. Elodie had addressed the packages to subscribers of the postal boxes and I handed them to the kid at the counter with a twenty-dollar tip. To be safe, I sat in a doughnut hole across the street until the kid locked up and climbed on a bicycle. Barry and his pal could sit in the parking lot and have a clear line of sight to the front of the outlet and the client table inside. I doubted too many people received bright red packages.

Elodie left a note saying she'd headed out for lobster, another preemptive strike to avoid the Vietnamese dinner she still owed me. I met her at a seafood joint a few blocks away and helped myself to her bottle of wine. She said the lawyers had called: no one got out that day. The Crown, they said, cited public danger, ongoing investigations, and fear of flight. They'd continue the bail hearings in the morning.

We ate lobster tails and I told her what I thought was going on, and pointed at the back-steps taken by the Shiv at the press conference. When I mentioned Michael Bailey she said he'd called and so had Carl Hanson. "*Mr.* Carl Hanson, he said," she said, "emancipated at last."

Hanson said he'd be around tomorrow, but Michael said he wanted me to call him back. I tried at the newspaper but he was gone. I called his cell with no result. When the lobsters and wine were gone, we wandered along Queen Street and listened to jazz, drinking amaretto and discussing various schemes.

She said, "I like you like this, Charlie. I thought I'd lost you for a few days there."

"Well, it was tough on the kids."

"But we're gonna get them, the fuckers, right?"

"Oh, yes," I said. "We already know they can get got, now we'll get 'em."

Leaving, I didn't see the Indian or the bum. But it was dark and they could have been anyplace.

The next morning I didn't have much to do. I stayed by the phone in case Barry White called. I didn't watch the news, staying out of the terrace with my weights, making a few of the tai chi movements I'd learned. But I was big and ungainly and I quickly became frustrated. Exhausted anyway, but feeling strangely uplifted, I flopped on a teak bench and read some Orwell, feeling in the warm sun as though I was in Rangoon, finally getting up to make fresh coffee when I heard the wheelchair creak through the open window as Elodie transferred from bed. When it was brewed I poured two cups and took them outside, putting hers at the farthest end of the terrace.

While she was struggling awake with her coffee, I made some mischief, using the cell phone to call Magda the K's secretary and leaving a message she should call Michael. I refused to leave a last name, but gave the number of the newspaper's switchboard. Then I had Elodie call the newspaper and leave a message with the city desk: it was Magda. *Call me back, my messaging system at headquarters isn't working so if I'm not in hit zero and my secretary will take the message. If I don't hear from you, Michael, call me at home later, you have the number.*

I wasn't doing anything, just laying down smoke to alleviate my boredom. There were further moves I could make but I resisted for now. I wasn't sure where Magda the K fit into the conspiracy, or even if she did. I'd have to resolve it one way or the other.

By noon I was walking in circles. Elodie sent me down to

have a swim, arming me with the cellular phone. After showering off I got into the dry sauna and baked. Through the wood door I heard the phone go off and stepped out into incredible cold.

"Stud? Your old guy just called. All done, he said, he wants to meet."

Upstairs I hit the stash and grabbed a few thousand dollars.

Someone was up on us when we left the condo. The giveaway was one of those dumb things people do: one of the cars was an old white Cougar, the kind with the reverse line at the back of the roof. They're not rare but they're scarce and you don't see too many of them around. I eased the Intrepid onto College Street and went east, taking the Cougar across the front of police headquarters. The trick was to lose the surveillance decisively, without being obvious about it, and letting them know we knew they were there until we were ready to dump them. If they thought they were burned, they'd call in other vehicles, or ride us so tightly we wouldn't be able to operate at all. I didn't have the other vehicles yet, and didn't expect to. The Cougar had the eye and was the only one visible: the driver would alert other players to our direction and location. There'd be one above us on Wellesley and one below us on Gerrard, both likely a little ahead of us. If we headed off onto a north-south street one of those vehicles would take the eye and the Cougar would take a new out-of-sight position, making a box.

Barry White had cryptically told Elodie to have me at the Chinese Jew's place in an hour—a deli staffed by Chinese waiters down on Front Street. It was south and west of where we were driving, in the opposite direction, and Elodie pointed that out. I told her I had to make a quick stop on the way. Most often it isn't the actions of the driver that tips off followers that they've been burned. It's usually the passengers, getting fancy with the rearview mirror, pretending to reach for something in the back seat and taking a peek.

I needed streetcars, the huge ponderous beasts of public transport with a specific and locked-in path, and I knew the place I wanted one.

At the end of Carlton Street the road T-s into Parliament; the streetcars go south, an awkward turn if you're in the curb lane and also having to go south. If the surveillance car on Gerrard Street to the south was a little ahead, they'd either have crossed Parliament or have swung north to begin setting up a new box. Same with the car on Wellesely to the north: it'd have to come south until it was notified by the eye which way I'd gone.

A streetcar was waiting to make the left on Parliament. I saw it from a few streets away. Northbound left-turn traffic on Parliament had an advanced green signal. Two blocks short of the intersection I pulled over and went into a convenience store for cigarettes and newspapers. I didn't look for the Cougar: it was there, likely still behind me, pulled into another parking spot. In the Intrepid I gave Elodie a paper and began reading Michael Bailey's piece on Pia. He'd obviously connected well with Petey, who was quoted as her fiancé. A sister living in Hamilton was interviewed and she told the sad tale of the mother committing suicide. Michael had managed to get a guard at the jail to say they couldn't talk, citing an investigation into how Pia's suicide notice had fallen through the cracks. In all, it was a tragic piece and there was a stunning photograph of Pia, her hair loose and thick, wearing a turtleneck sweater that made her face a perfect oval. She had the smile of a model in a milk commercial. The cutline said: "Terrorist or victim? Sherelle Filipina, 25, killed herself in a jail cell in Toronto this week. Fifteen years ago her mother killed herself in a jail cell ten thousand miles away. Is this the face of the new terrorism? Or a young woman with a social conscience that killed her?"

The streetcar was gone and as I flipped through the pages I saw another approaching. I started the car and crept along the curb so the streetcar was almost parallel, a little behind. I signalled south at the red light at Parliament. The advance green signal held back pedestrians and the northbound vehicles turning left entered the intersection. I could see the northbound traffic, but the Cougar, if it was still behind me, couldn't. When the last northbound car was in the middle of its turn I told Elodie to hang on and went ahead of the streetcar a few feet, then cramped my wheel, and spun a fast and noisy tight north turn. A half block up a man's pale face flashed at me from a southbound Jetta. I went east into the first street north and made sure he could see me in his mirrors. Just inside the street I did a fast three-point turn out of his view and barrelled out again, continuing north one block and then into the next east-west street. I took random streets back into the downtown core, catching stale yellows, and ending my evasions by driving into a one-way street for a block, then south to Front Street. I went into the indoor lot attached to the deli and we were able to make our way to the restaurant without going outside.

"Well, that was pretty TV," Elodie said when we were seated and she'd arranged her wheelchair at the table.

"They know we know, now." I felt pretty good. "You turned on?"

"Shoulda let me drive, stud. That would've turned me on."

We ordered coffee and a few minutes later Barry White walked in. I thought he looked like a pensioner out for his afternoon treat of strudel and tea, wearing an old cardigan and his dress shirt buttoned to the throat. His eyes counted heads in the restaurant as he made his way to the table. He ordered strudel and tea and I laughed. He very politely greeted Elodie and asked about research into spinal cord injuries. "You keeping up, young lady? Never give up. When I was young they said, you bust your hip, you're toast, it's a rocking chair and you'd need help to get to the shithouse, pardon me. Now I got a new hip and I move better than my wife. Of course," he laughed, "I don't weigh two-ninety. Or two-ninety-four with a dessert in each hand."

I told him what just happened, the white Cougar and the fast run through town.

He nodded. Everything's got a story behind it: "They got that Cougar, the white one, and another white one and three of the bronze ones from Parsons, the dealership where Connie Lombardozzi worked after he retired. I told 'em they were too distinctive, especially the white ones. That back window silhouette, it's a killer. The sale made Connie salesman of the month and he took us all out for beers on the bonus. Billy Tallhouse wiped out one of them helping the holdup squad take down some bandits, but the other white one somehow survived." He poked his tea bag into the pot to steep some flavour out of it. "So, they know you're heated up."

"Somebody's on us. No question."

"Well, it's an Intelligence car. No one else would take it. The budget up there, they'd still be pumping in leaded gas if they could." He drank his tea black and ignored the strudel when the waitress put it down. "You ready to write?"

He didn't use notes. "Ten-ten a.m. a couple come out of the postal dump, together, each carrying a red box. She opens hers on the way to her car and finds a big piece of white board. She looks at both sides. He's parked beside her; he pokes his hand into his, takes a peek and grabs 'em both, throws them away. He starts reading the street, every vehicle, every window, everybody passing by. This guy knows he just picked up a big smelly wad of shit, pardon me. Now this is good news and it's bad news. We got pictures of them, we've got their licence plates. The bad news is it's going to be impossible for me and Harry to take them both out of there. Your guy's heated up and he's going to be watching." Barry turned to Elodie. "I know you know a lot, and I don't mean to talk down to you, but let me tell you: it takes six cars, minimum, to do a moving box in the city, daytime nighttime, it doesn't matter, even when the guy you're doing it to doesn't know you're doing it to him. So, there only being two of us, we decide to do her. She wasn't smart enough to know what we'd just done to them. We'll play her loose, and if we have to dump her out, we'll dump her out. Harry and I got freddies with fresh batteries so we can keep in touch.

"We let him ride off and when she heads out, we take her. He's not dumb; he obviously calls her on her cell phone and gives her directions. He's going to trap us up, have her pass through a place he's got picked, see if he can get us. We don't. First turn she makes we keep going. We're south on Yonge Street, way ahead of where she went into the side streets. We're now down past the 401 and we've got a decision to make. The hell with it, this is all value added for our client here: we've put vehicles under them and we've got their snaps. We wait and wait and when a big block of traffic comes south, down below the highway, she's in it. We don't know where he is, he's got a brown Chrysler Sebring, rag-top, top up, but her Corvette is red and pretty distinctive. We play, nothing serious, and we take her into the downtown core. We're both actually ahead of her some of the time. At Gerrard and Bay, near your place, we get too smart and we lose her. Last seen," he said, "eastbound on Gerrard, signalling left, south, onto Bay Street."

While Elodie wrote, Barry recited descriptions and the licence numbers of the cars. He told me the hours and the mileage and gave me some one-hour photos in an envelope and I took a wad of bills from my pocket and paid him.

Work finished, he finally started in on the strudel. Casually, he said, "Guy's a cop, you know? Mr. Sebring. He's a cop, or he used to be a cop. I seen him around, I think, but I would've read it on him in the dark." He smiled at Elodie as she put away her notes. "Miss, did I ever tell you about my friend Connie Lombardozzi?"

I ordered more coffee.

At the apartment Elodie dug out a notebook of codes and passwords and went to work on the computer. I picked up calls from the phone: Michael, Michael, hangup, hangup. I took another charged blind cellular phone from the closet and when Michael answered at his office I told him he was a master storyteller. We batted around developments—there were none, really—and he said he'd received a message to call Magda the K; when he called her back she didn't know what he was talking about and hung up quickly. He said Jeffy called. He was going to resist bail on the Kensington crew.

"What else did Jeffy say? More about the shadowy offshore financier?"

"Actually, your name did come up. He said if you wanted, you should walk down the street and have a coffee with him. He said he'd hate to see you end up in trouble, trying to get your girls out of it. He said he'd do what he could for them, but that you guys should hook up, make sure things don't get fucked up."

"Well, Michael, I think maybe he's too late."

"But, Charlie, what I think he really called about was the questions at the presser about the informant. I was pretty specific, he said, in my questions. Gender, age, mental problems. How come I knew that?" Michael laughed. "He asked if I had someone inside the case, talking to me. To be careful with whatever they told me. That there are agendas on the go that I know nothing about."

"I think he's got that part right."

The Corvette came back registered to Brenda Harris, with a residential address a few blocks from the postal drop. The residence was purchased for $460,000 three years earlier by Brenda Harris and Gregory Johnson, spouses. There was a $355,000 mortgage on the place; Harris and Johnson, spouses, had to scrape hard to get anything above a minimal down payment. The mortgage was held by a chartered bank. The Corvette was a brand new lease and had no liens against it. There were no speeding tickets. Policemen's wives don't get tickets, any more than policemen do. Neither Brenda Harris nor Gregory Johnson had criminal records, again no surprise there.

Elodie had bought some credit bureau reports and Brenda Harris was deep in the swamp of credit cards. She'd declared bankruptcy several years earlier. She was a late-pay on several occasions, but always managed to scrape up payments. A previous entry showed her as operator of several businesses, ranging from a kitchenware boutique to a florist shop, to being a real estate agent. She was living on credit and waiting for the big break.

Gregory Johnson was on his credit report as a municipal employee. He had pretty strong credit, except when he gave his wife her own credit card on his account. Then things went to hell pretty quickly.

Both were twenty-seven years old, born exactly one month apart.

The Sebring came back leased to RJS Associates, Inc. with an address in Burlington, just west of the city. There was an RJS Associates on the telephone disk, on Lakeshore Road. It had been registered a year earlier. The names of the people listed in the registration papers were your basic Black, your basic Brown, and your ever-popular Green. Elodie had used a cellular phone and called the number and a perky woman answered with the company name and asked how she could be of service. I knew right away it was a front, a channel to move people and cars and even residences around, to screen them, and was set up to detect any outside interest and provide an early warning system.

"Did you trip any wires, hacking in?"

"Couldn't tell. You think they're looking?"

"Oh, yes. Now they know for sure we know. If not us, then somebody else. Is your credit guy protected?"

"He'll be okay." While she was doing Johnson and Harris, she said, she'd had tracked down an address for the missing witch, Gerry Adams. He lived out in Pickering, a half-hour out of the city.

"We have get out front on this now," I said. "We can't weasel around any more."

19

Elodie took a nap at dinnertime. Usually on Friday nights we'd go out and make a night of it, dinner, then a dance club, then an after-hours joint. But she looked at me sleepily, yawned, and was gone. I lifted her out of the wheelchair and put her on the sofa. I went down the street for a shawarma and beer and went walking, trying to decide my next move, although I think I already knew it.

I felt, more than saw, a bum trailing me. At Elm Street he almost lost me; I stopped at a phone booth and called the cell phone in my pocket and I pretended to talk. When the chirping stopped I left the pay phone and walked east, towards Yonge Street. I picked up my step and portrayed jauntiness and a purposeful direction. At an LCBO I bought a bottle of wine and had it put into a gift bag. Outside I went west and walked briskly, as though in anticipation, over past 52 Division. Someone had written FREE KENSINGTON 19 on the front of the building in black running spray paint. In red the 19 had been turned into an 18 by closing up the bottom of the 9. In the same red it said, ONE FOR ONE, A PIG FOR PIA. I cut down the west side of the building, on the street where a shopping complex had been turned into condos. On the west wall of 52 was painted NO JUSTICE NO PEACE and under it was the anarchists' symbol, an A inside a circle.

The condo complex down the street from the police station reminded me of when I was a boy in winter, after my mother vanished one day, sending the old man into his shed and off his routes. I took a cash job at a dye factory in the neighbourhood, reaching into deep drums and scraping the sludge from the bottom with a rubber spatula, to be reblended and repackaged, the fumes making me see kaleidoscopes of colour and pinwheels of light. My ears took to ringing after only a few days. Ever since, when I had to drive by the dye factory, long closed, the long-gone smells would fill my nose, like the old opium guys in Chinatown rub their noses into their coats to find a last sweet remembrance. The façade of the condominium building must have had the same looming presence over me as that dye factory. I shivered, and wondered if I was making a mistake.

I was aware I shouldn't be there even before my hand pressed buttons at the security gate. Her voice came out mechanically. My voice said my name, and after a pause the black iron trellised door clicked and I was floating across a courtyard, sure of my way, clutching my gaily packaged bottle of bingo. Her condo faced out onto the yard and had a tiny garden area where nothing could grow in the absence of sunlight. There were windows in the front, and at the back, facing onto the street that ran beside 52 Division, where I'd come in, was a perfunctory bathroom window of pebbled glass.

The door to her unit was ajar. From inside I could hear music and the rattle of dishes being unloaded from a dishwasher. She was humming along with the music. I smelled cigarette smoke, cigar smoke, and the flavour remnants of cooked meat. She didn't smoke and didn't eat meat. She was a vegetarian and an accommodating former smoker, though not of cigars.

When I closed the door behind me, she murmured, "Do you think this is a good idea, Charlie?" The evening was warm and the silks and cottons had given way to shorts and a baggy York University t-shirt. Photographs on the wall showed her bestowing awards upon reporters, sailing a Tanzer, and with a previous client, a truly obscene businessman who'd been caught up in an extortion investigation. I looked for the photograph I liked best, and found it in a cheap wooden frame, the kind you put diplomas into. Magda carrying a sign at an anti-nuclear demonstration, during her college years, her face determined and angry and beautiful.

I'd come here only once before, just after she bought the place, a winter's night—the worst of times for me, when darkness came early, the cold reminded me of hated childhood dawns. Elodie had been away with the family at a function in San Diego— I'd come here that night and like a normal visitor commented on the funky furniture that had failed to make the transition from her old place. I'd said how the new décor was superb, mentioned the tastiness of the wine. I'd asked her to take me to bed and she had.

But that was then.

"Do you think this is a good idea, Charlie?" she repeated.

The dishes from the dishwasher were put away; she turned on a fan to rid the place of the smell of seared meat and tobacco smoke. I put down the photograph carefully. I sat in the chair and she sat on a sofa.

"It's falling apart, Mag. What were you guys thinking?" I actually wanted to ask if she was doing the Big Chu. The cigar smoke and the meat suggested so.

She shrugged. "It's fine, Charlie. I'm sorry about the girls." She'd met them in our off-and-on year before I met Elodie. To the kids, she was Dad's date, a cool chick who could talk revolution, capitalism, socialism, counterculture. How'd an old guy get such a cool chick, they asked each other, my little puppets talking to me through each other.

"The girls have no problem, Mag, I think you know that."

"The course of justice," she said with cool, exaggerated pomposity, "will flow. Truth will prevail and the wicked punished and the good rewarded." She smiled. "Sayeth the Lord."

I put my elbows on my knees. "A quick story. I was in Rangoon not long ago, having a cold drink at a little café. Hot in there, so I went outside and sat on the broken air conditioner. You'd love Rangoon, Mag, corrupt military dictatorship, torture the folks, close the schools, tanks in the street. Clients galore, for you, a little international spin and you could make the place look like Switzerland, except there's no banks, there's no chocolate, and there's a really big army. Anyway, I was in a street I called Electronics Street—the Burmese name was beyond me—where all the stores sold electronic equipment. So, I'm sitting there and I see this guy stop at a stall across the street. There's baskets of old electrical parts. He picks up a tiny speaker, blows into it, examines it. He holds a finger up to the shopkeeper, like: back in a sec. He crosses to my side of the street where another store has all these little transistor parts. Again he picks up a couple of things, examines them, sees if they fit together. Says, I guess, hang on a sec to that shopkeeper and goes next door, carrying his components. At the next shop, again he rummages, comes up with something, I don't know what, but he sees if it'll fit with the other stuff. It does. He goes to each shopkeeper in turn and pays them a few kyat, pennies really. He sits beside me on the air conditioner and he takes a double-A battery from his shirt pocket and puts himself together a radio. He turns it on and there, presto, scratchy voices."

"He sounds like your kinda guy, Charlie," she said, smiling. "Remind you of anybody?" She'd listened to all the stories about my old man and had then clearly admired him, saw him as a warrior in the battle against waste and built-in obsolescence. That was then. Now, I suspected, he'd just be some bum fishing in her bins in the pre-dawn, making a mess. She went for it: "My question, Charlie, is: did you take the broken air conditioner and how much did you get for it?"

I ignored it but filed it away. "Thing is, Mag, I've got the little speaker, and I've got the transistor, in another couple of days, at most, I'm going to have the battery. And the little thing I'm putting together is going to talk. And I suspect it's going to talk like a guy with a Chinese accent."

"We could talk at this later, you and I, you know ... after?" She fidgeted. "I'm sorry, there, about the air conditioner crack. Cheap."

I found myself thinking about it. I had always liked her a lot, especially talking afterwards. She was cynical and smart and funny. She'd been snaffled up by the corporates after successfully turning around the public's thinking on waste disposal, lobbying for, and pursuing political support for a Green group that had for years been screaming into the wilderness. It was the last of her many successes in social policy. In fact, we'd met when Kent assigned me to write about this Canadian Gloria Steinem of the environment. Money was stacked upon her, a better boat than the old Tanzer, a better car than the rusted old Volvo she was proud of, with four hundred thousand on the odometer. But she was so different now from then that when I saw her on television I could easily fail to put together the real Magda. She just looked, in her cottons or silks, like a corporate bimbo shovelling someone else's shit.

Except for the eyes, of course. I made myself think of Pia, of my kids passing their nights in separate cells. I hid my disdain and acted indecisive. I had to get the condo's lights turned off.

"Tell you what, let's sit in the dark awhile, like we used to. See how it plays."

As a half-measure it appeased her. While she moved about flicking switches I unplugged the telephone cord from the wall, leaving it only partially in the socket. I gave her the wine and she rustled up a wrinkled old baggie. We spent an hour talking nonsense, laughing and smoking dope and drinking, she loosening up a bit and sending a strong beam, and me always just a millimetre from saying the hell with it, who'll know? Once I glanced at the clock; we were side-by-side on the sofa, her head on my shoulder. I'd been there an hour. When I next looked another half-hour had passed and my face was in her hair and her nails were lightly picking at the fabric of my pants. Then the wine and weed worked on her and, as happens to most guilty smokers who are confronted by themselves, she became believably teary and left the room to get tissues. I'd been in her apartment for two-and-a-half hours, long enough. I stood up and touched my hand to her hair. She misunderstood and ran her hands on my hips and made a humming sound.

"I gotta go, Mag. It's late."

"Stay. We can work through this."

"Can't do it. I'm too stoned and too drunk."

She nodded. "Okay. Charlie, don't do anything without talking to me, okay? It's pretty dangerous and there's a lot at stake."

"Why don't you tell me what I need to know, Mag? You can go back to mung beans and riding a bicycle. This thing is fucked."

"I'm going to, Charlie. I just need enough."

I touched a scar high up in her hairline, a policeman's baton swung in wild moments at the power plant. My kids had loved the brave story of Magda and her gas mask, Magda the strong, doing battle with impossibly overwhelming forces. Now my Allie had scars, too, two of them. Neither the Mouse nor Allie would look acceptable in silks and summer cottons.

"You know, I always thought you had a master plan when you went over to those fuckers. You were gonna bury yourself deep into the dark kingdom and chew it alive from the inside out, like a worm in an apple."

"At first, Charlie," she said, "that was the plan."

I went into the bathroom. Before coming out I found some lipstick in her cabinet and put a dab on the edge of my lips. She didn't look up as I passed the sofa. I touched her on the shoulder, but she was rigid. I said goodnight and told her to be careful. On the way to the door I untucked my shirt from my pants and made a bit of a show tucking it back in as I crossed the courtyard. When I hit the patch of brightness under a tall globe-light I pulled my handkerchief from my pocket and industriously wiped her lipstick from my mouth. I dropped the handkerchief into a tastefully designed waste container disguised as a clay planter.

The bum was there, I knew, a shapeless piece of grey in a black shadow.

At a pay phone I called Michael Bailey at home and asked him to call Magda at home. I said she wouldn't answer, but that he not identify himself and simply say: Hey thanks.

"What are you getting me into, Charlie? What's it about?"

"Big story, Michael. We got trust, right? You and me? I don't call you Mikey, right?"

"Okay. Give me something, something I can use."

I told him we were collecting documentation and would

share it all with him in a day or two. He asked if I had anything he could use, like, now. I told him I hadn't confirmed anything, but the *Star* reporter had called me back and asked if I'd heard anything about a federal investigation into the handling of the Kensington 19 project.

"They going with it tomorrow?"

"Dunno, Michael. Guy called me up, asked if I'd heard anything about an outside agency taking the project apart. You saw the Shiv today. He's shitting. You oughta call him up, Michael, ask him about it."

"Shiv's gone home, this time of night."

I found my pocket directory and read off the Shiv's home number. "There might be something to it, Michael. You saw how the Big Chu threw him the tough stuff today. When was the last time Chu gave anybody anything that wasn't going to have to be scraped off their shoes?"

I smoked a cigarette for a few minutes to give Michael a chance to leave a message on Magda's phone. The bum was out of sight someplace. I dialled Magda's number and it went to message. I said, "Mag, it's me. Look, I appreciate everything. And I had a great time tonight. When I'm not walking funny, I'll give you a call. This'll put my kids in the clear. I appreciate it."

Elodie was taking a break from her snooze when I came in. It was too late to use the pool, but we suited up and went down so she could vamp Jerome into giving us the night key. We swam for an hour and went into the dry sauna. I lifted her onto my lap and rearranged our swimming gear. Afterwards we showered together in the men's room. I wasn't sure why, but I was feeling pretty good.

20

It was mechanical the next day. I always wanted to tell people about the key moment in an engagement, that flashing understanding where the clues fit together and everything broke open. How my amazing intuition and intelligence allowed me to penetrate the heart of a conspiracy, using only a strand of hair and a hunch.

But it wasn't like that, there were almost no mysteries anymore, no surprises, no clues that I didn't have six months ago. Conspiracies were just people, people who were in on it with a passion, and people who knew there was something going on that they didn't like, but they went along anyway.

First, I had Elodie, using a phony accent, call Hanson at the station. He was out, so I had her call his home. When he picked up she said, "Hey Carlo baby I heard you finally quit. Let's get together, eh, celebrate?" They agreed to meet at her place in an hour. "Bring your little blue pills, man, 'cause you're going to need them."

While I waited I went down and got coffee and newspapers.

The coverage was predictable, with the outstanding suspects all detailed and described and there was a story in one about the Mystery Moneyman: International Financier Funded K-19, Cops Say. Citing sources, Michael had managed to get in a few late graphs about an internal investigation into *possible irregularities* in the K-19 project. He said a high-ranking officer confirmed an internal investigation was underway at police headquarters, but the officer refused further comment. The *headquarters* was key, and pointed away from the Shiv's intelligence bunker. Neither the police chief nor his senior information officers was available for comment.

I was feeling pretty good. I took my coffee upstairs and a few minutes later Carl Hanson, puffing from climbing the stairs, knocked on the door. I told him I was going to fuck the Big Chu, but I needed a little help. He made a telephone call on one of the cells and spoke quietly and insistently for a few minutes. He hung up. "He's pissed off and he's scared now. He'll want to get out in front."

He said an appointment was set up for me in the early afternoon east of the city. I showed him Barry White's photographs from the postal drop surveillance and the *Post* photographer's picture from the violence at Old City Hall. He looked at them for a few moments. "Same guy, Charlie. Gregory Johnson. I don't know the woman."

The house line rang and Elodie answered it. "It's a woman, for you. She's pissed."

It was Magda. "You know what you've done, Charlie?" Her voice was even and cold.

"I've fucked you, Magda. How'd you figure it out? The bum they had following me last night when we were in the dark for so long? The phone messages? Didn't you think they'd put something on your phone, once they knew you were talking to the media after hours? I told you last night,

Mag, it's coming apart. You had a chance. You still have it, if you want it."

"Cocksucker."

"Kee-a-zock Zee-a-zucker."

"What?"

"You wouldn't understand." I hung up. Elodie and Hanson were listening.

"Pardon me, Carl," she said, "but I have to ask my significant other here a question."

He said, "Go ahead," and looked away.

She said to me, "You saw Magda last night? Did you fuck her?"

"Well," I said, starting to laugh, "yes and no."

The ex-witch patted me down to make sure I wasn't wired up. His wife was inside the townhouse, rattling pans and humming sadly along to the radio. Gerry Adams said: "They got a thing now, they put it surgically under your skin, nobody can see it."

"Probe away."

He took me out onto the patio and went back inside, apologized to his wife and came out with a radio. He plugged it into the outside wall, dialled into the lowest and highest frequencies and ran the speaker over my body, listening for feedback. Almost satisfied, he found fast Latin jazz and we sat at a patio table with the radio playing between us.

"Bombs," he said, "are unique. Each constructor has a signature, whether he knows it or not. Counterclockwise twist on wires, a dab of adhesive, an extra layer of tape. Something. When I went to the DND bomb school there were twelve of us in the class. There were some coppers, like me, and there were some guys who didn't go out drinking with us afterwards, didn't stay in the barracks overnight, didn't pass much more than the time of day. After classes they just disappeared in the same blue van that had brought them in the morning. They were all named Joe or Bill or John. Amongst the cops, we networked. There aren't a lot of bomb guys in the country and we all know each other, it's like a fraternity. Guys with steady hands, who only get called in when there's something funny to fix.

"The class was all together for theory, all the Bills and the Bobs and the cops. For practical studies, the cops were taught in one room, the funny guys were taught in another, another instructor. I guess they had to learn some more sophisticated stuff.

"We had a guy teaching us, an army guy who could make a bomb out of snot, a blue fart, and a snap of his fingers. He could take a handful of manure, some peroxide, and a July 1 sparkler and level a room. This guy took us through a local drug store, spent less than twenty-five bucks and took us back to class, and he made a bomb containing a napalm-like goo, could light up a roomful of people in a heartbeat.

"This guy, we just called him Fingers, he taught everyone how to put things together. I mean, you have to know how to make 'em before you can break 'em, right? He had a quirk. When he had to wrap wires he'd go first one way, then the other, then he'd come back again and tie a wee little bow, using needle-nosed pliers. Neatness. Everybody he taught learned it. The Finger's Twist. Everybody did it, because what did we know? Maybe this is some technical thing, maybe it's just his own voodoo, his good luck charm. Thing is, he tied the bow and he still had all his fingers. Good enough for me.

"In the class, we were the LE, law enforcement guys, we all learned the same stuff, together. We made the same mistakes our instructor made, we made the same extra things he did. Everyone he taught did it the same: one way, then another, then back again and the little bow tie. A quirk. Made no difference to the bomb, but we followed him close, just in case, I mean: what's the harm? Like crossing your fingers, or not crossing under a ladder."

Gerry Adams was loosening up. He went inside to get some beer. I heard his wife whisper, Who is he? Is he an informant or something? He answered it was okay, I think he's okay. Carl said he is.

We drank beers while he organized his thoughts. "We get the call there's a device at the legislature. We suit up, we jump into the truck and we're up there in about fifteen minutes. The device is clearly live. This isn't some school kid forgot his homework and somebody got nervous. This is the McCoy and that's rare. We do a visual and there's no way we can shoot it with water. What it is, is a glorified pipe bomb, but the wiring is pretty sophisticated. Ninety-nine times out of a hundred we'd send the robot in on a suspicious package and blast the fucker, end up with a bunch of soaked underwear or some kid's wet lunch. But this is complicated. Water's a conductor. We shoot some liquid in there and it closes a connection, it's sayonara. So I go to look closer. And what do I see?" He looked at me, waiting.

"The Finger's Twist." I lifted my voice a bit over the Latin music.

"Yep. Wires get wrapped first one way, then the other, then back again and a tiny little bow tie. A signature. So, I think, how come Finger's little signature is in this package? He only teaches three kinds of people: spooks, army, and cops. I note it but it doesn't have anything to do with what I've got to do, right at that moment. I disarm it. I tell my commander and he goes to a guy that runs intelligence and they take me aside. Shut the fuck up, you're on a plane to England tomorrow, you go to inspector when you come back and you run a task force out of headquarters. You say anything you're jeopardizing a joint federal-provincial-municipal task force. Loose lips sink ships; the enemy is everywhere. Buy war bonds." He rubbed his hands over his face as though removing grease.

"How come you're talking to me? You got a cushy job, you got inspector. You can file your nails at headquarters and take long lunches."

"Jesus," he said. "You sound like Carl. Carl was my training officer, a great cop, not necessarily a good detective. He just took the wrong assignment and it did him in. You know about the child abuse stuff? Well, since then it's a different Carl. But in uniform he was aces.

"You know, I wish I could say I'm talking to you because I don't like what they're doing and I trust in Carl. But the real reason is: I'm a bomb guy, an adrenaline guy, and they've got me sitting in an office with a bunch of geeks who talk in pixels and megabytes and motherboards. Effectively, my career as I'd planned it is over. They're the ones, those Intelligence fuckers, who handed me the bomb. I took it. It went off and now I don't get to wear my favourite winter mittens to keep my hands happy. I don't need 'em."

I took the *Post* photograph and Barry White's picture of Gregory Johnson from a file folder. He looked down at them, then up at me. The radio started a Ricky Martin song.

I said, "Say anything you should say. If you want."

He looked at the pictures a long time. He tapped the newspaper's demonstration photo. "Maybe, maybe, Gregory, the guy in my class." He tapped Barry's surveillance photograph. "Gregory, the guy in my class, for sure."

He walked me back to my bike. As I put on my helmet he asked, "Can I stay out of this? I hate it, but it's a job and I'd like to keep it."

"There's going to be shit, I can't lie to you. There's

especially going to be newspaper shit, there's a guy who'll be stirring this stuff up. I'll keep you out of it. If he calls you, he'll use my name. I can vouch for him: if he says he'll keep it off the record, he will."

He watched me climb on the bike. "Carl said your kids are in the bucket over this. What you got? Boys? Girls?"

"Twin girls."

He had a vacant look on his face. "Girls. Break your heart, eh?"

"Yeah. But they're going to be coming out." I kicked the bike to life and spoke over the rev. "And maybe somebody else's going in."

He looked at the house. It was big enough for a dozen kids. There was a pool in the backyard. There seemed to be acres of lawn, trees to hang an old tire from. Two people of child-bearing age in a house made for a family.

I hadn't seen any sign of kids anywhere.

21

In Kensington Market I avoided the Krak Bar. Brenda Harris was on the phone behind the counter of Lucy's Juicery. A teenaged clerk was trying to find the price on a container of a Middle Eastern saffron. Brenda Harris looked up as I came in and we stared at each other. I nodded at her. She said into the phone, "Gotta go, honey, they're here ... I won't, I won't, don't worry."

She was a fit and attractive woman but she looked stressed and a little haggard. Without me saying anything, she said she wouldn't talk to me. She asked me to leave.

I invited her and her husband to the Red Lobster on Bay Street, a short distance from the apartment, at eight o'clock that night. "You can come or not, it's up to you. But tell Gregory the wheels are coming off and he should be thinking about rolling the shit back uphill."

I went to Mr. Liu's real estate office on Spadina Avenue. He seemed to have a lot of properties in the Market area, ranging from residential homes to office complexes. His window was crammed with pictures and signs in Cantonese, Mandarin, Vietnamese, and I think Cambodian. I told his secretary I needed to see him, it was police business. She disappeared into the back and brought him out. I thought I could hear a lot of footsteps back there; a door slammed shut.

"You're a policeman?"

"An investigator."

He asked for my badge. I said it was a private investigation. He folded his arms and told me to get out. I did, and walked six blocks to Harry Quan's place and told him I needed Mr. Liu to talk to me. Nothing criminal, just needed him to look at a picture. Harry said he had no influence anymore, he was an old retired gentleman, maybe once a gambler, but now a pillar of Chinatown. I promised to bring Michael Bailey, the esteemed food critic from the *Post*, in for the Szechwan noodles the following weekend. I'd give him a heads-up. Harry nodded and went into the back and started yelling into a telephone.

He came back. "Mr. Liu made a mistake, he wishes to be cooperative. He is very sorry."

Mr. Liu looked at the photographs and said the man was the one who had paid the year's lease in advance. The woman was the lady who now operated the vegetarian shop.

I walked back to Harry Quan's place and thanked him. We drank beers, looking out the window. We talked about restaurants along Dundas Street and he went back to the telephone and started yelling into it again.

Gregory Johnson and Brenda Harris came into the Red Lobster fifteen minutes late. They spotted me and looked with some curiosity at Elodie. We sat and had dinner, talking about Gregory's uncle who was recently confined to a wheelchair, about spinal injuries, about whether it was better to have been born disabled or to have some life with mobility first. Elodie clearly liked him. He was a good-looking young guy, compact and in very good shape. I chatted with Brenda Harris about the condominiums in Kensington Market, health food, and physical fitness. She said the vegetarian supply business was booming—a mega growth industry, what with the aging population and the trend towards fitness, she said—and she hoped to turn Lucy's Juicery into a franchise, first in the city, then the province, and then nation-wide. She was very avid; she reminded me of a girl I knew in the carnival, a caller like me, who had big wet dreams that hinged on a single lucky break. Brenda Harris gave me her card as though the act was a key part of her networking strategy. Lucy, it turned out, was Brenda's sister and the prime investor. When we finished eating I suggested Elodie take Brenda out up to the Advocate for a drink. Brenda looked at her husband and he nodded.

When she was gone he said, "Thank God, I'm fucking dying for a smoke." We went outside and he found a loose cigarette in his coat and lit it. I looked up the block: Brenda Harris slowing her brisk walk to accommodate Elodie's rhythmic arm pumps on the wheels. The Macedonian bum was weaving on the sidewalk and pedestrians made wide cautious arcs around him. I said to Gregory I wanted to give the guy a buck and walked over. He took the buck and asked for smoke. I gave him one and lit him. His eyes were clear and steady, at odds with his aggressive, swaying manner.

"Macedonia, eh? Interesting place."

He said, "The park, right, bud," and smiled.

Gregory and I went around the corner the other way. We stepped into a doorway and he meticulously patted me down, apologizing. He took the folded photographs of himself from my jacket pocket, looked at them, and shook his head.

"I'd be really lucky if these were the only copies?"

"Sorry. I made a dozen and one's addressed to the *Post*. You can keep those if you like."

He put them into his pocket. We went into a small Chinese bar on Dundas Street. It was Saturday night and the karaoke machine was getting a workout from a dozen couples celebrating something. The owner immediately made Gregory for a cop and took us through the crowd into a back room where he kept a beer cooler full of plastic pots of various foods. We passed through the room and out the back door into an alley, turned left and went a few buildings along to where the kitchen door of a restaurant was open to let the steam out.

"You know this place? Any good?"

He shook his head. "But they're all the same."

It was boiling inside, the cooks chowing vegetables in huge woks, some of them stripped to the waist, some of them with cigarettes dangling from their mouths. They held the long wooden handles of the woks with both hands and sent the food flying up in the air, catching it on the way down, banging the hammered metal onto the gas burners. They all had the choppy haircuts you got when all you could afford was a pair of scissors. There was a lot of shouting back and forth and even some laughter and singing.

I said, "Let's try this one. Or the next. You choose."

"This's okay. They're all the same."

We passed through and entered the crowded restaurant and found a vacant Formica table that was mostly blocked from view of the entrance. There was a sign in Mandarin taped to the wall above the table.

Gregory said, "When she opened the red package I knew it was over. You should've put something in them, advertising flyers or something."

"I didn't mind that you knew. Once I had the vehicles and

your pictures, I was happy. See, Gregory, I don't have to prove anything. All I have to do is make it look dirty. The Big Chu's got enough enemies in this town and on the police force to turn a whisper into a shout. And of course Chu's brushing off his credibility suit for when he gets his turn to talk to the press."

"What have you got?"

"Well, if you want to dance, okay." The waitress came by and took our beer orders. She asked if we wanted menus. We shook our heads. I said to him: "I got you. I got your wife. The leases, the setup at Tibby Kay's. Who thought of that, by the way? Big mistake then, and now another clue."

"One of the guys. Thought it was funny. Tibby Kay's. By the time the Shiv found out what we'd done, the sign was printed and up over the coffee shop. He was pissed. There were five of us. I won't give you their names. You've got me. Maybe you get the Shiv. But that's it."

"Don't need 'em, as long as I've got you. Also, I've got your signature on the bomb at the Park last year, I got the last-minute training course in London for the witch, I got the go-nowhere child porn task force, which is one guy and one broad and a bunch of computer goofs, play-acting, collecting salaries. I got the bums they're using for surveillance. Including, I have to tell you, that guy I just gave a buck and a butt to."

"The Indian?"

"Macedonian. I thought he was an Indian too."

He sighed and said, "Fuck. So I'm burned, anyway. They know I'm meeting with you. You burned me."

"No," I said. "He followed me, is all. Unless, of course, he was on you and your wife and you guys brought him on me. If he's following me, all I've got to do is walk around town and poison everybody just by nodding at them."

"Is there a hole here?"

"Well, we can look." I shook out some cigarettes and lit us. "You know this is about my kids, right? I'm not on some crusade, necessarily, put good cops into deep shit." I looked up and waved my finger in a tight circle. "This is all up there, and up there they're already walking backwards from it, they know there are too many moving parts, it's not going to fly much longer."

He was working things out in his head, remembering what his guys had done and what the brass had done. Who'd said what and what he'd said back. He understood about my kids. During dinner his wife had chatted lovingly and proudly about their three, two boys and a girl.

"You know," he said finally, "this all should have ended last fall when we stopped the bombing at Queen's Park. One of the guys actually thought we should've let it go off, really got things going. It was going badly fucked. I said if we didn't tip off security up there, I was out. I was never really a cop anyway, you know, they took me out of training and convinced me ratting bad cops was the best way to be a good cop. Only," he said, "most of the cops I ratted weren't fired or charged. The information I gathered let them make more and more rats. Now you've got guys turning in their partners, guys setting up their partners, guys who sit all day in a cruiser together and never, ever, say anything personal or not related to a specific call. All to make more rats until they start eating each other up."

"You guys set them up, the anarchists, you made the bomb?"

"Us? Fuck, no. We brought them together at the Tib's. There wasn't anything going on, a few demos, some sit-ins. Someone upstairs, either the Big Chu or the Shiv, decided there was something going on and we just didn't know about it. So we, I, went in first, we looked around, we did a bit of organizing, but no one was up for anything.

"Then one day we're in the Tib and this girl comes in, Corolla Carlson. She thinks we're cool and the guys she's hanging with across the road at the Krak are a bunch of wussies. I wanna do an action, she said, those guys are just into music and talk. I wanna make a difference.

"Well, I said, or one of us said, gee, are there any more like you at home? She brings in some pals, a couple of them are brain-deads, outpatients or runaways with bad habits. Suddenly we got our cadre, but we don't know what to do with them. Corolla starts with the music, you know, hey you fuckin' fags, let's do something, like in Berlin.

"So, somebody from us goes up to one of them at Dyas and says we got someone, she wants to do an action, but she doesn't know how to do it. How far should we push her, huh?

"And the guy up there goes like this, Well if she says she wants to, then she will, sooner or later. Some evil bastard's gonna come around and take her on a training picnic, we'll lose sight of her and when she comes back we're all gonna know about it pretty fast, especially the hospitals and the coroner's office.

"One of us said, How do you want to handle it?

"He says he has to talk to someone first, but he thinks we got a shot at a task force, at funding. He comes back and he says the guys upstairs figure it's better that we make her ours, so we got some control.

"So they move us out of the Bunker up to York Region and suddenly we've got DND guys around, we've got some Funny People, we've got trainers who explain the Black Bloc. We're now really deep under. Blood oath, cross-your-heart stuff.

"I'd had bomb training, but I guess you know that, when I had to lie low for a while. They sent me up to DND and put me through the paces, kept me away from some guys I'd turned into rats, give 'em time to calm down, get their minds right. So, I was the front man on Kensington, I was going to show them how. There's a place up near Bancroft and the OPP uses it to keep guys on ice until they can testify. Cabins, lake, no neighbours, lots of bears and bugs. So we created a training camp. They trained in ski masks and fatigues. We did some interrogation and evasion. I ran the explosives course. How to get the stuff, how to put it together. I told them tales the instructors at DND had told us about bombings in France, Germany, Belfast. We had clippings, news videos. Hey, that's us there, in the masks and the fatigues, and you can be too. We didn't do singalongs around the campfire or anything, but we brought speakers through, guys who looked like old hippies, guys we borrowed from the drug squad. We said they were the SDS and successful graduates of the Tibby School of Reaching Out and Touching Society."

"Who else was in it, can you tell me? Besides you and your guys. Anybody higher, headquarters or Dyas."

"Well, one day a guy came up. We told the recruits he was too notorious to expose his identity, even to us. Interpol red notices, flags in every computer in the world. He wore a ski mask, cammies, carried an alley sweeper on a cord around his neck. He looked everybody over, checked their technique, and pronounced them true believers. I'm not sure, but he had the physical shape of the Chu. His driver, also masked when we saw him, well, I'm not sure. But I think if you cut that guy's head off and put the Shiv's right on, you'd have a pretty good fit."

"So," I said, watching the waitress and signalling for some more beer, "you're all up there and the Tib is closed. No more recruits?"

"We had eight, small enough, we said, to keep the cadre close for security, big enough to break into two independent cells. Of course, one cell was us guys, all cops. I was the liaison between the cells."

"So you came back, down, when?"

"Near the end of last summer. We reactivated Tibby's, but we made sure everybody kept to themselves. We had 'em out and around the Market, at the clubs and at the demos. They kept their ears open for stuff we could use, you know, so and so's stockpiling gas masks, someone else is organizing an anti-poverty action. Bread-and-butter intell. We had them keep their eyes open for other recruits we might bring in, but we'd trained them too tight and they consistently found something wrong with everyone else. Like, we're the elite, we've been trained, we're in another world now."

"Then," I said, bubbling my new beer, "came the Park."

"That," he said, "was a fuckup, no question. See, even with the training and the secret cadre, Corolla was still a hard-charger. It wasn't enough, all this planning for actions, she wanted to go ahead and do it and she wanted to do it big. I told the guy up there, the Dyas guy, she was going to go off, what should we do. He said, stall her, give her advanced training. We're not ready, we want to light these people up in the springtime. Keep her head down until then. Well. Do you know Corolla?"

"Just by name and reputation. I know some of her family."

"Corolla," he said, looking over my shoulder and remembering, "she was your basic rich kid, too educated, too ... *needy*. She needed everything she thought she wanted and she wanted everything she saw. Her parents were dead and some old grandfolk tried to look after her, but she resisted mightily. A sister took her in and that worked out a little better, but it didn't hold. So we got her. I tell her there's an action, it'll take six months to put all the pieces in place. Six months, she said, that's like, wow, next year. I gave her the discipline speech, how we were under discipline and even if we didn't understand it, there was a big picture of coordinated actions, worldwide, planned. Oh, she said, cool, okay, I'm hip.

"But whether she got it or not, even us, the vast international terrorist conspiracy, wasn't enough. We were fags, we were talkers and bullshitters and, well, I guess she thought, pretty fucking lazy.

"The others in the cadre noticed she was strange-ing out. See, one of her little buddies was fucking her and she, I guess, told him she was doing an action, an independent action. By the time he came to us she had taken herself out of the Market and we couldn't find her. Absolute panic up at our headquarters. Fuck, find her. I go back to the kid who was jamming her and I said, You heard from her? We gotta find her, she's jeopardizing a major operation. He gets shifty, like they do, Uh, no. Now, this is bad. We've got this little douchebag out there. We've trained her. We've lit her up. Like, you get a pitbull, right? You train it for blood but before you can use it in the dog ring, it gets out of the backyard and heads for the nearby schoolyard. Yummy. And it's wearing dog tags with your name on them; not so yummy, that part." His voice was getting hoarse. He drank the rest of his beer and made a v sign for two more. He looked at his watch. He waited until the beer came before he resumed. "I go around and around with this little buddy of hers and finally he tells me she's made a bomb and she's taking out the legislature. They're screaming now, up the Bunker and at our place. Find her. Find her. Find her. The little prick doesn't know where she's at. She just shows up late at night at his flop, stays a while. They fuck, they talk, they dream the big dreams. But she got stupid a couple of nights earlier, last time he saw her before coming to us.

"You'll hear about it, she told him. Friday, she said, Friday is the first day in the days of rage. Black Friday.

"We notify Queen's Park security to keep an eye out and they come waltzing in, Corolla and a couple of pooches, carrying their little device, and they're grabbed up. The witches dismantle it. The handler recognizes the twists from his training, and tells his commander, commander tells a deputy, dep tells the chief and the handler is on the next plane to Scotland Yard's kiddie diddler training school."

"So what happened? Why didn't it end? After Queen's Park."

"It kind of did. We shut down the storefront, we all cleaned up, had our tattoos removed, took the metal out of our faces, grew our hair back. For about a month. The storefront was paid, cash, and Brenda goes: It's empty? It's paid? So in she goes. And then they came back, the guys at the Bunker, and said, It's Showtime, false alarm, we're alright. We've turned Corolla and she's put the finger on a real bunch of badasses in the Market. That included your kids, I guess. And away we went again."

"Who came back and said that? What'd they tell you?"

"I dunno. You'll have to ask your buddy, there, and his dance partner."

"Who?"

Not the right thing to say and certainly not the right time to say it. I'd leaned in a little and had spoken too quickly. He felt the edge shift to him and he was, suddenly, rat-like, angling, looking for his hole out of the box. I noticed his upper teeth were long and in my mind they took on a naked urge to gnaw.

"I'm out of it if I give it up, okay? And my wife and the thing with the lease. I can get charged, if the lease gets out, how she made out on the store. It's going to be fraud or corrupt practice."

I thought about it. I suddenly didn't like him and was glad

we were sitting here in dirty old Chinatown, sitting in this dirty old restaurant. It was the place to do this kind of thing.

Underneath the hearts-and-flowers about being a reluctant rat, he was indeed just a rat and they'd likely spotted that early, the Dyas guys and the Internal Affairs guys, when they went looking. He was a sharpie with no character. He was always the poor puppet: blame the puppet master. I could lie now and fuck him up later and there'd be no danger he'd come back on me. It would be someone else's fault; he'd lick his wounds and go into mindless businesses with his space cadet wife. He was never a cop anyway, as he'd said. I couldn't imagine Barry White or Carl Hanson or even Gerry Adams, the ex-witch, coming to this and still not standing up and taking it square. In any case, I could decide later which route to take.

"Deal."

He wanted to shake on it, a strange schoolboy ritual that he should have known wouldn't mean anything. But we were pals again and he was pleased. "Fox," he said. "And that prick from the Crown's office that's got more teeth than a bandsaw. Jefferson."

"When'd this happen? Where?"

He computed and came to a date. "I saw Fox coming up to the Bunker to meet Jeffy. Fox was all beat up, like he'd been in a wreck. He had some marks on his face and he was walking like he'd fallen down."

I worked it out. Even before making the deal for Corolla Carlson, Fox had begun his revenge. The slapping out by Aaron Bower, sounds like Aryan Power, and Enio Palma had put him over.

We found Elodie and Brenda Harris having an intimate girl talk over shooters at a corner table in the Advocate. There were eight glasses lined up on the table and both of them were pretty gone. Gregory and I sat for a few minutes with them, listening. It seemed Brenda thought Elodie would make a great partner in the franchise business. Think, she said, no offense, of an advertising program with Elodie in her wheelchair, looking healthy, shopping at Lucy's Juicery. They could market their own line of products, cutting out the middleman and buying directly in Asia. It conjured up fabulous trips, buying sprees, hustling those dumb Asians into fronting shipments of ginseng, curry powders, Burmese saffron. Buy in bulk from the moronic Asians, repackage under a cool label and flog the stuff through a chain of Lucy's Juiceries. A killing would be made, Brenda Harris said. She was a predator. I waved down the waitress and scribbled in the air. When the bill came Brenda Harris made a point of covering it with her hand. She slapped down a credit card and made another point of peering at the receipt, writing on the back and tucking it into her wallet.

Outside there were no Macedonians visible. We stood a few minutes saying goodnight and Brenda gave Elodie another card. Gregory said to me, "We cool?" I nodded and said I'd try to keep him posted. They walked off hand-in-hand, she chattering into his ear, him laughing with his arm around her. The rat's reprieve.

"Well, stud, a night of commerce."

"And, I suspect, a little sippling?" I took her hand and tugged her along the sidewalk down to Dundas Street. We went west into old Chinatown. The Macedonian was across from the restaurant I'd used for a screen. I waved and we went to the second restaurant, the one with the amazing chowing chefs.

Inside the waitress was leaning on the cash register. I gave her a fifty-dollar bill and Elodie waited while I went to the back table and un-Velcroed the micro cassette from under the table. The waitress came over and took the Mandarin sign—RESERVED FOR HONOURED GUEST—from the wall.

At the next two eateries I dealt out fifty-dollar bills and untaped unused tape recorders from under tables beneath signs with Mandarin characters scrawled on them.

22

Elodie and I went home. She was a drunken little frolicker and we didn't check messages until well after midnight. Four hangups, then Michael, Michael, Michael, Michael, then two hangups, then Michael again, the last message saying it was late and to call him at home Sunday before noon, he had to have a feature ready to go for the Monday paper.

We lay in the darkness with the terrace door ajar to let in some cool night air. From my pillow I could see the towering lights of the town. I thought again about the birds flying into the bright squares of glass, thinking they were meeting a sunrise, meeting a new day of promise or at least the promise of new day. I thought of my kids in their cells, still mourning Pia. I thought of the Mouse in her orange jumpsuit. Cool, eh, Dad?

On the terrace I heard a noise, a soft thump, then a subtle clicking sound, then silence for a few minutes, then a rustling sound. Elodie slept. I eased from the bed and opened the safe and took out the Glock. I went down the hall to the end room and slipped open the other set of doors, silently, silently. I was naked and the terrace was full of dark cold shadows.

The neighbour's cat was there, feasting on a mess of white and grey feathers. It looked up at me aggressively for a moment, then went back to playing and chewing and pawing. I laughed and it looked at me again, this time longer. It reminded me of the placid stare of the bum who'd taken my five-dollar bill, who'd been laughing at the demonstrators being arrested at Old City Hall.

In the books and movies, I thought, sitting on a stone bench, the flagstones icy under my bare feet, the renegades would come after me, creeping ninjas flowing over the terrace wall with long swords and garrotes, hunting down and killing the man who was too dangerous to live. But that was an evil that had form and shape and a beginning and an end. TV evil. Cheap literary evil. Real evil isn't like that. Real evil is invisible and pervasive and it makes you listen to a cat eating a bird and you think it's a squadron of killers, afraid for yourself instead of happy for the cat or sad for the bird. Real evil puts a gun in your paranoid hand and sends you creeping, naked.

It's like leaving towers full of lights ablaze at night for no reason at all, pulling birds from their paths, killing them while offering a false sunrise.

Evil is indifferent.

In the end, we jammed everybody as best we could. It wasn't perfect and it wasn't conclusive. Sunday while Elodie slept through the tolling of bells I headed out on the bike to meet Michael Bailey. He lived outside the city and I gave the bike a good workout, roaring along in the fast lane all the way. He showed up at the Holiday Inn in Oakville wearing a neat, sombre suit, his hair combed, and his eyes alive and glistening.

I put my helmet on the floor under the table and laughed at him. "Hey, bud, I get you out of church, or what?"

"No problem, Charlie. I only missed the collection plate." He looked pious and bland and I laughed.

After putting the Glock back into the safe I'd spent much of the remainder of the night at the computer, making point-form notes, some cryptic, like "Don Connie Lombardozzi"—and printing out Elodie's report. I made a hasty transcript of the recording of my conversation with Gregory. I put together the photographs. I used the fax machine to copy all the documents. Without identifying Adams as the source I briefly outlined the Queen's Park bombing incident and the fallout. I went to a Kinko's and put together four packages, some with documentation and notes left out.

There was work to be done, but I wasn't going to be the one to do it. I didn't have a client and all I wanted was my kids out. The Mouse had a boyfriend to drive crazy and Allie had her songs to write. I wouldn't get Jeffy and would probably never know why he schemed with Cornelius Fox to keep the thing going. I knew why Fox did it: his fragile ego was hurt when I battered his head against the window of the Renato and then witnessed his humiliation. Simple. A stupid simple thing.

First, I told Michael the Connie Lombardozzi story. He laughed at all the right parts and said he wished he'd been a cop reporter in those days, he loved guys like that. "I can use this, Charlie. Not for the paper, but there's a movie in there. I love it."

I told him they did it again with the Black Bloc. Someone, he'd have to find out who, the Big Chu or the Shiv or maybe even Buddy the Buddy, maybe all of them, maybe with Magda the K orchestrating, got a great idea to open a hangout for anarchists. They set it up in Kensington Market, a place they saw as a radical hardcore place where the disaffected and depressed could vent their anger. They set up one guy, Gregory Johnson, as a fugitive from the cops in Europe and he brought them all together, nurtured their funny little busted psyches, identified the most useful and trained them in bomb making.

"Likely what happened," I said, "is Corolla Carlson fell hard for it." I pushed an envelope at him. "I'm giving you this now, so I can't go back on it. But I want you to wait a couple of days because there's some stuff I've got to do. I don't give it to you now, later I might say the hell with it and let it all go, once my kids are out. I've got your word?"

He took a Book of Common Prayer from the side pocket of his jacket. He held it in his hand and said, "I swear, Charlie."

I felt like an asshole.

I'd never spoken to Jefferson before, had never heard his voice, so I was surprised it was so low and toneless. Probably he had a courtroom voice, one he used to essay authority and certainty to a judge or a jury, but on Monday afternoon at the bar atop The Rooftop Lounge it sounded like a nasal drone. We sat outside on the deck with drinks. He was very specific about his Scotch and I just ordered a beer. I said it was too windy and he said he liked the wind. He'd listened to enough tapes made off sensitive little hidden microphones to know the sound of the wind was something we don't notice until it's howling through a headset, obscuring words and phrases, puzzling the jury.

He leaned against the wall and cupped his hands to light a cigar. "How much do you know?"

"Jeffy—can I call you Jeffy? All the people I've talked to tell me they call you *Jeffy*. *Jeffy* this, *Jeffy* that. *Jeffy* knew this part, *Jeffy* knew that part. Be careful, people told me, *Jeffy*'s dirtying you up, going to make you the back-end man, the architect of it all. Big money you've got, *Jeffy* says, must be offshore, maybe from Libya. I actually thought Jeffy was your name, until people started writing and signing their statements and putting in Jefferson." I hated the cigar and I hated how he held it like a dart, how he dressed like a politician bringing in a budget. His hair was blond and long and kind of whipping when the wind gusted. His eyebrows were blond and a little feminine. He had an ambitious jutting private school jaw that I could imagine him thrusting at the ladies on the jury, a wide thin mouth that seemed ready to grin boyishly, and he wore glasses with gold frames. "And you can call me Charlie, okay?"

"Whoa. Statements, whaddayamean, statements," he said, holding his cigar up beside his face. "Look, look, your kids'll get clear. You've got my word on it. Clearly something went wrong in the system. We've decided that to continue the prosecution would bring the legal system into disrepute. Charges dropped in the interest of justice. That'll be tomorrow morning, I've got some stuff to do to set it up. We'll have an investigation and the guilty parties, probably ambitious low-level cops who watch too much television, read too much Le Carré, will be punished. To, of course, the full extent of the law, what else? So, let me ask you, Charlie, what else? What else do you want? It's over, just about. There's going to be a czar of anti-terrorism appointed next week. Me. And, if you want, you can be ... something. Like, what? Chief investigator? We can do a lot of good together."

I told him about Pia. His face didn't change, except to become a little impatient. I told him about Pia's mother making a noose, about Pia alone in a cell without friends or support and making a noose. He just looked at me, like: so?

"You lack," I told him, "imagination. You have to make yourself a mental picture. I can help you. Imagine this: a bunch of cops take some emotionally fucked girl and turn her into a bomb maker."

He stared at me and held up the hand holding the cigar. "No no no no no. Sherelle Filipina wasn't part of this. She was just collateral damage."

"Not Pia."

His face lit a little. "Ah, that what this is about? Corolla Carlson? Fuck, Charlie, that's your pal Fox. Our office played square in that. That's long over."

"Tell me about it. Don't tell me the Youth Act. Don't tell me confidentiality, just tell me about the deal Fox made."

His manner changed significantly; he took on a posture of easy self-control and became businesslike. He was on firm ground here and wasn't in any way guarded or defensive. This, I thought, he could defend by putting the hat on Cornelius Fox. "Straightforward. We had the daughter of a very wealthy family, caught with a bomb. Fox got her bailed. We negotiated and agreed she'd go into psychiatric care, set a long date for trial. She comes back to court, her head straightened out, and the psychiatrists say she was brainwashed, like Patty Hearst. Emotional gun to her head, she melts down. It's an episode, she's a victim. She makes full disclosure, makes a full statement about the other two—who by then were bailed and have fucked off—and she agrees to a couple more years, treatment, getting her head really rinsed out. And it all goes away. That's it."

"That's it? No more from Fox?"

"Well, yeah, it was a little funny after that. The deal's done, the fix is in. And then Foxy shows up and says—remember, this is after we're all on the same page—and Foxy says: wait a minute, hold on. We'll give you more. I go, what more? Fuck more. No, Cornelius, we're okay, we're fine with this. The old Carlsons pull some weight in the province, the son-in-law raises donations for the party. We're cool, Cornelius, go fuck off okay, it's lunchtime, c'mon, we'll buy. But Cornelius goes: no, listen to this. My client told me there's a bunch of people in the Market, going to make more bombs, going to wreak havoc. It'll be raining bodies, fruits, and vegetables down there. She wants to help the cops, show she's really rehabilitated. Well, we go, so what? More business for you, unless they blow themselves up."

"Who's the we?"

"Well, me. It was me and Cornelius, that time. Cornelius's now a hundred grand richer and the Carlsons, well, they just want to blow him once a day and serve him his favourite foods. He did the impossible, which, come to think of it, wasn't impossible at all. If a law student came to me with the Hearst defence and the psychiatric treatment deal, the connections, I'd've gone for it. Who wouldn't? Anyway, I tell him I don't want to know. If you want to be a good citizen, get some brownie points, go up to the Bunker, they're interested in that kind of thing. Take her up there and if they like her, she's in business. Then, if they go ahead and they want to dedicate a Crown to it, I'll take it."

"That's it? No more?"

"Last I heard of it until the Kensington 19 and they put me out front on it."

"When was this?"

"Last fall. I've got to admit, Cornelius and I were in negotiations about partnering up, if I quit. But, Charlie, that wasn't a factor here at all. Cornelius's getting on, you know, needs a guy to do the heavy lifting. We were talking, that's all. He said he was slowing down and I believed him. He had some bruising on his face and when I asked he said, that's what I mean, Jeffy, see I was playing racquetball the other day and got hit twice in the head. Come in with me, you'll learn to defend and

I'll have more time to keep my fucking face out of the line of fire." The cigar was out and our glasses were empty. The waiter lurked inside the glass behind us. He was wearing a bad toupée and really didn't want to have to come out in the wind. I shook my head and he looked relieved.

I was thinking: when I swung Fox into that window at the Renato I was in the red mist; I must have dinged him a couple of good ones without really knowing it. Then Enio gave him a couple of taps. And the undercover cop. He was humiliated. He took his battered face to Jefferson after dealing away the Carlson charges and ended up using Corolla Carlson, the girl everybody used and would one day use up. First he'd used her to collect long dough off the Carlsons, then he used her to get my kids, so that I'd get got too.

"Did he go to the Bunker?"

"I guess. I mean, the jail's full of people now, right?" He made a tight cup of his hands and relit the cigar and led me across to the balcony overlooking the city. If I leaned and read the buildings and sightlines right, I could see a top corner of our condominium building poking at the sky. Clouds skidded and scudded. A high-away jet plane scratched an arcing silver line across the bottom of the blue sky. He said, "You know Magda the K, right? You know she was fired? Resigned to seek broader opportunities in the private sector, they said, but actually they gave her two in the back of the head and a decent severance. How'd you set that up, how'd you fuck her?"

"Was she in this?"

"Magda? Fuck, no. When she saw your kids were in there she went, Whoa, go for someone else. Their old man's gonna come down like hammers, leave 'em out of this. But they didn't listen, those smart Intelligence guys in the Bunker." He turned away from the city and with a careless flight of his wrist fired his cigar stub over the balcony. "I guess she was right, eh?"

23

After that it was clean-up, housekeeping.

Enio told me he owned about a hundred grand worth of Cornelius Fox's pasty white ass. We were sitting in an outdoor café on St. Clair Avenue and our conversation was continually interrupted by passersby who wouldn't insult Enio by passing without a greeting. Enio, who still thought of me as a journalist, introduced me to many people as a reporter writing a profile of him and his good works in the Italian community. No one laughed at him. I thought of the old gangster Harry Quan, scheming in Chinatown to rehabilitate a lifetime of one thing into a memory of another. We all of us, I think, try to rehabilitate ourselves, if for no other reason than we like to see how we look in different lights.

I told Enio about Cornelius Fox's moves, how he went after my kids.

"Jew prick," he said, shaking his head and making a spitting noise. "Even we don't go after kids."

I thought of shredded children's bodies I'd seen on a

beach in Calabria, a family picnic that ended with dad, a short-weight dope hustler from Locri, and two kids being caught up in a burst of machinegun fire. But I didn't correct him.

"Cal-o-gero, this isn't my business. He's a fuck and he's a degenerate but he owes me a lot of money. Anyone who takes action on him owes me that money. If you buy his debt, say, fifty, fifty-five percent, then ..." he shrugged, "perhaps."

I said I had about fifteen thousand dollars, but I wasn't looking for Fox to get whacked. "What if, if, you had a guy I could give the money to and he played against Fox for me in a game? What if he was ..." I rubbed the fingertips of both hands together, "... and Fox lost and lost?"

"You're sure, Cal-o-gero? It's a very expensive revenge."

"Mr. Palma," I said. "It's only money. And we don't live for money, do we?"

He began laughing.

The Carlsons returned from Europe, stopping on the way from the south of France and picking up a freshly laundered Corolla on the way home. We heard they were back and after a week or so ran into them at the Club, where the Grays were having a homecoming party for themselves. I was starched out in business attire and I saw the Carlson and Appleby clan, elegant old Mr. and Mrs. Carlson, sleek Janine and her dour-looking husband, and a calm and beautiful young woman having chateaubriand prepared table-side. I kept an eye on them while I listened to David Gray hold forth on energy stocks and old Colin Gray agree with his analysis. Elodie and I were side-by-side and holding hands under the table. Martha Gray noticed and kept smiling at us, seeming to want to ask a question. David Gray, as was his habit when old Colin was around, ignored Sharon. Elodie,

Martha, Sharon, and I talked about the Grays' trip to London.

When I saw Janine Carlson-Appleby take her purse and leave the table, I excused myself and followed her out of the dining room to an outside portico, where she was smoking a quick cigarette.

"How's your sister?"

"She's alright, all things considered. She was brainwashed or something, by those people, that Black Bloc gang." Her voice was remote and cool and she stared at me without blinking, like: no thanks to you.

"Well, I'm glad she's okay."

"She isn't yet, but she will be. I didn't know your daughters were part of all that. You should have told us."

"When Corolla was arrested, I didn't know. They tried to help her. They tried to help her but she was too far gone."

"You must feel so ashamed of them, your kids. I've always believed it's the parents' fault. They don't listen, they don't care."

"My daughters are nothing for me to be ashamed of."

"In any case, Mr. Fox was able to expedite Corolla's freedom, to make the judge understand she was a victim. He could have, Mr. Fox could have been greedy, but he said he'd just accept the retainer and if it wasn't enough, well, he said he'd pursue the case at his own expense. He knew right off it was a miscarriage. He saved us."

"Cornelius is a master lawyer," I said, "and a great man."

The last contact I had with the Carlson-Appleby family was when we took my kids to the Market for a long-anticipated Vietnamese dinner. We sat on the edge of a patio. Elodie looked suspiciously at each dish as it was put down but she tasted everything. The Mouse had brought along her boyfriend, whose name turned out to be Martin Fox. No relation, he hastened to add, to the lawyer who had been found beaten and brain-damaged the week before in Little Italy.

"There's Ola!" Allie was gone from the table. She crossed Baldwin and hugged Corolla. They stood on the sidewalk while the Mouse, the good Fox, and I ate cold rolls, mystery meatball soup, and picked at a vegetarian plate. I watched Allie constantly, keeping some kind of physical contact with Corolla, as they talked. I watched as Corolla dropped her head down in what looked like shame; I watched as Allie glanced at me and then hugged Corolla to her. Allie used her sleeve to wipe tears from Corolla's face. Then, behind them, came Janine and Ted Appleby, carrying shopping bags. They pried Corolla from Allie and Ted Appleby spoke to her sharply, and the three were gone.

Allie came back across the street and sat down, looking at the ravaged plates. She used chopsticks to pick up a lonely wad of noodles. "They called me a terrorist. He said I was a little bitch bomber and should be in jail. And so should my sister ..." She looked at the Mouse, grinning, " ... my sister, the Rat, and my old man, the criminal."

The Mouse asked how Corolla was doing.

She said, "You know what she asked me, what Ola asked me? She asked where Tib was, she said she and Gregory were together a lot, and she had an abortion. She asked where he was, had I seen him, and could I get in touch with him. She's looking everywhere for him."

I thought, Ah, Gregory, you little shit.

Over the years Elodie had taken pains to civilize me. Use this fork, hold this chair, sit down after the ladies, examine the wine like this and then this. But, I told her after I found Gregory Johnson one night jauntily coming out of the newest

Lucy's Juicery outlet in the Beach, sometimes there's no civilized way to do things.

A few months after it all happened, after the kids were free and we had our feast, after the night with Gregory Johnson in the Beach, after Cornelius Fox was found in the laneway, Jerome called up and said a gentleman was in the lobby to see Mr. Tate. I turned on the closed circuit channel on the television set and there was a trim, well-shaven man in a dark business suit. He didn't look dangerous. I went downstairs and we went to the sofa by the south windows. He handed me a five-dollar bill. He didn't introduce himself, but I recognized his eyes.

"We didn't know which way it would jump," he said. "When you turned up at the Krak after I saw you on the Russian security team, we couldn't figure it. For a while there, you were everywhere. You just have an interesting life. Then we found out the Tate girls were your kids. I tried to call you a few times, but I couldn't get through. I was going to call the reporter, but you know reporters, you can't trust any of them."

"No shit. You were working out of the Bunker, right?"

"Right. They had this project going and they needed money. They weren't going to get money unless we had a piece of the action, some control. So they seconded a few of us and we mostly were observers, monitoring the case, auditing what they were doing with all the federal money they received. What we really wanted was to take the chief, the Shiv, and the mayor. The chief is going to run federally, sooner or later, and the mayor, unless he goes completely nuts, can be useful to us, too, someplace down the road. The Shiv," he shrugged, "well, we'd just like to have the Shiv for our very own."

"So," I said, "why come out now?"

"You're going to get a case, tomorrow or next week, a, what do you call it? An assignment?"

"An engagement."

"Yeah. It's a Russian guy wants to invest in a diamond mine up north. You and your wife are going to do due diligence on this guy and you're going to find a lot of stuff. What we'd like is, if you didn't find that stuff. No anomalies, no red flags. The source of the guy's money is going to be clean, the allegations of his criminal activities in the Ukraine will be proven false as you do your investigation. Your engagement, whatever. We need this guy in play and you can fuck us up. So, we ask a favour, and we all know the world runs on favours, right?"

"Two favours."

"What?"

"One for later, but for now, who's the Indian? The Indian-looking guy who's actually Macedonian? In the park across the street?"

He got up and looked at me, genuinely puzzled. "Straight up, and I can tell you this because I monitored the surveillance shifts on you, we didn't use anybody looked like that. You want to be careful, Charlie. Maybe you've got enemies?"

As I said, in the end we fucked everybody we could, one way or another. Except Michael Bailey and GerryAdams, the witch. Elodie became convinced she could turn Michael straight and after a few dinners at our place where she brought a seemingly endless line of young women, she gave up. He did, however, come to be quite fond of Jerome, the night concierge. There was nothing headquarters could do about Adams: Hanson had retired and when he heard they were circling the defrocked witch, Hanson met him for drinks and gave him the list he'd picked up in the corruption case.

Michael's story ran for about a week and then was smothered by the usual flood of scandals and rumours. But he was okay, for all of it. The Big Chu apparently gave up on trying to shift the weight onto the Shiv, and at the intelligence bureau he remained, a placid, massive, mean cop with a head full of the most hateful of secrets. The weight ended up on a detective-sergeant I'd never heard of, didn't even know existed, but he must have had something very nasty in his package because he resigned before the investigation was complete and went to work with Carl Hanson at Bobby Clarke's crew.

Buddy won another civic election, an unprecedented landslide, even though he took a swing at a reporter during a scrum about his personal finances. He was the people's guy, and a guy of the people. He'd hired Magda the K, and the smart money said that that was what did it for him: the male voters loved the K and in some twisted way thought if they dumped the crazy little bastard, Magda would be out of work. I saw Magda one night at a fundraiser David Gray took me to, and she refused to acknowledge me. I felt bad about it, but I told Elodie I thought she should have stayed with the tree-hugging bicycle riders and made the environment safe for all of us.

Elodie said: fuck her.

Jeffy just vanished into the quiet corridors of the Crown's office, his hopes of becoming the terrorism czar crashed and burned. Cornelius Fox sat on his porch for a few months screaming at passing cars and barking like a dog. One day he was lucid enough to load a shotgun and aim it at some passing schoolchildren. His lawyer used the stress defence to keep him out of jail.

Allie and the Mouse went back into the Market. For a while they were newly minted heroes who had defeated the forces of injustice and darkness, but there slowly came new, younger people crowding that scene, and my girls were seen as old-timers at twenty-three or -four, I always forget. Their lifestyle, the leathers, the metal in their faces, and the music began turning up in television advertising for hip clothing shops. The Krak Bar lease went to a franchise and was sold and became an expensive coffee house for the yuppies who moved into the new lofts in the area, where they could read their *New York Times*, their *Elle*, their *Wallpaper*, and feel like they were ahead of some cool curve. Allie stayed over there anyway and became a cook in a vegetarian restaurant; the Mouse managed to hook up her string-bean and they live together up in the Annex. He's got all the ideas and she's got all the energy, as it should be.

Afterword

On the way home from a Gray family function one midnight later that year I realized it was a harvest day, one of those rare days when householders could put anything out for pickup except tires, batteries, toxic household waste, and anything else that would irritate the environment. The front edges of the dark lawns were cluttered with broken furniture, old fridges and stoves, washers and dryers, pieces of trellis, chairs with three legs, busted stools, rolled-up carpets, exhausted air conditioners, and cardboard boxes full of treasures that were no more.

Elodie leaned against me as I drove, yawning periodically, sometimes fiddling with the radio when the music stopped and the pitchmen came on, dozing. Heading down Avenue Road we passed the reuse where the Gone Wong had re-established himself. As I passed the dark McDonald's outlet I realized I was hungry and I started looking for an open restaurant. I tried to think if Elodie still owed me a Vietnamese feast of mystery meats and suspicious broth. Or had I negotiated it away for less filling but more substantial and satisfying mysteries?

I glanced into a side street and saw a white fridge, its door off and lying flat on a lawn beside it. The fridge glowed and beckoned for someone, a piece of melancholy abandonment under the streetlights. I swung into the next left without signalling. The street was straight and well lit and well treed, the lawns spacious and unfenced; the houses dark except for the odd blue television light brightening a window or two. I travelled about halfway along the block, my speed barely above an idle, looking, looking. I slowed to a stop in front of a darkened gabled brick house with two identical silver Audis in the driveway. On the lawn were a narrow stove, the twenty-eight-inch kind you find in apartments and kitchenettes, a small bar-sized freezer, the freezer door on top of it, a couple of chromium-legged stools with leatherette seats, a lamp with no shade, and cardboard boxes full of junk. Full of stuff. I felt my heart race.

I shut off the car and pulled the key out of the ignition a hair to kill the alert buzzer. I slipped Elodie off my shoulder and balanced her in the middle of her seat. Her hair had come down and the streetlights reflected gold strands; I gently rubbed the side of her face with the knuckles of my hand and she made an indecipherable sound.

Outside the car I stood on the sidewalk and looked around, breathing in that absolute cleanness of the autumn night, a little cool and lacking pollution. And a scent: someone had mowed their leaves into mulch, rather than raking them up. The trees were fragrant with sap.

The boxes were full of cracked bricks, some old LP records and a clock stopped at 9:33, the glass face splintered. I flipped through the records, recognizing Louis Prima and Keeley Smith, Webb Pierce, Hank Snow. There were two Elvis

Christmas albums, a Herb Alpert and the Tijuana Brass, some polkas with a faintly recognizable fat guy with an insane smile, armed with an industrial-size accordion. I picked up an album cover and touched it to my nose: cardboard. Cardboard and old dust. Who would throw such stuff out? Who would put their past into cardboard boxes and just ... toss it? Jesus Christ, I thought, I'd keep it just for the smells.

"Charlie, where are we?" Elodie was dozy, leaning across the driver's seat, watching me through the window.

"Go back to sleep, El, I'll wake you when we get home," I whispered. "I'll just be a sec."

I leaned into the car and pulled the lever to pop the trunk. I took the garbage bags and odd disguise clothing, old notebooks, a pair of boots, and other stuff out and put it all into the back seat beside the dismantled wheelchair.

Elodie said, "Charlie?"

I found an old bungee cord under the front seat and hooked it into my belt. The stove was no problem at all, once I got my hands under the sharp edges and tilted it, accommodating myself to the cutting pain. I got it up onto my knees and walked, bent legged, to the rear of the Intrepid. It jammed in nicely on an angle and I secured the trunk with the bungee cord. I fitted the record albums in around it.

As I drove off I saw a blood, smear, purple-black on the steering wheel. I wiped my palms on my pants, one at a time, and placed them back on the steering wheel, in unsticky places. I couldn't stop looking at them, my old man's hands.

Elodie had her eyes closed. "We already have a stove, Charlie. What're we going to do with that one?"

"Well, El," I said, feeling pretty good about myself, "we're gonna sell it. I figure it's one of the coils. When a coil goes most people figure the thing's busted, and usually when the coil goes the thing ain't so new anymore and they figure it's time for a new one anyway. But you know what? You can buy another coil; take the old one out and put another one in. I'll pick up a used coil tomorrow at a junk shop, get some stuff to buff up the chrome, maybe a little white touch-up paint: ten bucks, tops. I'll sell it at the second-hand place on Queen Street, twenty-five bucks, minimum." I thought a moment. "Thirty. Not a penny less."

"Twenty dollars, clear profit." She repositioned herself on my shoulder, snuggling. "Oh, Chah-Lee," she said, sounding like a breathy Hepburn talking to Bogie in *The African Queen,* "we made some money tonight, didn't we? We made the long dough. Twenty beautiful smackeroos."

"Well, kid," I said, slowly passing a prowling cop car, the Intrepid's springs squeaking under the weight of my stove, "one of us has to."

Thanks to Lucy K. White and Katy and Michelle Lamothe, for making things interesting for a long time to say the least.

To the Ross family who provided a tranquil place to write in the early mornings when the coffee was hot and the children were asleep.

Thanks to the crew at Turnstone: Jamis Paulson, publisher, Christian Mazur, and Sharon Caseburg, who, for any writer, is the best kind of editor: a poet; Wayne Tefs who suffered through the sometimes contentious edit, and Heidi Harms, who did the copy edit. The proposal for the Charlie & Elodie series was originally accepted by former managing editor Todd Besant.

And my agent, Robert Lecker.